Summer Secrets

Jean Stubbs is a frequent lecturer at writers' summer schools and seminars and in 1984 she was writer-in-residence for Avon. Her novels and short stories have been translated into eight languages and have been televised and adapted for radio. She lives in Cornwall with her second husband.

Jean Stubbs

SUMMER SECRETS

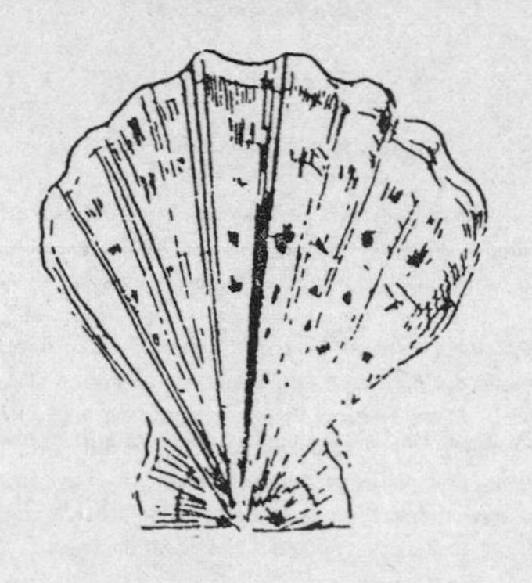

Pan Books

First published 1990 by Macmillan London

This edition published 2001 by Pan Books
an imprint of Macmillan Publishers Ltd
25 Eccleston Place, London SW1W 9NF
Basingstoke and Oxford
Associated companies throughout the world
www.macmillan.com

ISBN 0 330 31916 7

1 3 5 7 9 8 6 4 2

A CIP catalogue record for this book is available from
the British Library.

Printed and bound in Great Britain by
Mackays of Chatham plc, Chatham, Kent

To Felix, Trewin,
and fifteen Cornish years

Old Lizard exists,
but the story, people and places
can only be found within the pages of this book.

ACKNOWLEDGEMENTS

My thanks are due to Stephen Ivall of the *Helston Packet*, for allowing me time and space in his office to study the newspapers for 1975; and to my editor Kate Jones, for being a corker!

The author and publishers wish gratefully to acknowledge the following for permission to reproduce material: Unwin Hyman Ltd for an extract from *The Hobbit* by J.R.R. Tolkein; Faber and Faber Ltd for lines from Canto IV from 'Autumn Journal' in *Collected Poems of Louis MacNiece* and lines from 'Marina' in *Collected Poems 1909–1962* by T.S. Eliot.

ONE

February 1975

I would not have believed I could cry so much, but I must not cry now. If I begin I shall not be able to stop, and this rack of a day is only at the first turn of the screw. A merciless winter wind searches me. The daffodils bend and blow wildly, helplessly, but do not break. A miser's powdering of snow whitens the mounds of earth by the graveside. Cold intensifies my pain.

The ritual observers are frozen in sorrow and silence: women in retreat behind their dark veils; men tallow-faced, gloved hands clasped before them, bared heads bent to receive benediction. The funeral has taken us over, transformed from a quiet family affair to a public meeting. A family affair. These chief mourners are strangers, related to each other only by marriage. They congregate only on life's three great occasions. Weddings. Christenings. And now death.

Should we have had her cremated? But, then, what does one do with the ashes? Theatrical to scatter them, and where would she have liked to be scattered? On what wind would Sarah like to ride? And afterwards where can you keep the urn, so that it looks neither conspicuous nor neglected?

And yet, to putrefy. The flesh is not grass but corruption. A stench of lilies that fester. Obscene. And worms shall try. But Sarah's undoubted virginity was not long preserved, did not even reach the stage where it might be tried. My daughter was only nine years old.

My mother Ethel, who barely reaches my shoulder for I am a tall woman, grips my arm and gives one short rough sob as the coffin is lowered. I shall not look at her. Nor at Mrs Tavey, who took care of the twins while I went out to work, and is grieving for Sarah as for her own child. I am grateful for the fine black fluttering of chiffon between myself and the world. To keep my lips stiff and my eyes dry, I stare beyond the pit and the crowd of people to the yew trees at the other side of the churchyard.

He is still there, the tall young man in a sober suit and dark overcoat, who removed his hat as the cortège passed and revealed a fleece of fair hair. I thought at first that he was on some sad errand of his own, and merely paid us passing respect. But he has remained in the same place, head bowed, throughout the service. Since he appears to be taking part at a distance, is he someone we should know? Someone connected with Sarah, whose face and name and importance I have forgotten? Should we invite him to the house afterwards? I have no wish to offend anyone, and there are so many who could be offended, for Sarah collected and attracted friends throughout her life. Her bright brief life.

My lips tremble. My mother would like me to cry with her, but I will not. I look at my husband instead. His face is as mild and gentle as Madox Brown's *Light of the World*, but he is slighter, warmer, browner than that. A subtly handsome youth masquerading as a man. Technically younger, I seem far older than he. People instinctively like and trust Giles and treat him as a favourite brother, whereas I know they fear me a little and try to impress me. In his profession as a teacher of boys Giles reveals an *alter ego* and wields considerable authority. In private he raises no eyebrows, causes no strong currents, is more peaceable than me, and the easiest of companions in the good times. But in our present crisis we have become strangers.

To be kind and thoughtful is good, and is appreciated. But when kindness stops short of frankness, when thought is extended no further than filling a hot-water bottle and making a whisky toddy, the heart of the relationship is lacking. We had shared confidences in our early years together, made our aims one. And if, looking back, those aims were largely material, limited to making life an aesthetic experience, they were at least a fair beginning. But they had no answer to a child's mortal sickness. And when we sought that answer in ourselves we could not find it.

Giles's reaction to Sarah's death is to retreat into total silence on the subject. He will massage my neck when I am tense, but if I try to tell him why I am tense he will evade the conversation even to the point of leaving the room. So there is no communication, and my grief freezes me.

Between us stands our son. We hold his small hands firmly, to reassure him of our love and to remind him to match his behaviour to the occasion. For Joshua, who was Sarah's twin, has refused to accept his loss. Even before her illness he was a problem to us, though not to her. Now, unable to cope with this winter world, he has retreated into the summer of their old contentment. Of course, he is in a state of shock, as we are. But in sorrow, as in all else, appearances are of paramount importance. To forgive, it is necessary to understand.

My rigid composure, Giles's mute white silence, my mother's tears are understandable. But no one will understand a plain bespectacled little boy smiling secretly to himself, as if he were in bed on Christmas Eve and knew that a bicycle waited for him downstairs by the lighted tree.

He was always a second-hand version of his twin. Sarah's dark-brown eyes were large and brilliant, his shy and shortsighted. Sarah's flowery pink mouth paid a compliment to her femininity, his was too soft and full for a boy. Her hair was a rich black mane like mine: his clung to the skull, fine and silky. She held herself like a wand, he stooped like a scholar.

Now Joshua's lips move in silent conversation. He whispers to himself, catches a chuckle or an exclamation before it escapes. In this joyful communion, despite the spectacles, he bears an uncanny resemblance to his sister. Feeling my fingers tighten on his, he looks up at me quickly, half afraid, interprets my message and is solemn again.

Ashes to ashes. Dust to dust.

It is over. One by one the chief mourners shovel a little trowelful of earth on Sarah's coffin: my mother and Mrs Tavey crying openly, Giles and I in numbed disbelief, Joshua carelessly as if it does not matter. Some earth falls on his shoes but he takes no notice. It is I who bend down and brush the soil away with a handkerchief. He pays no attention to that, either. His face is once again transformed, and as I come close to him a faint hum is audible. He is actually humming to himself. Oh, Joshua, Joshua.

My mother Ethel, who monitors and ministers to all my humours, realises that I have had more than enough of my son.

She turns to him, as to a knight errant, and says, 'Here, my lad. Come and take care of your old grandma for a change!'

Her smallness, her unimportance and her dependence divert him. He returns to this moment, gives her one of his rare smiles and proffers his arm. Thank God, he has learned some manners at the preparatory school. Pray God he will learn more at boarding-school.

They walk off together slowly: an odd couple. Was he her favourite grandchild? I wonder. She had doted on Sarah as on me, but related far better to Joshua. Perhaps she found his inadequacies more comfortable than Sarah's gifts.

Giles and I have a few words with the vicar: one of those robust and modern pastors who encourage pop groups to perform in church, and have laughing games of table-tennis at the local youth club. He has correctly placed us as present-day non-believers, using the church as a traditional background against which to act out our baptisms, marriages and deaths. We have nothing in common.

He says to our frozen incredulity, 'Of course, I realise that is difficult for you to believe that Sarah is with God, but indeed she is. Only her body was interred today. Her soul is free and joyful.'

He ventures further, watching us carefully for signs of hysteria or disapproval. 'We cannot explain why a beloved child should be made to suffer as Sarah did, and be deprived of life so young. I can only say that if we have faith in a power greater than ourselves, and a destiny which is meaningful even though we cannot interpret it, then comfort will come. Mourn, and ye shall be comforted. Were you churchgoers I should say – trust in the Lord.'

Which is the last thing I shall do.

I never knew my own father, who died in the war, and my mother's God was and is a narrow-minded, unforgiving and unsociable deity. So God the Father meant nothing to me, though I paid Him lip service until I left home. An adult in a sceptical age, married to an intellectual man, I had no need of religion. Now, as far as I am concerned, He has blown any chance He ever had. In my judgement the Lord, if He exists, has proved Himself to be either incompetent or sadistic.

Sarah died bravely and died slowly. A quicksilver child, she had never been patient. Leukaemia taught her patience. Endless, unbelievable patience, with treatment, with pain, with the knowledge that all this suffering could not save her. She forgave us our ignorance, who could not lighten her darkness. In the end she was bald and blind and beyond our reach. My daughter.

My eyes sting and I clutch my husband's arm. To hold tears at bay I remark upon the young man who has shared the service with us, and is still standing beneath the yew trees. Giles turns his head and glances covertly at our uninvited mourner, puzzled and perturbed.

'Do you know him? Is it someone we've forgotten?' I ask.

'*I* don't know him!' says Giles emphatically. 'But I suppose he must be here for some reason.'

He hesitates, thinking. He is irresolute. Then he makes up his mind.

'Stay here a moment, Rina,' he says. 'I shall have to find out.'

I brace myself for unwanted conversation with passing mourners who desire, or feel obliged, to stop and speak to me.

'Marina, my dear, what can one say? That lovely little girl!'

I should have liked a private funeral, but Sarah's long dying became a public concern. They are all here. Our friends, her friends. Adults, children.

'Such wreaths, Marina. I never saw such wreaths!'

Against my express wishes, against my very grain, they send their pierced blooms to flutter and freeze and die on my child's grave. We, too, have had to give a wreath, because it would look strange if our tribute were less imposing than the others. Our cushion of white and yellow daffodils is set in Oasis, and has Sarah's name picked out in scarlet tulips. It is intensely pretty and she would have loved it. But best of all I like the large and small bunches of spring flowers sent by children, because they can be collected afterwards and given to the local hospital, so that someone can enjoy them. Flowers are for the living, and should be enjoyed in the lifetime.

'You must come and stay with us, Marina, as soon as you feel able. We promise to wait on you hand and foot, my dear.'

And after this ordeal comes another, the funeral feast. If it is called a feast. Up north they call it a funeral tea. 'They buried 'im with 'am!' Is that a saying or a song? I can't remember. Well, we shall bury Sarah with an especially splendid cold buffet and excellent wines. As hostess to such an event, how shall I strike the balance between private desolation and social warmth? What more will they expect of me?

'Darling Rina. So wonderful. You've been so wonderful all along. I say no more, darling. You know how we feel. You know where to find us.'

If only they would leave me alone. If only I could be left to lie on Sarah's grave and cry for her, call for her. Sarah. Sarah.

But I continue to mouth platitudes and to remain composed.

The meeting between the two men takes only a few minutes. Giles gives the impression of being courteous but firm. Our mourner receives his words with suitable mortification, bows his head, replaces his hat, and walks quickly away. My husband stands there for a few moments, looking after him, seeing him off the premises, as it were, and then returns.

Apparently the reason for his presence is neither

mysterious nor poignant. At any other time Giles would be jaunty, grinning at the absurdity of the situation. But his face is sallow, his smile a mere grimace.

He says, for my ear alone, 'No one we know, or who knows us. Just some nutter who likes attending other people's funerals! I asked him to have the goodness to leave us alone.'

This news gives a final air of unreality to the occasion. My husband takes my arm and we walk away, leaving our daughter by herself for eternity in an ocean of flowers.

TWO

March 1975

I have been up in Lancashire, nursing my mother through a sharp bout of bronchitis. She caught a cold at Sarah's funeral and was really ill at one stage, coughing and crying, 'They might as well bury me with that little lass!' An attitude which helped nobody. As soon as our Dr Guthrie said she was fit to travel I drove her home and stayed with her for ten days while she convalesced. This was easier on all of us.

Quite apart from the pall of misery hanging over the entire household, Giles's kindness, Joshua's devotion, and my most hospitable efforts can never disguise the fact that my mother is not at ease with us, nor we with her. This is only partly due to our different life-styles. She is not at ease anywhere but on her own ground, so much of a hermit has she become. Her insularity is further complicated by a total lack of trust in herself and others, and her conversation is laced with worries. She doesn't want to be a nuisance to anyone, she says for the hundredth time. And for the hundred and first, 'I should never have left Mrs Greenhalgh in charge of the shop!'

The corner shop in Salford has been in my mother's family since the turn of the century, providing a modest living for two generations of widows and fatherless daughters from two world wars. Virtually a museum piece in a run-down area, it is certain to be demolished sometime in the future and replaced by an office block, council flats or a supermarket, but I hope that will be after my mother's death. The shop is Ethel's home and her being.

So I took her back, and also took myself back, because I could find no solace in my immediate circle. Mourn, and ye shall be comforted, said the vicar. But people have different ways of mourning, and none of them seem compatible. Friends avoid the subject of Sarah, lest they upset me. Giles is taking out his grief in work and silence. And if I see Joshua's secret smile or moving lips just once more I might be driven to slap him.

Inwardly Ethel is delighted to have me to herself for a while and to vaunt me and my apparent devotion before her neighbours. Outwardly she bemoans the trouble she is causing, and frequently leaves her bed to do so. Clutching a crocheted shawl modestly to her throat, she displays the skirt of a winceyette nightdress, a pair of old blue-veined ankles and scuffed carpet-slippers.

'As if you hadn't enough without this. And to think of a lady in your position, serving in a shop. Whatever will Giles say . . . ?'

'He'd think it was amusing, Mother. After all, I'm used to serving the public. An estate agent's office is only another sort of shop.'

'A sight posher shop than this!' she replies tartly.

Despite years of failure and exasperation, I try to bolster her self-image. 'Shops are shops are shops, Mother. I don't mind and Giles doesn't mind. Now, please will you go back to bed instead of shivering on the stairs? I'll bring you a cup of tea as soon as the rush-hour's over.'

'Rush-hour! What rush-hour?' she cries scornfully.

'Between the children coming out of school and the mothers doing last-minute shopping for high tea. I'd call that rush-hour, wouldn't you?'

I have pleased her. The shop has a rush-hour, like London traffic. She stands there smiling tentatively, in her sick-pink nightdress, small and old and cold. God knows where she bought the thing. I sent her a couple of enchanting Welsh red flannel gowns with tucked bibs and frilled collars and cuffs, and have never seen them since. This garment is strictly utilitarian and devoid of style and charm.

'Off you pop!' I say humorously, covering my impatience.

She drives me dotty at times and we have nothing in common apart from the blood tie, which too often constricts. But because I loved my daughter and know how much my mother loves me, I feel guilty that I can't return her love in adequate measure.

Curiously, I find life more bearable here than in London, though a dozen times a day I am reminded of the chasm between her standard of living and ours. The front parlour upstairs is set aside for a myth known as 'visitors'. In this she keeps her uncut moquette three-piece suite, her floral carpet, framed photographs of her wedding and mine, and a sprigged china tea-service in a glass-fronted cupboard. Though everything is dusted each day, polished once a week and spring-cleaned annually, I can only remember it being used on one occasion, for Grandma's funeral. My wedding reception was held in a chic little restaurant near Putney, and Giles and I paid for it.

There is one other sacred place in the household. The back parlour sideboard has been set up as a shrine to my father, who died for his country in 1943. We never knew each other, and I have felt the lack of that vital relationship since early childhood. For years I pretended he was alive and would one day march round the corner of the street and claim us. But I was roundly discouraged from such fantasies, and gradually relinquished them. He was not a local man, so no one really knew him. There was no family on his side to remember him for me, nor were my mother or grandmother imaginative enough to re-create him. Instead they set him up as a symbol of his generation, an unsung hero, and made him a mere obituary notice in my life. Set on a lace doily and flanked by a couple of matching vases, his image stares uncompromisingly at the viewer. His brows are thick and dark and straight. His mouth beneath the dashing moustache is firm. An intensely masculine man with a hint of recklessness. I wish I had known him.

The rest of the house is a muddle of draughty passages, narrow stairs and chill rooms, of worn lino and odd rugs, and the sort of beaten-up furniture you see on a rag and bone cart. She lives in the back parlour behind the shop, stuffy and cosy, uses unmatched crockery bought from market stalls, nibbles and sips like a church mouse, and grudges the purchase of a new dishmop. Her income is small and her independence great. Giles and I would like to give her an allowance, but this she will not permit. When we try to help her unobtrusively she treasures our presents but does not use them. Yet it is not poverty which forces her to deprive herself of comforts but lack of self-regard. My mother is not worth much in her own opinion. She has always been like this. With great difficulty I persuade her to turn on the one-bar electric fire in her bedroom, pleading her bronchitis and the wintry weather. I expect she turns it off as soon as I go out.

But in her eyes I am the most wonderful person in

the world, and on the rare occasions that I visit her she casts economy to the winds. All the luxuries we have given to her she saves for me. The electric blanket, the feather duvet and pillows, the pretty sheets, are on my bed. The dressing-table displays linen and lace mats I brought her from Belgium, a set of tortoise-shell and silver brushes. Her own contributions, on the bedside table, are a blue pottery bowl of assorted fruit, violets in a jar which (judging by its shape) once held Shippam's Paste, and (until I gave up smoking last year) a packet of my favourite brand of cigarettes, a Present from Blackpool ashtray and a box of matches in a red silk knitted cover.

In my youth I accepted this homage as of right, and lived up to the image she created. Even my name set me apart. Marina, after the Duchess of Kent. Lancastrians do not take kindly to airs and graces. Local children called me Lady Muck to my face. I was not allowed to play with them. Unfortunately, the sort of children my mother regarded as proper company were not allowed to play with me. So I worked my way up and out, in solitary pride and self-regard, and re-created myself, and married a man who was also on his way up in the world. As they say round here, I did well for myself.

Usually I am regarded as an exotic stranger and the social exchange is stilted. But this time my mother is ill, I am running the shop, and I have lost a child. Service and suffering make us temporarily equal. There is genuine compassion for me, as well as a sneaking satisfaction at watching me weigh out their goods and give them change with a smile and a thank you. Conversation improves.

And for me it is a distraction from the void I must confront when I return to London. I have some sense of identity here. They remember me as I used to be. They admire and envy, even if they dislike or despise, what

I have become. Hourly, daily, I can present myself to this old looking-glass and receive its compliments, know that I exist.

I see also what I might have become. Old classmates slop into the shop, shapeless and hopeless with family responsibilities. I treat them with what I hope is cordiality but fear is kindly patronage. Take Betty Hurst, for instance, who once sat at the same school desk, and now weighs thirteen stones and looks at least ten years older than me. To serve her with twenty Players Medium and a block of Toblerone is intensely reassuring, because for a few moments I can relax, knowing I was right to give up smoking, to keep my figure and make the most of myself. And I have done well with that, too. At seventeen I was a reasonably good-looking but forgettable girl. At thirty-five I give the impression of former beauty.

'What a stunner Marina must have been!' a new acquaintance once said to Giles, who reported the past-tense compliment, knowing it would amuse me.

'Of course, I agreed,' he told me, 'but actually, darling, it wasn't your appearance but your potential that was stunning.'

My husband, for whom teaching is a philosophy and hobby as well as a profession, has been my schoolmaster. I wanted to study at university. I didn't particularly mind what. Any arts degree would have done. English, languages, history of art. I was good at them all, and social segregation at the high school had turned me into a swot. But there was no money for further education. Ethel scraped herself to the bone even to send me to secretarial college for a six-months' shorthand-typing course, which I accomplished in just over half the time. I must admit that secretarial work gave me my first taste of freedom, and the training has been useful in many ways. But ambition made me hungry for much, more more than that. I was famished for learning. Giles laid the table before me, and I have dined at it ever since.

And he, coming from a suburban background with greater pretensions but no more style than mine, longed for beauty, order and refinement. He instinctively knew what looked, felt, sounded right, yet had no notion how to achieve it. Strangely enough, I did. A magpie, I pick up anything that shines. A starling, I mimic amazingly well. My eyes and ears are alert for ideas. My fingers are nimble. I am a compulsive worker. Within months of coming to London I knew exactly what I wanted, and what I wanted to be. I have spent the last seventeen years achieving it.

So, although no marriage is perfect, ours is considered so among our friends. I would have called it symbiotic, for what one lacks the other provides. Giles feasted me on education. I created for him an elegant home and life-style. And the children, of course. Though Joshua was often a problem, and then Sarah died.

Here, among contemporaries who allow life to happen to them, rather than using it for their own purposes, I am somebody of importance who has nothing to prove. In London I must run to stay in the same place, and I am constantly on the alert for deficiencies in this and that department. Have I read, seen, listened to or attended, the latest books, magazines, films, plays, concerts? Was Greece the best choice for our holiday last summer? Wouldn't Yugoslavia be more fashionable? Should I try transcendental meditation? Are aerobics preferable to yoga? Am I too formally dressed, or is that quasi-Indian style really as tatty as it looks?

Years of observation, application and imitation have made me what I am. Never call me vain. I was humble, and anxious to learn. I knew that art and study could improve on nature, and they did. But sometimes I do wonder whether I exist at all, or am merely a collection of fashionable items cunningly assembled under the name of Marina Meredith.

THREE

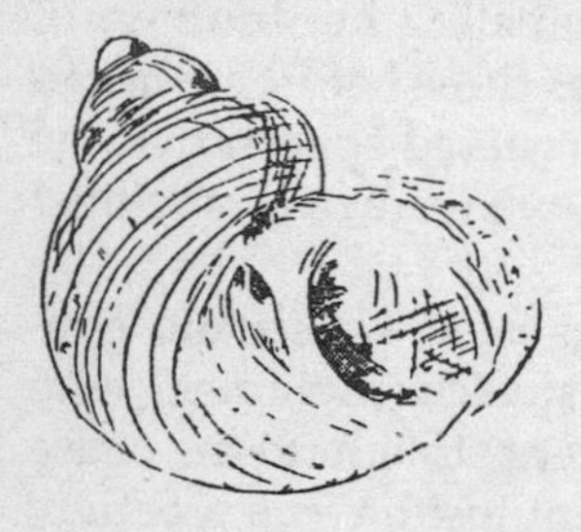

March–April

Easter came cold and early this year. Home again in time for the school vacation, I scorch my legs by the fire and wonder who can help me. In my hand I hold a tactful and kindly letter from Joshua's headmaster, which I have read until I know it by heart, and still cannot answer.

After the usual condolences over our tragic loss, he says that Joshua's behaviour has reached new heights of eccentricity. That he believes this to be due entirely to shock, but wonders whether we should seek professional help for his troubled state of mind. He suggests that we keep the boy at home until the edge of his grief is less keen. Possibly an extended holiday will settle him down? And he does venture to think that our decision to send him to a boarding-school in September may perhaps be premature under the circumstances. He offers any help we think he might be able to give, concludes that all shall be well, and assures us that we have his understanding and sympathy at all times.

Sarah has taken not only herself away but my image as a successful mother. With Sarah in the foreground I could almost forget Joshua in the background. My vital and delightful daughter obscured his failings. The fact that my son lurked in her shadow did not matter so much. Giles and I told each other that he was a shy boy and a late developer. We had deprecated, more in pride than anger, Sarah's way of dominating her brother, of holding the stage. But Joshua was three before he began to talk, and no sooner had he mastered speech than he developed a stammer. Instantly, we were overwhelmed with advice.

His kindergarten teacher suggested we should consult a speech therapist. The speech therapist, who treated him for some months, went straight to the cause of the problem. In her judgement Joshua was woefully hampered by Sarah's strong personality, and until he could extricate himself the stammer, or its behavioural equivalent, would persist. In this she was backed by our darling Mrs Tavey, who had looked after the children since they were two years old. Neither of them thought that Joshua was abnormal, but both of them advised us to separate the twins when they left kindergarten, and encourage Joshua to pursue his own course.

Guiltily, obediently, we sent them to different day schools. Yet on the first report his form master wrote, 'Joshua does not concentrate and finds it difficult to mix with other children', whereas Sarah was the most popular girl in her class and always among the top five pupils.

We had them assessed for intelligence and aptitude. Surprisingly, the tests revealed that Joshua's IQ was higher than Sarah's.

Now thoroughly confused, we turned to our family doctor: a man of humour and common sense. Who said, 'In my humble and old-fashioned opinion you are compounding the problem by correcting Joshua and showing him that you worry about him. Leave the boy alone, and let him find his own feet.'

So we stopped fussing and tried to ignore his little eccentricities.

I sip tea, and long for a cigarette, and watch my son in his absorption, building a house of cards on the carpet. He smiles to himself. His soft ripe lips move in silent conversation. The eyes behind his spectacles are dark and gentle and worlds away.

By his side sits Webster, a contrary-minded marmalade eunuch of dubious ancestry and no grace, a misfit if ever I saw one, but fortunate with it. His Providence brought him to our garden one Sunday morning six years ago, a forlorn and bony outcast trying to steal bread from the birds. The twins insisted that we adopt him, and called him Webster. I don't know why. Overfed, well-housed and spoiled to distraction, the animal has remained mistrustful and, to sum him up in one word, cantankerous.

I return to the headmaster's letter, which Giles gave to me the morning after I arrived home, speaking almost breezily. 'Oh, and by the way, Rina, will you deal with this well-meaning epistle? I'm awfully busy with end of term, and you're off work at the moment and always so marvellous at this sort of thing. I rang him up and told him you were away and I'd discuss the matter with you when you got back. Actually, there's nothing to talk about. I have no intention of changing my mind about Josh going to Jefferson's in September, because I'm convinced that's the answer. There's a much more open approach there, with emphasis on individual development. Though from the tone of the letter you'd think we were sending him to Dotheboys Hall!

'As for eccentric behaviour, the boy's in a state of shock and grief, nothing to do with behavioural problems. In another few months he'll be a different fellow. By all means let him have a holiday at home.

You're on extended leave from work, so that's no problem. But if you think we should consult anyone else then go ahead. Darling, just do what you feel is best.'

Giles has not been able to talk about Sarah since she died. Now I know that he is not prepared to discuss Joshua either.

At the sixth storey the house of cards falls down.

Joshua reddens with anger, muttering furiously, 'Leave it *alone*, Sarah!'

I have had more than enough. Despite all kind advisers who say I should ignore the Sarah-fixation, I pull my son up from the floor and shake him with savage emphasis as I make my points.

'You *stupid* boy! You are *not* playing with Sarah. Sarah is *dead*. We *buried* her six weeks ago. And if you ask me you know *very well* she's dead. You're just *pretending*, to attract attention. I'm sick of your *nonsense*. So just you *stop* this minute, or I'll *slap* you!'

Webster heads for the door in terror and scrabbles at the immaculate white paintwork, but for the moment I am not concerned with him.

Joshua and I face each other in stunned silence. Then I let him go, and smooth out the headmaster's letter, which has been crumpled in my hand.

He says nothing, and begins to sidle backwards towards the door. There is an air of cunning about him that infuriates me further. I advance, brandishing the letter, saying all the things I think about him and have been advised not to say, and am nearly thrown down by Webster who dashes through my legs, seeking safety under the sofa.

'Out!' I am shouting. 'Out! Both of you. Out!'

From his sanctuary Webster howls dolefully. But Joshua, now struggling with the door-knob, gives a shrill, thin shriek like a rabbit in a trap. The howl I can ignore, since Webster is a shocking old ham, but the shriek stops me instantly in my tracks.

I say as calmly as I can, 'Sorry, Josh. I didn't mean all that. Just play somewhere else for a while, will you? I'm a bit jangly this afternoon.'

And walk away from him and sit down, trembling.

'You, too, Webster. Off you go. Go with Josh, there's a good cat.'

The animal gives a terrible performance of cringing past me. Joshua grabs him and retreats. I hear him sobbing all the way to his room, calling on Mrs Tavey as upon a benevolent mother-goddess, and begin automatically to gather up the cards which Sarah scattered. I am no good at anything, no good with anyone, any more.

' . . . and I have this tension in my head, like a band pulling tighter and tighter. Is it just nerves? Or could it be a physical symptom? Giles, are you listening?'

Our domestic bliss, so lovingly created and sustained, has vanished. Our supper was an indifferent Chinese take-away. My present catalogue of woes and fears has prevented Giles from enjoying his evening drink and evening paper. He has put both of them away from him and is sitting opposite me, hands knotted between his knees. His expression is hunted, worried, exasperated, and wary.

'Darling, it's simply tension. Let me make you a hot drink. Or you can lie down for half an hour and practise deep breathing . . . '

I am not to be put off the scent. 'But there's something wrong with my head. My mind won't work. I tried to write to Joshua's headmaster for hours, and I simply couldn't put the words together.' Pathos becomes protest. 'So I haven't done it. And I don't want to do it.'

He sighs and says, 'Then I'll do it. Rina, darling, I have essays to mark . . . '

But I will not let him escape. 'Darling, can't you take an evening off just for once? Why don't we go out? Mrs Tavey would sit with Joshua for us.' I reach across him for the entertainments page, saying, 'There are loads of things we ought to see!'

'But not this minute on a whim!' he cries, understandably annoyed. 'Certainly, we can go out, Rina, but it needs to be arranged . . . '

I relinquish the *Evening Standard* at once and am off like a hound on a different trail. 'Then talk to me. Simply sit and talk to me for half an hour. It's not too much to ask. You've hardly spoken a word since you came home.'

'I haven't had much chance,' Giles says, with truth. 'What do you want to talk about?' He attempts to reason with the unreasonable. 'Darling, this sort of nightly inquisition is becoming a habit, and it isn't like you.'

I know it isn't but I cannot stop. I intend to hunt my quarry down.

'No, I was very convenient, wasn't I? You could leave everything to me. And I did it all beautifully, didn't I? But if I'm not well and life isn't perfect you've got no use for me, have you? Have you?'

His face is full of concern and disbelief. He comes over to put his arms round me and I push him away.

'No! Don't touch me. I won't be mollified.'

This stings him and he shouts, 'For God's sake, Rina. What *do* you want? It's like living with a total stranger.'

Tears, now. And with their release comes the truth. I cry, 'We're *both* living with strangers. You might be on the moon as far as I'm concerned, and I need you. I want you to want me, and to be with me, and to talk to me properly – not about the school and the weather.'

He stands apart from me, hands in pockets. He is in safe hiding, and I have lost the scent.

He says stiffly, 'We've suffered an appalling loss, Rina. We can't expect to be the same as we were. Things will get better in time. So long as we're together we'll pull through.' Since this is no comfort he makes a show of picking up the evening paper and saying, 'I suppose I could mark the essays tomorrow. Let's see what's on at the local cinema.'

I wipe my face and hands, trembling, thinking. Then I give up.

'No,' I say very calmly, in quite my old manner. 'I'm going to bed, Giles. Probably for good.'

I am staying in bed and keeping the world at bay. We live on frozen food. I refuse to answer the telephone or to receive visitors or to go out under any pretext whatsoever.

I hand over all domestic responsibilities to my twice-a-week treasure Mrs Pettit, who is only too anxious to oblige me. Mrs Pettit, red-cheeked and boot-button-eyed as a wooden Mrs Noah, broad of beam and bosom, eloquent with Cockney phrases, loves death, funerals, major operations and gloom. Up to now I have kept at a cordial distance from Mrs Pettit, but tragedy makes sisters of us both. I need to indulge my grief. She encourages me to wallow in it. For the moment it seems that Mrs Pettit is the only person who understands me.

No, perhaps Joshua does, since he is behaving in a similar manner. Released from the pressures of school he also retreats, though his fantasy world seems happier than mine. We are both slightly mad, he and I, and this graceful white house at the edge of a green is our private Bedlam.

Our family doctor, Ralph Guthrie, stands at the foot of my bed, looking nonchalant, as if he happened to be passing by and thought he might look in. Which is nonsense, because nowadays doctors only call on serious cases.

He has been announced very confidentially and intimately by Mrs Pettit, who is no doubt lingering outside the door listening on the landing. Giles must have asked him to see me. We both like Ralph, who was so wonderful with and about Sarah. So I suspend my rule about no visitors and prepare to hear him out, just on her account.

He comes to the point with admirable promptness. 'I understand how you feel, Marina,' he says, sitting in a chair by my side. 'You're at the end of your rope and can't make any further effort. But you're worrying Giles to death, and this sort of behaviour can only encourage Joshua to backslide as well.'

I say factually, unemotionally, 'I'd die if I could, but I don't know how to.'

'I've known you for several years. You're not the suicide type,' he replies briskly. 'Too much of the ringmaster about you for that.'

I need him to understand my position. 'I wasn't talking about suicide. I meant that I should *like* to die.'

'And leave your husband and son to fend for themselves?'

'I'm no use to them anyway.'

He tries another approach. 'I know you don't like the idea of Valium, but I can prescribe some other tranquilliser to help you over this bad patch.'

'I don't like tranquillisers of any kind. They can't take trouble away and they'll make me too woolly to deal with it. Like having a nightmare and not being able to wake up.'

He is doing his best, despite me.

'Look,' he says, slightly uncomfortable with the suggestion, 'I know you're not a religious person – like most of us nowadays – but I do find that people who have a faith deal with grief far better. Isn't it worth asking your local vicar to call in?'

'No, it certainly is not,' I say positively. 'Nor, in case you're about to suggest it, do I want to talk to a psychiatrist.'

Opposing him makes me feel less of a victim. But just as I think I'm in charge of the conversation twin rivers of tears, unpredictable and despised, pour down my face.

I cry out in desperation, 'If only I could be left alone I'd heal in my own way in my own time, but no one will let me.'

The tears keep pace with my sudden eloquence.

'If someone breaks an arm you don't expect them to use it. But I've broken a main spring somewhere inside me, and yet I'm expected to think and talk and make plans about a thousand things, when all I want to do is to work through my trouble. No one taught me how to lose a child, and I don't know how to do it. I'm having to find out how to do it, every minute of the day and the night, don't you see? I don't want to be bothered with people and meals and laundry. I just want to *hide*. A cat hides when it's sick, for God's sake. Why can't I?'

That seems to sum up my case.

'Sorry about this,' I say, quite sensibly, of the tears, 'I can't help . . . '

He makes a little gesture of reassurance. I reach for the Kleenex and stem the flow. 'It happens,' I say, and dry my eyes.

He has made up his mind about me. His voice and face are decisive. 'This is the age of the easy answer,' he says surprisingly. 'We expect everything to be instant. But without tranquillisers and antibiotics to fall back on, your old-fashioned family doctor used to let nature take its own time and its own course. Now you and Giles are literary-minded people. How would you describe your present condition, in Victorian terms?'

For a moment I return, intrigued, to the present. I think of Elizabeth Barrett Browning decoratively arranged on her sofa.

'Not in quite such vigorous health as we could wish?' I suggest, smiling.

'And what, as your Victorian doctor, would I prescribe for that condition?'

A whiff of enjoyment has re-entered my life.

'Sea air?'

'Exactly so. A month at least. Longer, if possible. Why not spend the whole summer getting well again? Take young Joshua with you. He needs time to adjust as well. Remember that Sarah was more than his sister. She was his twin. They shared the womb. He's lost half of himself.'

But I am reluctant to take Joshua, who is part of my trouble, and seek delicately to evade this responsibility. 'I'm sure he'd much prefer to live between Giles and Mrs Tavey. To be quite frank, Josh and I get on each other's nerves at the moment.'

Ralph Guthrie is brisk with me. 'If Joshua feels that you're walking away and leaving him he'll be in serious trouble. Going off on a special jaunt together should help you both to readjust, and will give the boy some confidence.'

As I hesitate, he says sharply, 'For heaven's sake, Marina, he's not a demanding child. He'll be perfectly happy to potter about on some beach while you sun yourself in peace, or read a book.'

I am in the wrong and have no option but to agree. Still I must quibble.

'But how would Giles manage?'

'Presumably as he's managing now, with your Mrs Pettit to look after him. And with the added bonus that he needn't worry about either of you because you're both getting better. Besides, if you choose a south coast resort he can come down every weekend.'

Thinking about it, I am not sure that I want Giles to come down every weekend. I need a long cure of uninterrupted time and space. Nor would he be allowed to come alone more than once or twice. The prospect of a trip to the seaside would be too great a temptation for our circle of friends. They would begin with the suggestion of popping in for the day to cheer me up. 'You won't have to do a thing for us, darling. We'll bring a picnic lunch and be off again after tea.'

Nevertheless they pack sleeping-bags in the car, just in case, and stay so late that they have to use them. The next visit will blossom into a full weekend. By the summer I shall be spending Fridays getting ready for everybody, Mondays getting over them, and three days in the middle planning for the next assault. As the summer holidays begin I can expect weekends to become weeks.

Naturally, I don't say this. Instead, I thank Ralph Guthrie who has given me life and hope, and run an aromatic bath and soak myself in it for half an hour, working out my escape and a delicious evening menu. Mrs Pettit does some late shopping, with many disappointed murmurs about being glad to see me looking more like myself. I send her home and cook the first really good meal in several months.

Seeing me occupied and apparently sane again, Joshua emerges from his room and asks if he can draw at the kitchen table. I say yes, but not to ask me a lot of questions because I am still jangly. Webster, who never gives a feather or a fig for anyone's jangles, winds round my legs, claws my tights, and jumps up on the draining board, begging for a taste of everything I prepare whether he likes it or not. Irritation further renews me.

By the time Giles comes home I have changed

into an exotic house-gown embossed with dark-green leaves and strange blue trumpet flowers. I am in charge of myself again, recognisably Marina Meredith. Joshua, who prefers plain, quick, or take-away food, has been fed on chicken and chips. But for Giles and myself I have seethed the chicken in peaches and ginger, made saffron rice, tossed up a green side salad, poached plums in port and partnered them with rich almond cake. A bargain red Rhône from Oddbins comes to room temperature. The meal is prayer, placation and apology. I want my husband to give me leave to go, and when he does I shall fly far, far away.

In my childhood, holidays were few, cheap and local, except for one. My father was killed in Italy in 1943, and Ethel took his death badly. Theirs was a brief war-time marriage, to be reckoned in months, and he had been drafted abroad before I was born. So her memories were few and emotionally extravagant. Shock and grief provoked her lungs, always weak, to succumb to bout after bout of bronchitis. She took to her bed all winter, and the doctor said she must convalesce in a kinder climate than the North Country could provide.

When money is short, blood ties become strong. My father, whose own mother had come from the West Country, still had a cousin there. She was informed of his death and Ellen's plight, and persuaded to have the pair of us for a pittance while my mother recovered her health. I was then three years old. Grandma stayed in the shop and earned our small allowance, and Ethel and I set off for Cornwall early in 1944 and stayed there throughout the spring and summer. She used to start crying suddenly, silently. As I have cried, as I am crying still, for Sarah.

We travelled back by night, almost a year after my father's death, and the journey took eighteen hours. I was the only child in the compartment and the passengers made much of me. I remember our train standing in Penzance station, parallel to another train. They were blacking out the windows, preparatory to starting, but our blinds were still up and so were those of the sleeping carriage opposite. In a narrow space, in an oblong of light, I saw a young army officer and a girl with a long black bob of hair standing opposite each other, laughing as if in triumph. He put his arms round her waist and pulled her to him. They kissed. Then he saw they were on view, said something to her, laughed again, and drew down the blind.

It happened in a few seconds. I was sitting on my mother's lap and squirmed round to look at her. All my questions boiled down into one.

I said, 'Why are those people laughing?'

'I expect they've just got married,' she said, and gave a small shuddering sigh and added, 'in spite of everything.'

For a moment I was afraid she might cry and disgrace the pair of us, but she was past that phase. Her face was sad and yet exultant, and I knew she could now think of my father in peace.

That image, one of my earliest, burned in. When Giles and I married I wanted to honeymoon in the West Country and take a sleeper overnight, to re-create that moment of laughter, of life being at its peak. But we went to Brittany for a week instead, and journeyed prosaically by day.

I have often wondered what became of the officer and his black-haired girl. They will be in their fifties and grey now, their children grown and gone.

On an impulse I ring up my mother, ostensibly to ask how she is.

Fair to middling, she says stoically.

In truth I am searching for roots of a kind, for an excuse. I say that Dr Guthrie advises a change of air for Josh and me, and I was wondering about

Cornwall. Whereabouts did we have that holiday, so long ago?

It was a farm on a place called the Lizard, says Ethel, but she can't rightly recall where. After all, I mustn't forget that I'm talking about thirty years back. She used to send my father's cousin a card and a letter at Christmas for quite a while after. Then the lady died very sudden, and of course the husband wasn't what you could call related. So they lost touch. She can't even remember their name now. But the farm began with a Pen- or Pol- something, and ended in a -gelly or a -genza. Or was it -glaze or -goose? Can't have been -goose, surely? Now, what was that farm called?

I have a map of Cornwall spread out before me on the telephone table. With what my boss calls my customary sharpness, and Ethel calls being too clever for my own good, I connect two disparate facts.

'Mother, if we were down somewhere on the Lizard why did we leave from Penzance station? It must be fifteen or twenty miles away,' I ask.

'I wanted to make sure of a seat, my lady,' she answers with some asperity. 'It was war-time, you know.'

My search for a hiding-place, circling closer and closer, has settled on one small patch, but I am booking at the last minute and my requirements are too specific. Surrounded by holiday brochures, I run up a large telephone bill getting nowhere. That evening after dinner, sitting on the carpet, waiting for Giles to make the coffee, I draw a red ring round the last advertisement.

> ATTRACTIVE COTTAGE Lizard Peninsula. Secluded situation overlooking picturesque cove. Superb views. Will sleep four. Comfortably furnished. All mod cons. Telephone 0933 . . .

Giles, returning from a short absence in the kitchen, is flabbergasted. In the twenty minutes or so that he has spent stacking the dishwasher and making our after-dinner coffee I have booked Mrs Harvey's Hendra from mid-May to the end of August.

'Just now?' he keeps saying. 'While I was out, just now?'

I realise that I have become a difficult person to live with. I pretend not to notice that he is astounded and slightly hurt. As if he were as thrilled as I am, I chatter on, feeding him sippets of information.

'It was quite incredible. The cottage I wanted was only available for three weeks, but the owner recommended me to try a Mrs Harvey, who had inherited a similar sort of place belonging to her father. Father died last month and left it to her. She's thinking of doing it up and selling it, but there are various family complications. Meanwhile it's standing empty. So I rang her. And, Giles, when she lifted the 'phone she just said, "'Es?" – no name, no number. Just " 'Es?"?

'I have never in my life known a more reluctant landlady. She said Hendra was in "some awful state" after Father died, and she'd cleaned him through but he needed smartening up before she could do anything with him. It was a while before I realised that she meant the cottage, not the father! All very macabre. Then she launched into a long tale about Mr Tozer – isn't that Dickensian? – who is a builder and decorator. Mr Tozer has promised to smarten Hendra up, but he is busy at the moment and he cain't get to it!

'I couldn't help asking why she didn't find another builder who *could* get to it. And she said, "Oh, I cain't do that, my dear. John 'Enery Tozer be my mother's second cousin!"

'At this point I thought of our phone bill, and while she drew breath I asked her whether the cottage had running water, electricity, a kitchen and a bathroom. And yes, it had, and it overlooked a cove and was "some pretty". So I persuaded her to let it. She didn't know how much to charge and we finally agreed on a price which suited both of us. An absolute bargain, as far as I'm concerned! I've said that Josh and I will go down on the tenth. And I'm expecting, darling, that you'll join us the following week for Whitsun half-term, which will be lovely.'

I am expecting no such thing. Giles is not impulsive. He likes time to make up his mind, time to plan ahead, time to savour the idea. This is much too sudden. He shakes his head in negation and wonderment. I offer more sippets. He tastes them gingerly, swallows them incredulously, and endeavours to understand what has come over me.

'But, my darling Rina, no telephone at all? Not even a shared line? How are we going to keep in touch?'

'Mrs Harvey says there's a kiosk in the village, less than a mile away. I can take a brisk constitutional and phone you every evening if you like.'

He fears for me, away from the security of street-lamps and people.

'But, darling, surely you won't leave Josh by himself in an isolated cottage, and walk down some lonely country road in the dark?'

'It won't be dark before nine o'clock. I shall be ringing you around seven or eight, and I'll drive to the village, if that makes you feel happier, and bring Josh with me.'

'But suppose there's an emergency? How shall I reach you?'

'I'm sure Mrs Harvey would take a telephone message and pass it on. A village grapevine works faster than light! I'll ask her, anyway.'

'No television! No hi-fi! Not even a record-player? What on earth will you and Josh do in the evenings?'

'We've both got portable radios. And you were always on at Josh about watching too much television, anyway!'

To soothe him I proffer a piece of news that does not please me.

'Actually, we shall have neighbours. There's a large house nearby called Trenoweth, and they've got a telephone. It isn't her property but she keeps an eye on it and acts as go-between for the owners, who are living in the Far East at the moment. Apparently, what Mrs Harvey calls a handsome family has rented the house for the summer. The husband is an actor and he's making a film in Cornwall. They share a private path down to the beach with us. I'll have to get acquainted, of course, before we're on telephone terms – but no doubt that will happen.'

The handsome family cannot prevent Giles from being practical. 'Darling, have you considered the disadvantages of being a mile from the nearest village and several miles from the nearest town?'

'Mrs Harvey did say we should need our own transport. But that's no problem. I shall drive down in the Ford.'

He looks into the distance we must travel. 'The journey alone must be three hundred miles or more.'

'Darling,' my 'darlings' don't sound as affectionate as his, 'it's no further than driving to Lancashire, and there are plenty of good stopping-places. The West Country is absolutely littered with cafés serving cream teas.'

Still he tries to keep me within his orbit.

'Rina, I can understand your objections to, say, Brighton. People dropping in and so on. But if you must go to the West Country why not Dorset? Dorset is still reasonably near. Weymouth? Lyme Regis? Lulworth Cove?'

'I have a particular attachment to the Lizard,' I say

positively. 'Ethel and I had a very special holiday there during the war.'

Giles says, 'But, darling, it cuts out all hope of my popping down for weekends. It would take me a day to get there and another to get back.'

'Darling,' a very tough 'darling' indeed, 'there's no reason why you shouldn't come for Whitsun. And it will hardly be any time at all before the summer term ends.' Two months, in fact. 'And then you can join us whenever you like for as long as you like.'

I know that he is tied up until mid-August, because he is taking a party of boys to Switzerland for a fortnight. Nevertheless, the offer is there.

'But that gives us no choice of a holiday anywhere else, does it?' he enquires, reasonably enough. 'What about the Goddards' suggestion that we share their *gîte* in the Dordogne for a month? I could leave you and Josh there safely while I was away. And they'd be company for you.'

My tone is waspish. 'I don't want company and I don't want a holiday with the Goddards or anyone else. I'm trying to get away from people, not take them with me.'

He pours our coffee and offers chocolate mints, trying to come to terms with me and my cottage on the Lizard.

I say repentantly, 'Sorry, Giles. I know I'm not easy to live with these days. But it *is* what I need. And I promise you faithfully that Josh and I will sort ourselves out and come home happy and normal.'

Giles says, with a touch of humour, 'Since when has Josh been normal?'

Sipping coffee, he finds my future residence on the touring map, and is again filled with dismay.

'Good grief, Rina, you're going to the end of the world!'

FOUR

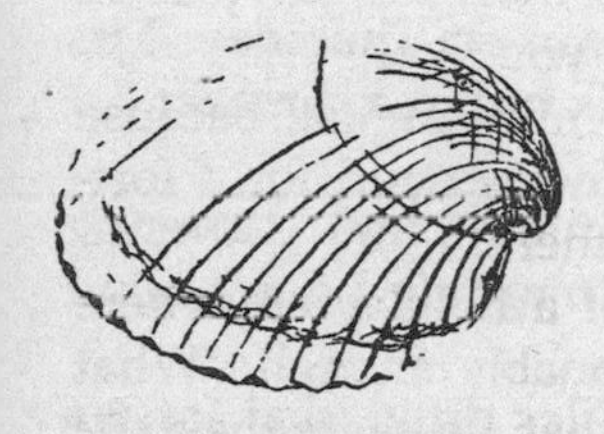

I have come out of that cold dark night in which I dreamed dreadfully, and emerged into everyone else's day. On a fine cool May morning Giles and Joshua and I breakfast together with a degree of normality which has long been absent. Webster, who is not allowed to eat before the journey and is consequently more bad-tempered than usual, writhes round my legs yowling, and then nips my calf with painful precision.

'He doesn't m-mean it,' says my son quickly, picking up the cat.

'While you've got him, Josh,' says Giles,. 'we may as well give him that sedative. Hold him by the scruff of his neck. Rina, grab his front legs. Keep still, you awkward old cuss. God, he's got the strength of ten!'

'D-don't w-worry, W-Webbie,' says Joshua.

He would like to say more, but cannot get his tongue round the words, so strokes the animal and kisses his flat head passionately.

Giles closes the cat's jaws together until the tablet is

swallowed. Released, Webster scratches Joshua's arm and escapes into the garden.

'Leave all this,' says Giles, of unwashed dishes and unmade beds. 'I'll do it when you've gone.'

An air of holiday excitement is about us. Giles brings my car round to the front of the house, and as I pack the picnic basket he stows our suitcases in the boot. We check our separate lists to make sure that nothing is forgotten for him or us. Mrs Pettit's cleaning days. Laundry van on Thursday. Mrs Harvey's telephone number. Milk ordered. Freezer list on wall. Our route, mapped out.

Joshua comes downstairs, humming and chattering to himself, or to Sarah, but this morning I don't mind as much as usual.

'Have you noticed,' I say to Giles drily, 'that Joshua doesn't stammer in his own world?'

'I expect,' says Giles sadly, surfacing for once, 'that we all communicate perfectly in our own world. It's this one that makes us stammer.'

And now I don't want to go away. I want us to make coffee and sit down and talk together. But the moment is over. Giles's stiff upper lip is in place again, and he says something sensible about stopping every two hours, even if we only get out of the car and walk round for a few minutes.

'Accidents happen when you're tired,' he says.

I can get this sort of information from the AA, and consider it a waste of time since I know it anyway. So now I am anxious to leave him, but Webster, in a fit of rage and cunning, has hidden himself. We hunt all over the garden and disturb our neighbours. Eventually the wretched animal is found fast asleep on our bed. We stuff him in his basket where he complains most dismally. We say our goodbyes over his howls, and laugh a little, and once again feel like a normal family.

'Ring me tonight, as soon as you've settled in,' Giles says.

'Make sure you eat proper meals,' I remind him. 'No snacking.'

'Come down as soon as you can, Daddy!' Joshua cries.

Not a s-s-s or a d-d-d in the sentence. Wonders never cease. Oh, yes, they do when he addresses me.

'C-can't I s-sit b-by y-y-y-y . . .'

'No, you can't,' I say crisply. 'It's not safe for children to sit in front. Stay in the back with Webster, and see if you can make him shut up. He's supposed to be sedated, for heaven's sake. I've no intention of listening to that appalling noise all the way to the Lizard!'

Joshua subsides instantly and obediently. I hear him crooning to the cat, who croons back dolefully. I switch on the radio to shut them out and retreat into my own world where, as Giles rightly says, I communicate perfectly.

Once away from the suburbs and onto the M3 we make good progress as far as Popham. The prospect and responsibility of a long drive to a strange place is exhilarating. I become my old self again, and decide that the day shall be a series of treats. I reflect how I must sound to my son, and am ashamed. When Joshua was part of Sarah-and-Joshua my tone used to be loving and funny and friendly. I must pretend that he is both of them.

My caustic self then reminds me that indeed he is, and I have been punishing him for just that offence.

I say in my twins-voice, 'Are you OK in the back, Josh? Shall we stop soon or press on to Salisbury?'

He manages, with a struggle, to say Salisbury. I notice that the cat's song of complaint has dropped an octave, though still disagreeable.

'So goodbye, Hampshire, and hello, Wiltshire! We're on the A30 now, Josh,' I say in my adventure-voice, '"and roads go ever, ever on" – remember *The Hobbit*? – all the way down to Penzance.'

I hear him retailing this information to Webster. Later he sings 'and roads go ever, ever on' very quietly, without stumble or hesitation.

In Salisbury we have coffee and orange juice, and I offer my son a choice of cakes because the morning is late, though still too early for lunch. I have brought the road map into the café with me, and consult it for the next possible stop, stalking my fingers across the page, counting up the miles.

Joshua wants to ask me what was the fastest speed I drove on the motorway. For once I interpret his question, instead of letting him struggle through it and wishing I could smoke a cigarette or have a drink.

'Ninety miles an hour,' I tell him, man to man.

His 'N-n-n-ninety?' is the greatest compliment he could pay me.

'And I know I shouldn't,' I add, 'but it was a good clear road and I didn't take any risks. Just don't tell Daddy!'

He shakes his head vehemently. His face is all admiration. He has an Eccles cake with his orange juice, which casts flakes all over his jersey and shorts. Afterwards he goes to the men's loo by himself, with pride.

Webster greets our return with such an anguished and piercing yowl that I look round anxiously, in case there are any RSPCA officers about to charge us with cruelty. Wavering, I endeavour to keep up our holiday mood.

'On we go! Lunch in Somerset!' I announce gaily.

But as Joshua falls over his Ps in excitement, and Webster continues to waul dementedly, I relapse into my testy self and say, 'Yes, yes, we'll find a nice field and have a proper picnic, Josh. Now let's be off, for God's sake, before that animal gets us arrested.'

And turn up the radio, and take my wrath out verbally on other drivers, who are all without exception either too slow or too fast. But gradually the day and the distance soothe me, and I have recovered my equilibrium long before we find a nice field and lay out our picnic in style. The coffee has kept well. I drink two cups and have a one-sided conversation with Joshua. My affability restores him. He manages to explain, without his usual difficulty, that Webster thinks he is being taken to the vet's, which frightens him, and also he probably wants to go to the loo.

In a fit of well-being I let Webster out for a pee and a few minutes' sociable chatting and stroking, so that he knows we still love him and mean him no harm. He is grateful for these attentions and very interested in his new surroundings, but runs away as soon as we show signs of returning to the car, and we waste half an hour capturing him.

'You s-see he's f-f-f—' Joshua begins, as I clamp the wickerwork lid down on Webster's cowering head.

'Yes, I know he's frightened, but you insisted on bringing him and now he's got to put up with it.'

Crestfallen boy and whimpering basket are stowed away. We resume our journey under a cloud which once again disperses. The miles and the afternoon draw on. It is nearly four o'clock when I fill the petrol tank at a Plymouth service station. We need another break, preferably with lots of hot fresh tea, but I can't see a handy café and daren't leave the road in order to find one. The coffee left in the flask is not worth drinking. So we share the last of the orange squash, visit our separate loos, and I buy a bag of barley-sugars to keep us going. In Cornwall, I promise Joshua, we shall have a cream tea. And at the Saltash bridge we experience a tremendous high. So far signboards have told us that we are entering a new county, otherwise we should never have noticed. Here the broad river, the towering bridge, the line of tollbooths, all proclaim that we are crossing over into the last West Country stronghold. Entering Cornwall is an event.

In homage to the moment I say, 'Goodbye, Devon! Hello, Cornwall!'

And Joshua tells Webster that we are almost there, which is a mistake. This is only the beginning of a distant end.

So far the roads have varied from good to excellent. Now they alternate between reasonable stretches and bottle-necks, and the traffic increases. We endure a particularly straggling two miles before Liskeard through a built-up area. At Bodmin we put on a spurt but dawdle behind lorries again afterwards. My neck and arms and shoulders ache. At Indian Queens I see a café and pull in. It has just closed. We pull out again, wait our turn to join the queue of cars, and wander on.

The villages come upon each other's heels now: Fraddon, Summercourt, Mitchell, Zelah. We trail in and out of them, one weary unit in a winding ribbon of cars and trucks, with the occasional tractor slowing everyone down to ten miles an hour. At Blackwater I pull into a lay-by and we assess our situation.

Webster has nothing more than a subdued meow left in him. He expects the worst and is ready and willing to die. I know exactly how he feels. It is nearly six o'clock. We should have been there by now. I walk up and down, easing my neck and shoulders, taking deep breaths to clear my head, looking at this new country. After the lushness of Devon it seems disappointingly hard and spare. The trees are low-growing, windblown, the landscape fairly flat, dotted with derelict engine-houses. Not what I expected. Joshua has been studying the map, and as I am tired and silent he becomes voluble and articulate.

'Not far now, Mummy. Only about twenty miles. See?'

I put my arm round his shoulders because he is trying to encourage and help me. He looks pleased and self-conscious. We start off again in better heart, and Joshua sings softly, faultlessly, 'We're off to see the Wizard . . . '

Then changes it to the Lizard, and sings louder, so that I shall marvel at his wit. ' . . . the wonderful Lizard of Oz!'

I join in. We miss the turning at Redruth and go on to Camborne, through which grey town we drive slowly, finding our way out to a winding road and scattered farms, through a village, which is simply a double terrace of stone houses, through two hamlets, which are mere clutches of cottages. Now and then we wait for a herd of cows being taken home late. Joshua directs me accurately and without a stumble. Fork left by the school. Turn left again by the garage, and down the hill into Helston.

Here we are momentarily confounded, since Meneage Street is one-way and not our way, but on arriving at another crossroads garage we find that the Lizard lies straight ahead and we cain't miss it.

We have the petrol tank topped up, and as we set off again I hear Joshua saying over and over to himself in rapture, 'No, you cain't miss et, my 'andsome!' for this is not only a new country but a new tongue.

In his enthusiasm he offers hope and comfort to Webster, who revives sufficiently to claw his master's hand through the grille in the basket.

On this cool May evening there is little traffic. The locals are all at home, no doubt consuming Cornish pasties and cream teas, and how I wish we were doing the same. Joshua, wide-awake and fascinated, is saying, 'Look, Mummy!' every few minutes.

'Look, Mummy! Culdrose! Where the helicopters are.'

Obligingly one comes in low, as if to salute us.

'Look, Mummy! The new satellite station!'

Listening saucers, on Goonhilly Downs.

Yet in spite of these modern intrusions we have entered an inner sanctum. This part of Cornwall is more remote than anywhere we have seen so far, and very tranquil at six forty-five on a Saturday evening, communing with itself.

'Look, Mummy! Smoke coming through chimneys!'

Joshua, child of a smokeless zone, finds the idea of an open coal fire irresistible.

Cars are few. I have entered upon that state of fatigue where I drive automatically and well. The road still goes on and on, with one or two perilous bends, but I know now that we are arriving.

'We stop at the next crossroads,' says Joshua, 'and Mrs Harvey's house is the big bungalow on the left, called Shangri-La.'

'Dear Christ!' I say under my breath.

I praise my son for his clear instructions. His stammer has disappeared. He sits bolt upright, observing everything, and is full of confidence. But when we enter Shangri-La, and I introduce us, he does not risk his errant tongue betraying him. He smiles and gives a little bow, which makes an excellent impression.

Mrs Harvey, as I see from the wedding photograph on the sideboard, has been a black-eyed, black-haired Cornish beauty in her heyday. Now she is short and stout with white fluffy hair, a brown weathered face, and a bad leg. Her demeanour is amiable, and when I tell her how long we have been on the road she treats us as tenderly as if we had come from another planet. She tells me that tea is waiting for us, but if we would like to wash our hands first then the bathroom is at the end of the hall.

We avail ourselves of both offers. I ask her if I might telephone Giles from here, as we are rather late and he may be worried. She gives gracious permission, and will not accept payment for the call.

Mrs Harvey's bungalow is large, light, modern, and sparkling like a television advertisement for furniture polish. She gives us its brief bland history as she pours tea into flowered china cups, and hands round the Cornish Fairings. This house, which I find so unexciting, is indeed Shangri-La for Mrs Harvey, who was brought up in Hendra on a joiner's wage, with six brothers and sisters, early in the century, when the cottage had no running water, no electricity, and a cess pit.

'Course, 'e aren't like that now,' she assures me. 'After the First World War my eldest brother 'Lias was working, and he built on and made improvements for Mother. Some smart! And when he and Willum went overseas they bought the cottage for Mother. But she died soon after, and Father warn't never one to spend tuppence when a penny would do, so he didn't bother no more. I give him our old 'lectric cooker and 'frigerator when we had new 'uns. But I don't think he used them much. So 'Endra aren't cabby, but he aren't as eyeable as he will be when I've finished with'm.'

Joshua's eyes are pink of lid and dazed over his steaming cup, and I expect mine look the same.

Mrs Harvey tells me that everything I ordered has been delivered, and the ice-cream put in the freezer compartment of the refrigerator. I shall find a list on the kitchen wall telling me where to buy or order food locally. There wasn't the special brands of tea and coffee I asked for, nor the cheese neither, so Mrs Martin put in what she stocks and hopes that will be all right. If I want something special I can get it in 'Elston. Mr 'Arvey lit the Cornish range for us two days ago to warm the place up, and her daughter went over this afternoon to dust round, make up the beds and lay the parlour fire. I can use the coal in the shed because it was Father's, but if I need extra I shall have to pay for it, prices being what they are. The beds have been well aired, so I needn't worry, and there are more blankets in the wardrobe and hot-water bottles in the bathroom.

Her litany, like the road, goes on. I sip my tea and fade blissfully away. Joshua watches and listens absorbedly. He is taking it all in and will probably remember more than I do tomorrow. At length I rise and thank her, accept the cottage keys with a little tingle of pleasure, and climb into the car for the last time that long day.

'Is Webster still with us?' I ask sardonically, of the unusual silence.

Hearing his name, the cat meows piteously.

'It's all right, Webs,' says the charitable Joshua. 'We'll be in Hendra soon, and you can have a double supper because you didn't get any breakfast!'

And still the road goes on and on. We miss the turning on the right, about which Mrs Harvey was perfectly explicit, coast down to the bottom of the road and are half-way to nowhere before Joshua calls a halt, suspecting a mistake. We retrace our route, crawling along at fifteen miles an hour, searching.

'There's the turning!' Joshua shouts urgently, as we almost pass it for the second time.

Trees mask it from the road. It looks like the lane to a farm, with its gate drawn back in permanent welcome, and is not in good repair. We bump carefully along in second gear, and pass Trenoweth first: an imposing, slate-roofed, granite building of classical proportions, no doubt suitable for the handsome family of whom Mrs Harvey evidently approves. Certainly it would be much too large and grand for us, and is not what I seek. This is a gentleman's residence, a place in which to be gregarious, and from which to dispense gracious hospitality. All I want is somewhere humble and remote where I can cower in peace.

'Thar she blows!' shouts Joshua in true whaling fashion.

Why Mrs Harvey referred to Hendra as he I will never know. Hendra is definitely a member of the female sex. She faces the sea in permanent contemplation, and her back is primly turned on us. If ever I saw a fixture growing from its native earth it is this sturdy cottage with thick walls and small windows irregularly placed, as if someone built her when he felt like it, and to suit his needs and fancy.

Joshua and I, tremulous with fatigue and in a state of unbelief, smile at each other in delighted silence.

I say, 'Shall we let Webster out first?'

Joshua desperately wants to go in, as I do, but says, 'Yes, let poor old Webs out. He's been in his basket all day.'

So we do, and watch him scurry old-maidishly behind a bush. We catch him as soon as he reappears and before he can escape again, and to prevent a mauling I wrap him firmly in my car coat, and hold him while Joshua opens the front door. The animal wails like a banshee.

Hendra's house-plan could hardly be simpler. Directly facing us, so that we almost walk up them when we walk in, is a short steep flight of stairs. A living room is to the right of the front door, a parlour to the left. Above is a bedroom apiece, built into the roof, with sloping wooden floors and low-set deep-seated windows looking out at the sea. In many places, being a tall woman, I have to stoop.

A single-storey extension at the back has been made into a small square bathroom and rectangular kitchen, scrupulously clean but sparsely furnished. On the flagged floor of the bathroom stands an old-fashioned iron bath with ball and claw feet. The inside has recently been repainted and the brass taps are brightly polished. A lavatory of the same vintage and a washstand complete with china jug and basin stand opposite. Between them is a scrubbed wooden duck-board. The little window is demurely veiled in crisp white net.

'I think Brother 'Lias did rather well for them!' I remark drily.

But remembering Mrs Harvey's luxurious turquoise bathroom suite I can see that such simplicity would not impress her.

In the kitchen I assume that the deep white glazed sink and wooden draining-board beneath the window were also the gift of 'Lias, but would guess that Father built in the cupboard and shelves. An old-fashioned electric cooker and refrigerator have been squeezed in along the same wall. In neither kitchen nor bathroom is there space for more than one person at a time, and that one moving sideways.

'No, 'e aren't cabby!' Joshua murmurs, and I smile.

In the living room a shining black-leaded Cornish range warms the cottage and provides hot water and an air of comfort. Father's furniture is plain, probably home-made, and in keeping. His walls were too rough to be papered, thank God, and have been Duluxed white. The parlour curtains and chair covers are in a pleasantly faded chintz, which Mrs Harvey has attempted to smarten up with quilted satin cushions. I put these away in a cupboard, and am content.

We minister generously to Webster's needs and make sure that he is shut in while we unpack the luggage. Then we butter his paws, brew another pot of tea and think about supper.

The cat, replete, washes himself all over, lies alongside the Cornish range, and winks at us with malign green eyes.

'He won't run away now, will he?' asks Joshua, concerned.

'I don't suppose so, but we must take a chance on that. We've done all we can, and I'm pretty sure he prefers comfort to adventure.'

Believing that boys need to be as domestic-minded as girls in whatever future lies ahead of them, I have brought up Joshua to be handy in the kitchen. He never had Sarah's innate gift for knowing what should be done, but learned by rote, followed instructions, and waited for further orders. Still, he makes himself useful. Now he peels potatoes neatly and slowly, and cuts them into thick even chips while I put away the groceries. Later he will lay the table in the living room with equal care and deliberation. I cook a quick meal: mixed grill. Joshua chooses Cornish ice-cream and tinned pears to follow.

Upstairs is sparsely but quite cheerfully furnished. There are war-time covers made from knitted squares on the single iron bedsteads in Joshua's room, and my room is dominated by a double brass bedstead with a cotton patchwork counterpane. We bounce on the mattresses speculatively, and remark that a hard mattress is good for the back.

A slip of the tongue mars the last few hours of companionship between my son and me.

Joshua says, 'Sarah wants the bed by the window. She *would*!'

Then he flushes, and to conceal his embarrassment he hums as he puts her teddy-bear on that pillow, and his bear on this one.

I ignore the reference to Sarah but say sharply, 'You won't be able to take those bears to boarding-school, you know. The boys will laugh at you.'

He averts his face and mumbles, 'I kn-n-ow, I kn-n-ow,' to forestall a lecture.

I am ashamed of myself for snubbing him, and say

hastily, but I fear ungraciously, 'It doesn't matter here, of course.'

I wish we could have left Sarah's bear at home. Personally, I would have buried the creature with her, since it was her constant companion throughout months of degeneration, but she bequeathed it to Joshua. That damned bear is a source of grief and misery to me, a constant reminder of my daughter. The twin bears play an active role in Joshua's phantom games. I suppose, at bottom, I am grieved that Sarah should manifest herself to him and not to me.

Downstairs, washing up furiously, I ignore the chuckles and muttered conversation overhead. This is a house without privacy. In Hendra you would have to quarrel in a low voice, and still the repressed anger would seep through the walls and up and down the stairs. So I hear Joshua murmuring to his twin, though I cannot distinguish the words, and I clatter our supper plates into the white glazed sink, to remind him not to talk too loudly. The dishes stacked, dried and put away, I nurse myself and my grief, make coffee and take it into the parlour. And there see a sunset so beautiful that it is almost ridiculous.

The window acts as a picture frame. Through clouds of fire a golden light streams down in benediction on a bright metallic sea; plum-blue cliffs and rocks flank either side. It is the sort of scene that Victorians painted, using its drama to point a moral to the tale they told. I could imagine this composition, with a ragged sailor on his knees in the foreground, being entitled *Delivered From The Vasty Deep*.

Glad to find an excuse to be friendly again, I call up the stairs, 'Josh, do look out at the sky. Have you ever seen anything like it?'

A boy of nine is not interested in sunsets, but my son understands that I am apologising. May God forgive me for being rotten to him. If God exists.

'G-gosh!' he cries. 'Can we g-go outside and s-see it p-properly?'

He is responding with gratitude, but also taking advantage of my guilt, for it is way past his bedtime. Still, this is a holiday and I owe him something. I owe him much.

'We'd better put our coats on,' I say. 'It may be a bit nippy outside. And we needn't lock the door. Mrs Harvey says that we're perfectly safe here. Isn't that different from London?'

At home we have twice been burgled, in spite of every precaution.

'There's our private path to the cove,' says Joshua, pointing.

But tonight we are new and strange to place and space, and do not venture out of our territory. Beyond the hedge at the end of the garden is a long drop to the road and we keep a respectful distance from it. It is enough to stand and look and sniff and listen. The air is cool, fresh and salty. Our new and constant companion, the sea, rushes forward and trails back, greeting us.

'S-some s-smart!' says Joshua, to make me smile again.

Gradually, the sky puts out its fires and the heavenly rays recede. A chill descends. Less than a hundred yards away we see the lights of Trenoweth one by one declare that their children are also going to bed late.

'Some' 'andsome family,' Mrs Harvey has said. 'The gentleman's an actor come down here to act in a film. I seen'm on the television. Moment I set eyes on'm I said, I seen you on the television. Conrad Gage, his name is. Well, you'll know'm when you see'm. He's English,but I think his wife's a foreigner. Some lovely woman. Very natural. And three dear liddle maids, and a dear liddle chap in arms. And a foreign nursemaid. The liddle maids have lessons from Miss Benney in the village, so they don't fall behind in their learning. Some fine teacher, Miss Benney is. Taught at the village school for nearly forty years. Retired now. You don't see so many 'andsome families like that these days, do you?'

Assessing my only child. Assessing me, my London clothes and London voice and London ways. Some selfish, she will think.

She doesn't know about Sarah, of course. I don't tell unless I must.

I say, politely but without enthusiasm, that we look forward to meeting the Gages, and hope one or two of the children might be of an age to play with Joshua.

I shall, while being amiable, protect my privacy. The beauty about any large family is that it is usually sufficient unto itself. The parents will not be yearning to meet kindred spirits. Provided I am nice to their children they will surely not mind if I keep my distance.

T-tomorrow,' Joshua says, 'can I g-go d-down to the b-b-b . . . ?'

The beach is too much for him.

My kinder self says, 'Yes, of course. Directly after breakfast. But you must be careful crossing the road, you know. Even though it seems so narrow compared to London it is a main road, and just as dangerous. And there are no pavements, either.'

The lack of pavements, or even a grass verge, is disturbing. More than Joshua's safety concerns me. I am concerned for myself. I cannot sustain further grief.

'I'll t-take c-care,' says Joshua. 'And I'll t-train W-Webster.'

We stroll back to the cottage in a mellow mood and find that we latched the door carelessly, in our trust, and it is now standing slightly ajar. Webster, never one to miss an opportunity, has departed and is probably trying to commit suicide to spite us. We woo him by name. 'Web-Web-Webbee!' We appeal to his subtlest feelings. 'Fish, fish, fish!' we cry in dulcet tones. But the cat, overfed and bloody-minded, does not respond.

We go to bed in total dejection, and I am relieved to hear Joshua talking to Sarah. I wish I had someone to talk to. The sea keeps me company until I fall asleep, and dream the journey all over again, with the endless road leading deeper and deeper into nowhere, and Hendra at the end of it like a child's house.

But God is merciful, as Ethel says. And sometimes she is right. I am wakened at three in the morning by my delighted son.

Crying, 'Webster's back. He *called* me, Mummy. He stood at the bottom of my window and *called* me. Like a *person*. And he's caught a *mouse*. Ever such a *fat* mouse. And he wants to sleep on my bed.'

This is strictly forbidden, but the three of us have been through so much together in the last twenty hours that I give permission readily, and even come in to tuck the pair of them up. On Joshua's bedroom hearth, as upon a pagan altar, is laid Webster's offering.

I leave it there. In thanks, or propitiation, to Cornish gods.

FIVE

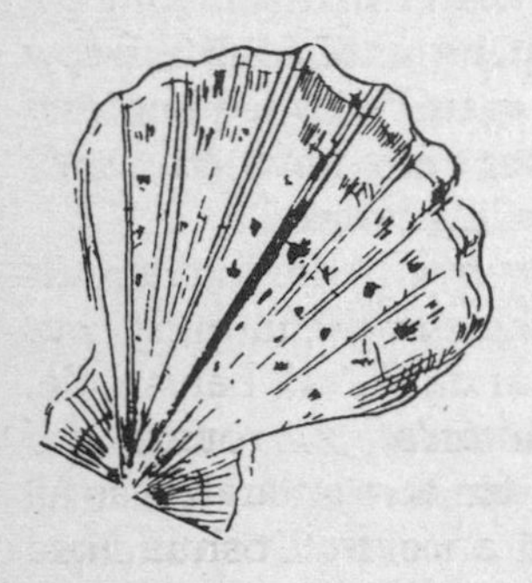

The day dawned cool and bright and clear, and we woke feeling that life had begun again. Joshua was too excited to eat breakfast, so I made him hot Ribena and packed a bacon sandwich in a greaseproof bag. The hedge, which protected us from a long drop, was thick-set but low, and I could look down on the cove from the parlour window. I laid down the house rules before he left.

'Always use the traffic code, even if the road seems empty. Watch the tide. You can be caught and stranded. Don't try to climb the cliffs. Take your watch with you, and remember meal-times. Half past twelve for lunch. Six thirty for high tea. Don't go off with *anyone*, man, woman or child, under *any* pretext, without telling me. If a stranger worries or frightens you, come straight home or blow your whistle and I'll hear it. I'll be keeping an eye on you, anyway, and I'll come down myself from time to time, to bring you a snack and see that you're all right.'

He nodded fervently while I was talking, shifting from one leg to another, longing to get away. Finally I released him, and watched him run down the path, bucket and spade clanking against each other, his bacon sandwich swelling the pocket of his red bomber-jacket. The latter part of the path and the road itself were hidden. I held my breath until I saw him emerge safely on the other side. He paused, looked up and waved, and then ran shouting onto the empty Sunday beach. My heart leaped in memory.

When he was but a little tiny boy he had loved our Saturday afternoon walks in the park. The entry was from two sides of a paved veranda with a balustrade, and beneath it trees, lake, children's playground, golf links and tennis courts spread for acres. Sarah was all for charging down the steps at once, but Joshua liked to savour it first. For his sake I used to pause, holding both twins by their hands: Sarah restive, tossing her long dark hair, Joshua quite still, gazing at the gardens below and on to the far horizon.

Then one day, as Sarah tugged me forward and he contemplated, my son had addressed the universe in reverence and with rapture. At three years old he was not as articulate as his sister. He said, 'O Park!' I reported it to Giles with glee that evening, and the phrase became a private joke if anything particularly delighted us.

Now, watching Joshua run free on the pale sand between the dark cliffs, I said, 'O Park!'

Then I made toast and tea and took it on a tray to the parlour and sat at the small deep window where I could watch him building a sandcastle. From there I could not hear him talking to Sarah, so I didn't mind.

I am not a monster. I do love my son.

At eleven o'clock, picking a bunch of wild flowers, I remembered that I had forgotten to look at Joshua and ran panicking to the hedge. But he was in good company. The sandcastle had come on apace and my son was standing lordly by it, spade over one shoulder, holding forth to an audience of three little girls with ash-blonde plaits. A few yards away on a plaid rug, a sultry young woman of statuesque proportions settled down to read a paperback book in peace. I could not make out at that distance whether she was the foreign wife or the foreign nursemaid, but provided that Joshua was safe I didn't mind and wasn't curious. His preoccupation with them set me free.

I had unpacked, sorted out and tidied round. Lunch and supper would be picnic meals. Tomorrow we should drive into Helston and find a good butcher, a good wine-shop and a good grocer who stocked Oxford marmalade, Earl Grey tea and coffee beans. I had no intention of being inconvenienced in my hermitage.

My mother, who brings her deity into every aspect of her life (and a very prosy and intrusive presence He is), used to say, 'Man proposes but God disposes'. In this instance she was right, because Joshua plunged into the kitchen as I was about to crack the first egg for our lunch, to say that he had made friends with three of the Gage children and their au pair girl, and they were following him up, and wanted him to eat with them, and could he, please, oh, please? And where was Webster, because he'd told them all about Webster and they wanted to see him.

'He ate a second breakfast, and caught a second mouse, and went out again,' I said caustically, putting the egg back into the bowl. 'Probably hunting a third mouse. The Lizard will be depopulated at this rate.'

Then, as the Gage party flocked into Hendra's kitchen and stuck there in single file, I cried with false camaraderie, 'Hello? This *is* a nice surprise!'

The au pair girl was built on a majestic scale and

lightly tanned. Her long muscular legs were capped by very brief crimson shorts. A navy blue and white striped T-shirt strained and wavered over two generous breasts. Her chestnut-brown hair, roped into a thick plait, was ornamented with pea-green plastic butterflies. A pair of large gilt hoops swung from her ears. Yet in spite of her daunting appearance she seemed a biddable creature.

'Would you like to bring the children into the living room?' I asked her, trying to sound my old hospitable self. 'And then we can breathe out!'

My humour and meaning were lost on her. Immobilised between the wall and the refrigerator, she regarded me in noble silence while the three little girls queued up behind her.

Joshua said, 'Mum, this is Dagmar. She doesn't speak much English.'

Then loudly, enunciating each word for her benefit, pointing a dramatic forefinger at me, 'Dagmar, this is my mother. Mrs Meredith.'

His forefinger changed direction. 'Dagmar, go in that room!'

Dagmar smiled splendidly upon me, crushed my hand until it ached, and stalked into the living room where she awaited further orders.

'In there, you three!' said Joshua.

Solemnly the girls filed past him, and stood, hands behind their backs, waiting to be introduced. They were clad in identical blue dungarees, blue gingham blouses and Clark's sandals. They resembled a row of matching different-sized dolls.

Joshua whispered to me, 'This is what happens when they're introduced, Mum, but don't laugh!'

Raising his voice, he said, 'Mum, this is Bibi, who's eight. This is Karin, who's six. And this is Elisabet, who's four.'

As he spoke her name each child spread out her

hands, bobbed a curtsy, and said, 'How do you do, Mrs Meredith?'

Joshua was grinning like Webster with a mouse, but all I could think, looking at their ash-blonde pigtails and clear grey eyes, was that they were someone else's daughters, and she had three of them.

Smiling widely, stiffly, I said, 'I'm very well, thank you, and how are you? Have you had a nice morning? Would you like some lemonade?'

Bibi, the eldest girl, glanced scornfully at Dagmar, who was staring out of the window, and took it upon herself to act as the party's spokeswoman.

'Thank you, Mrs Meredith, but we aren't allowed to eat or drink anything just before a meal.'

Her tone was grave and confidential. I endeavoured to match it.

'I quite understand,' I replied.

Bibi glanced at Dagmar, who could have been deaf and dumb, and spoke again for herself and her sisters. 'Please, may we see Webster, Mrs Meredith?'

'I'm afraid he's gone out exploring, but you can meet him another time.'

Conversation languished.

'Please, can Joshua come back for lunch with us?' said Bibi.

This time I looked at Dagmar and received no help, so turned back to Bibi.

'Shouldn't you ask your mother first?' I said.

The three little girls spoke at once, shaking their heads in emphasis.

'No, we needn't, Mrs Meredith.'

'No, she doesn't mind, Mrs Meredith.'

'No, we don't have to, Mrs Meredith.'

Joshua was saying, 'Please, oh, please, oh, please,' in prayer, and jigging up and down by my side. I was intensely irritated with all of them.

'Well, of course. It's very kind. Yes, certainly.' I

nerved myself. 'And then you must all come back this afternoon and have tea with Joshua.'

They dropped another curtsy and thanked me in chorus, while my son put one hand over his mouth to hide a grin. And in an instant all four of them had scampered away.

Dagmar came unhurriedly to life. 'Goodbye,' she said, and strode after them in her seven-league sandals.

Alone, which was how I wanted to be, I cracked two eggs and beat two tablespoons of cream into them, and went into the garden to hunt in vain for herbs. I was still exploring, and inwardly cursing because if I can grow a window-box of mixed herbs in South London they should be able to grow fields of them in Cornwall, when Bibi scampered back and stood to attention to deliver a message.

'Yes, Bibi?' I said, as politely as I could manage, while thinking, Oh, for God's sake, go away and leave me in peace.

'Mummy says, please, won't you join us for lunch, too?'

They had me there. At home I should have been spoiled for choice with excuses. Here I had none. I rose slowly to my feet.

'How very kind,' I said. 'Will you say thank you to your mummy, from me? And I'll be along in a few minutes.'

She bobbed her head and scurried away. Admittedly a dear little girl, but not my own.

I washed my hands and wound up my hair into a tidy knot, and put on some lipstick and rouge to make me look healthy and happy. From my suitcase I took a bottle of Scotch. I had not liked to order it from the village shop in case they thought I drank, which I do, rather, just at the moment. And as I poured myself a double I thanked God that I had not exposed myself to avid speculation, because undoubtedly the village shop did not stock alcohol, and I should have been left high and dry as well as disgraced. Afterwards I sucked a breath-sweetener, picked up a box of chocolates I had not yet opened, as a present for my hostess, and walked to Trenoweth on legs of lead.

The house was built for a family such as this. On the second Sunday in May we stand at the long table in the dining room, five children and four adults, and bow our heads. As well as teaching her daughters old-fashioned good manners and polite curtsys, Harriet Gage, daughter of a Swedish pastor, also says grace before a meal.

As an honoured guest I have been placed on her husband's right. Dagmar sits opposite between Bibi and Karin. Elisabet is next to me, and Joshua by his hostess. Holding Harriet's hand, two-year-old Leopold fidgets.

'You will please be quiet, Poldy!' she says.

As she gives thanks, he stares round fearlessly from beneath his flaxen fringe. His eyes are a brilliant blue, his cheeks and lips a vivid rose red.

At the head of his table, Conrad Gage conducts the conversation, making sure that everyone plays their part. I wonder if his wife cares for the way he manipulates people like puppets, or whether she feels resentful as I do. He is not a man you can ignore, and he is intensely self-aware.

Though I was late in arriving on the scene, he arrived later still, and made an entrance. I did recognise him instantly, as Mrs Harvey said I would, though my first impression was one of disappointment. In real life he seemed smaller and more ordinary than I had expected. In a crowd I would not have recognised this pleasant-faced man with thinning brown hair and a thickening waistline. But the moment he had our attention he literally clicked into life, as if someone had switched him on. He has the gift, or the art, of making each person in the room feel unique. When we were introduced, he bowed and kissed my hand, and said what a lovely name I had, and quoted Eliot so beautifully that I was afraid I might cry.

'What seas, what shores, what grey rocks and what islands . . .'

Which ends 'O my daughter' and I beseeched whatever masqueraded as a benevolent God to spare me that line.

Either my prayer was answered or Conrad was perceptive, for he stopped there and said lightly, 'What romantic parents you must have had to choose such an evocative name!'

Years ago I decided that truth and humour were the best way to deal with an embarrassing explanation. Though I could have kicked him, I answered drolly, drily. 'Not only romantic but excessively royalist. The name was my mother's choice – after Marina, Duchess of Kent.'

His eyes are light hazel, with a devilish green gleam. Bedroom eyes, we schoolgirls called them in our giggling teens. Did they flicker momentarily? I can't be sure, for he was laughing at himself and encouraging the others to laugh with him.

'If I am to be corrected so early in our acquaintance,' he said, in high good humour, 'I see I shall have to watch my step with Ma-ri-na.' He caresses the middle syllable of my name. His voice is a superb instrument on which he plays like a virtuoso.

At this moment the humour is quiescent. He has taken upon himself the social education of his family, and keeps the bubble of conversation nimbly aloft, blowing it from one to the other along the table.

Obediently, and in turn, Bibi, Karin and Elisabet contribute news of their morning on the beach. But Poldy, who has stayed at home with his mother, crosses swords with him, answering boldly from the fortress of Harriet, 'Shan't tell you. Shan't.'

This is my mamma, Poldy's eyes say.

Conrad's jealous gaze answers, That, sir, is my wife.

At the foot of the table Harriet caters to the appetite and monitors the pulse of the occasion. She is very attentive to me and already holds my son in thrall. Certainly, she and her daughters have had a magical effect on Joshua in a very short time, and my reaction to this is ambivalent. I ought to be grateful to see him so easy and normal, with his tongue untied, but their success reflects on my inadequacy.

She is a woman of my own age, and obviously the mother of Bibi, Karin and Elisabet. Her ash-blonde hair is caught up in a loose coil. Her grey-blue gaze is serious and direct, her full pink mouth unpainted. She is smaller and prettier and more feminine than I am, and strong in her femininity. She wears her air of wifehood and motherhood with great pride, as if she had graduated with honours, as no doubt she has; and she gives me the welcome due to a gracious guest, which I am not because I would rather be eating my scrambled eggs on toast in peace at home.

Everyone present is under her wing, even Dagmar who is probably twice her size. Poldy has climbed onto his mother's lap, though surely he is old enough to sit on a chair? His personality is far stronger than those of his sisters. He commandeers his mother as by right, and makes his demands upon her with many a sly glance at his father. Out-distanced in terms of manhood, he has nevertheless taken on the challenge of Conrad Gage, and one can only wonder at his temerity or his innocence. For the father of this family is not the sort of man to brook rivals, particularly in his own home. He is a man who likes to hold the stage in life as in art, and sometimes he directs a frown at his only and hopefully beloved son.

Although Harriet is Swedish, the Sunday lunch is superbly English. We eat roast lamb and fresh mint sauce, new carrots and peas, new potatoes and good smooth rich gravy. Afterwards there is apple tart and cream. The addition of wine to the meal is Continental. So is the way in which it is served. The adults drink it unadulterated. The children's glasses are diluted with mineral water according to age.

'Do you mind?' Harriet asks me, as Joshua proffers his glass. 'You approve of a little wine for children?'

I do approve. In fact I cannot think why we haven't adopted the same practice, for we have often admired the French habit of taking the entire family out for a midday meal and dispensing wine in just the same fashion.

Joshua, as both guest and eldest child, is served first. Perhaps a quarter of a glass of burgundy is topped up with mineral water. The other children's glasses come paler and pinker, according to age, until Poldy has three drops of wine in his tumbler, and smacks his lips over them like a connoisseur.

Skilfully Conrad draws out my son, who responds with such trust that I fear the seventh veil may be dropped, and Sarah appear in all her ghostly glory. However, she does not, which is fortunate for me since all my energy is being used up in eating a meal I do not want and talking to people who will not leave me alone. In dull pain, in gnawing apprehension, I sense trouble ahead: cosy family picnics, Dagmar taking care of the children so that we three adults can chat together. Having to confess that I had a daughter who is now dead. And other horrors of which I have not yet dreamed, but surely shall, and will as surely torment myself with them.

My part is rehearsed by the time Conrad turns his attention to me again. I reckon to be as skilful as my host at this game, so I give a brief and flattering portrait of my husband, mention my former work in the estate agency, and instancing Trenoweth I move immediately to the subject of old properties, about which I can talk fluently for hours. Conrad is quick to realise this, and lest I oblige them with a discourse he shifts the conversation to Dagmar.

One mark to you, and one to me, I reckon.

The Amazon is eating heartily, in rapt silence. Conrad's light eyes regard her for an instant with genuine amusement. Then he leans back in his chair, wipes his mouth with his napkin, and sets out to woo her. His voice is as lazy and tender as his smile. He speaks in her mother tongue.

'Dagmar. Dagmar. Wo bist du?'

The effect on her is electric. She flushes, shows her excellent white teeth, and answers him in German. Her voice is dark and deep. They joke together. She chuckles intimately. She laughs openly. Dumb Gulliver, towed in the wake of smart Lilliputians, has vanished. A Valkyrie emerges, sensual but chaste. The transformation is so astonishing that I glance covertly at Harriet to see how she copes with Conrad the Courtier.

She smiles serenely back, saying, 'My husband is so good with Dagmar. It is difficult for her, speaking so little English. And my German is not fluent.'

Harriet speaks with the too-perfect pronunciation of a cultured foreigner.

'How long has she been with you?' I ask.

'Two months only. It is very isolated here and she misses her boyfriend, Klaus, who is in Germany. Poor Dagmar.'

'How long is she staying with you?'

'I hope two years. Usually, two years. It is not good for the children to have many changes. But when we go back to London Dagmar will make many friends and have much fun.'

I can tell that Conrad is becoming restive because he has lost our attention, and I pursue the conversation deliberately and diligently, to annoy him.

'So you're Londoners, too? What part of London?'

God help me. Why couldn't they live in Scotland?

'North London. Mill Hill.'

'Ah! We're way down south. Near Richmond.'

Far enough away, thank God, to forget each other when we return home.

Conrad drops Dagmar, who returns to her former self and accepts a large slice of apple tart and cream in consolation. He turns to me instead, though he is wasting his time. 'You should have arrived earlier, Ma-ri-na,' he says, in gentle reproach. 'Last Thursday was Flora Day. It's unique, you know. One of the few remaining medieval festivals in Britain. People come from all over the world to see it. I am making a film – you may have heard – someone may have told you. And we even stopped filming for the day – partly because we lost all our extras, I admit! – but also because we were curious to see it. Yes, it was an amazing experience! And then yesterday was my birthday and Harri gave me a wonderful party, with forty-three candles on the cake. So you have missed two great events.'

'Happy birthday for yesterday, Mr Gage!' says Joshua, deep in pie and cream.

Conrad turns the beam of his attention on my son, and smiles at him. 'Joshua, you are a good fellow and we shall be great friends.'

My son's dark eyes are vulnerable behind his spectacles. His florid mouth quivers. Warm approval makes a baby of him. He says, 'Thanks,' briefly, and colours.

Conrad notes that he has conquered one member of the Meredith family at any rate, and makes much of him.

Afterwards, Dagmar takes the children away. Even Poldy is parted reluctantly from his mamma for an afternoon nap, and the three of us drink coffee at the dining-table. I continue to fence off any topic which might lead to mention of daughters, death, or our next meeting. When the clock in the hall strikes three I feel able to make my excuses, and thank them for their hospitality. I say that Joshua won't be able to play tomorrow morning because we must buy some things in Helston, but that the girls must come to tea with him in the afternoon.

'That is no problem, Bibi and Karin have lessons with a lady in the village, and Lisbet goes too, to learn her alphabet and numbers,' says Harriet, half smiling. 'We are here for some time while Conrad makes his film, and they must not fall behind with their school work.'

I had forgotten that point in my anxiety to put barriers between us.

'Is Joshua to learn lessons, too?' she asks. 'Miss Benney is very clever. Very kind. She would teach Joshua, also.'

'Thank you, but Joshua has been recommended a term's break. He's had certain personal problems,' I say, letting him carry the burden for both of us. 'Nothing serious. Nothing that a long holiday won't cure. I'd rather this wasn't mentioned, of course. The idea is to take his mind off himself.'

She looks at me so closely, though kindly, that I wonder if I sound odd. But her answer is reassuring. 'We shall not speak of it. And you must not have the girls to tea so soon,' she continues. 'You are only just arriving. Perhaps one day next week when you have settled.' Her smile is wide and white and generous. She says frankly, 'Let us not be formal with each other.'

She makes no attempt to detain me. She is full of grace and understanding, and Conrad follows her lead. I am forced to assess my own attitude, and find it wanting.

'But do not take Joshua with you,' says Harriet. 'The girls like him so much. Let him stay here until it is time for bed. He can eat high tea with them at half past six. Our food is plain and wholesome. You need not worry, Marina. Dagmar will bring him home to you safely.'

I walk back to Hendra with relief and a bad conscience, and find that Webster has eaten something he caught, and left one eye and its bowels on the back doormat. In solitude I pour myself another double Scotch, and contemplate the sea, the shore, the grey rocks and the islands.

O my daughter.

SIX

I am relieved that the Gage girls are being tutored by Miss Benney. Had they been at liberty Joshua would undoubtedly have defied me. As it is he behaves in a most truculent manner when I mention shopping in Helston. He wants to play on the beach, and says he will be quite safe by himself. Didn't I say this was a safe place, and didn't Mrs Harvey say so?

'Josh!' I tell him. 'It is unlawful to leave a child under the age of ten alone in the house. I wouldn't have a moment's peace, worrying about you.'

Defiance makes his stammer worse. 'I'll be t-t-ten s-s-soon!'

My authority is not to be denied. My tone is emphatic. 'Joshua Meredith! We are going to Helston. Together.'

He subsides, but not a hundred per cent. 'Well, I just hope you don't get us lost again, that's all,' he says unkindly.

Upstairs, where he is supposed to be changing into a clean jersey and combing his hair, I hear him telling Sarah exactly what he thinks of this expedition. As everyone has advised me to ignore Joshua's Sarah-world I cannot scold my son for being rude. I believe he knows this and takes advantage of it.

Nor does the grumble let off sufficient steam from Joshua's engine of wrath. 'B-blooming w-waste of t-time!' he mutters, as he throws himself into the back of the car.

'Are you going to map-read for us?' I ask, to mollify him.

Pride struggles with the desire to shine. Desire wins. 'Oh, all r-right,' he says sulkily, and guides us to the main road.

In Helston it is market day and the car park at the top of the town is almost full. We squeeze ourselves in, and as further mollification I send Joshua off with two tenpenny pieces to buy our parking ticket from a slot machine. It would have been sensible to ask Harriet Gage's advice about shops, but I was afraid she might suggest coming with me, so now I must hunt alone. My son returns, looking stubborn, and says he hasn't had his S-Saturday's p-pocket m-money y-yet. I hand it over and promise to buy him two comics and an ice-cream as well. I am aware that I have temporarily lost ground and status with him, and blame this entirely on the Gages. At the same time I must admit that Joshua being bolshie is a healthier sign than Joshua having secret compacts with the dead.

I walk, and he canters and clicks (to annoy me) down Horse and Jockey Lane, and we arrive in the middle of Meneage Street where I study my list of exotica. He stands ungraciously by my side, scuffing his sandals on the pavement, hands shoved into the pockets of his bomber-jacket, bottom lip thrust out. His twin seems to have endowed him with her volatile moods as well as her teddy bear. Remembering Sarah both hurts and helps. She always responded well when put in charge.

Offering the list, I say, 'Find the right shops for me, will you, Josh?'

He changes colour and stance, adjusts his spectacles, and smiles unwillingly.

'And what about an orange squash first?' I ask, marking but not mentioning a striped blind just down the street which he has seen also.

'There's a café!' he says instantly, pointing.

From then on we spend a pleasant morning tracking down everything I want, buy coloured postcards to send to Giles and my mother, and head for Hendra in a fine good humour together.

Joshua chooses hot dogs for his lunch, and hurries down to the beach immediately afterwards on a ditching operation. He is building a channel to his castle moat so that the sea will pour in at high tide.

'If you can't beat it, use it!' I say to myself, watching him digging and talking with equal energy.

I turn away. I rearrange the flowers. Read *Cosmopolitan* to make myself feel young, smart, and with it. Long for a whisky, but decide not to drink so early in the day. Brew more coffee and wonder if I should change to decaffeinated. Glance through four library books, which I have been allowed to borrow on a temporary ticket, and wonder why I chose any of them. Look out of the window to check on Joshua and find him still digging and chattering, absorbed in his self-appointed task. He seems to be doing better than I am.

The trouble with being me in grief is that I can't please me. I crave solitude, go to absurd lengths to achieve it, and cannot abide it. I admit that I needed to get away from London, but already I regret the lack of distractions here. There's not even a newspaper delivery. If I want any paper at all, local or national, I must give a regular order to the village shop and walk or drive there every day to pick it up. The highlight of local entertainment is the Flora cinema in Helston.

I spend the rest of the afternoon baking scones and gingerbread, and wondering whether we should have gone to Brighton after all.

A survey through my parlour window at four o'clock shows me Joshua demonstrating the beauty of his channel to the Gage girls, and Dagmar once more deep in her paperback novel. Harriet and Poldy evidently lead separate lives together. I decide to be sociable and make up a picnic basket of orange squash and buttered scones for the beachcombers. Dagmar is wearing a black T-shirt with WOW ME! printed across the front. The letters undulate exotically in green and yellow like snakes. Purely for aesthetic reasons, I really do think that big-breasted girls should wear brassières. The children greet me with an enthusiasm I do not deserve, and I admire Joshua's engineering skills before returning to my hermitage.

This gesture of hospitality was probably a mistake since they all troop into the cottage at six o'clock to thank me again, and Joshua announces that we have both been invited to join the Gage family next Sunday, for a picnic luncheon to be followed by an afternoon service on Tregonning Hill.

'And it's a very special service, Mum, because – guess what! – it's been held for a hundred and thirty years on the very actual place where Wesley used to preach, and please, please, oh, please can we go, oh, please?'

It is time to make a stand for my privacy.

I say firmly, 'Certainly, *you* can go, Josh, but Methodist Sunday Services aren't really in my line, historic or not, and though I appreciate the offer I'd rather stay at home.'

He is disappointed in me. He droops and says, 'Oh, all right.' And then, 'The girls would like me to have high tea with them again. Can I, please?'

A second refusal would border on rudeness. I say firmly, 'If this is all right with Mrs Gage.'

I am assured in a chorus that Harriet is waiting with bated breath for Joshua to arrive. Trapped, I say as pleasantly as I can, 'Then you three girls really must come here for high tea tomorrow. Will you ask your mummy, please, Bibi? And say I do insist.'

I can see that this holiday with the gregarious Gages is going to be uphill, uphill all the way. Already a pattern of events is emerging. Meals here, meals there. He'll be staying the night next.

Bibi gives the half-curtsy with which she responds to adult requests, and Joshua comes up with number three question. 'And please can we take Webster with us to Trenoweth? Dagmar will bring us both back at eight o'clock.'

'You can take Webster to the moon as far as I'm concerned,' I say caustically. 'That is, you can if you find him.'

But I am a child in the hands of these children.

'We caught him in the garden, Mrs Meredith. He's in the beach bag outside,' says spokeswoman Bibi.

Her sisters come to garrulous life.

Karin, confiding in me, '*All* of us had to push him in, Mrs Meredith. And he scratched me. Look. Here on my arm. And he's very cross.'

Elisabet, reassuring me. 'But you mustn't worry because he can breave, Mrs Merediff. Because we tied the knot round his neck and left his head sticking out.'

Defeated, I say, 'Oh. Good.'

And hope that Webster chokes.

By the time I march up the road to make my evening telephone call to Giles the emptiness within me has given way to panic. I am terrified of being taken over. What I need from my husband now is support, reassurance and advice, but I cannot ask for it. How and why should he comfort me? After all, if I had listened to him I should have been within easy distance of home, and furnished with a dozen excuses, whereas now I am alone at the end of nowhere unable to avoid convivial neighbours.

I am further disconcerted by the feeling that Giles is managing rather well without me. He says he has had a good day at school: something about changing the mind of a committee, which brought forth a personal commendation from the headmaster. He tells me that Mrs Pettit has cleaned up, that he has fried himself ham and eggs for supper and enjoyed it. That he thinks of taking up photography again, and do I mind if he turns the box room into a dark room? Finally he says it would be best not to telephone tomorrow evening because it's his squash night, and he doesn't know what time he'll be back.

In turn I describe the difference in Joshua, making the day's events lighter and funnier than they really were. He says, 'Oh, good, good!' which seems less than adequate. And instead of asking how I am, and giving me the excuse to tell him the truth, he tells me that I sound much brighter.

To approach our states of mind and soul from another angle I ask him how *he* is, how he *really* is. 'Oh, pretty good on the whole,' says Giles, and evades serious conversation by talking of school. I put down the receiver and walk back along the road, hands in the pockets of my white wool jacket, head bent, thinking that we must both have died with Sarah, and need something new and challenging to bring us back to life.

Perhaps we should move house?

As I hurry past Trenoweth I see Webster streaking ahead of me. Clearly he wants no more to do with them than I do.

Back in Hendra I try to soak my worries away in Father's iron bath, and change into a yellow linen dress to cheer myself up.

Again I am invaded. As I sit at the window with my first double Scotch of the evening, Webster hurtles past me with a living sacrifice clenched in his jaws, and takes it under the sofa where I can hear it squeaking and scrabbling for freedom. Then Joshua darts in excitedly, saying, 'Mummy, Mr Gage has brought me home and he wants to speak to you.'

I stand up, glass in hand, as Conrad enters, endeavouring to give the impression of easy hospitality. I hear my voice greeting this intruder with seeming sincerity, and wonder if his actor's ear can detect the lie beneath the welcome.

'But how very kind of Mr Gage!' I say, laughing. Then, gesturing towards yet another unbelievable evening sky,' 'I'm having a sundowner and watching the sun go down. Can I offer you a drink, Conrad?'

He is relaxed and gracious, smiling in the doorway, one hand resting on my son's shoulder. His presence dominates the room. His pause is deliberate: the pause of an actor waiting for his audience to recognise and acclaim him. In my mind I hear many fervent hands clapping. Then he moves centre-stage, still smiling, scratching one cheek lightly. It is a gesture I have often seen used by method actors, and I deplore it. Joshua glimmers at him worshipfully as he speaks his first lines.

'Thank you. That will be delightful.' A glance at my glass. 'I'll have whisky, too, if I may.'

Sits down in response to my gesture, and crosses his legs negligently. He is dressed negligently, too, but with a careful negligence that bespeaks considerable thought. His open-collared shirt and khaki drill trousers are beautifully cut, his soft black sweater is cashmere, his carelessly knotted black neckerchief looks both silk and Italian.

'I apologise for bringing Joshua home a little later than usual,' he says, 'but the children were playing a game that had to be finished. You know these important games that are always begun just before bedtime?'

His gaze moves with quiet deliberation from Joshua to the tick-tock mantelpiece clock, and my son takes his cue like a veteran.

'Gosh, is that the time? I'd better go to bed, Mummy.'

He dabs a kiss rapidly, shamefacedly, on my right cheek, says goodnight to us both, and thunders up our short, steep flight of stairs. Webster wriggles from under the sofa, sacrifice in mouth, and lollops after him.

The next couple of minutes are quiet as I pour Conrad a large Scotch and refill my own glass. He is taking in me, the scene, and possible props, while I silently resent and mistrust him. But we settle opposite each other in Mrs Harvey's overstuffed armchairs, smiling like old friends.

'Ma-ri-na,' he says caressingly, 'Harri has sent me to speak to you in the role of family ambassador.'

I cannot resist saying, 'Oh, I'm sure you'll play that part to perfection!'

His light eyes flicker with appreciation. He gives a slight nod as if to say, *Touché!*, and continues unperturbed. He has decided to be courtly.

'Ma-ri-na, we shall be desolated if you don't join us on Sunday.'

'Con-rad,' I reply, in the same vein, 'I shall be desolated to desolate you, but to be quite truthful I don't care for Sunday services. I'm a heathen.'

'And so am I. But Harri is not, and this will be a very special occasion.'

'Then you go – and perhaps Harriet will pray for me.'

We both smile spontaneously, pleased with ourselves. He lifts his glass to me, swallows, and switches tactics. His voice is now friendly.

'Look what I've brought you, Marina. A little booklet on Flora Day. Full of the most charming photographs.'

He leans forward in order to drop this offering in my lap and sits back, smiling and watchful.

Politely I turn the pages over. White-clad children dancing in pairs. A brass band playing. Gentlemen stepping forth in morning dress. The ladies on their arms wearing diaphanous summer gowns and picture hats. The shopfronts transformed into bowers of evergreens. I close the book and hand it back.

'Charming,' I say. 'Charming. How kind of you.'

I have closed the subject. He nurses his drink, pondering the next move. Then smiles so broadly that his eyes narrow to mere slits. When he speaks I listen in spite of myself, because his diction and delivery are a delight.

'We are the children of darkness you and I,' he says. 'They are wiser than the children of light, but not so agreeable. For instance, I came here as an actor. To me Cornwall is simply a temporary backcloth. When I finish my work I shall leave this place behind me, and forget it. But Harri is a child of light, and although she is only here for a few months she puts down little tender roots. Already, people know and like her in the village. She learns their names, enquires after their children. She reads her local newspaper from cover to cover, and always knows what's going on. When Harri goes home she will leave something of herself here. She will be remembered kindly. She would even have braved Flora Day without me, but that was not necessary and we enjoyed a great event as a family. Now she tells me, "Conrad, we must go to the service at Tregonning Hill!" Left to myself I should never have heard of it. But I'm willing to wager that it will be an experience I shall remember.'

As I remain unmoved, he says persuasively, 'So, Ma-ri-na, what am I to tell Harri?'

I reply resolutely, 'Tell her, Conrad, that I truly appreciate her kindness and her invitation. I'm willing for Joshua to go, and I'm sure he'll love it, but please leave me out of your plans.'

I do not say 'now and for ever more' but the firmness in my voice suggests exactly that.

Conrad is intrigued, amused, and undefeated. He makes no comment on my appearance, but his look registers that I am prepared to dress up even if I have nowhere to go.

'You seem such an unlikely hermit!' he says, leaning back.

He is making himself comfortable and at home and I despair a little. Shall I, shan't I, tell him the reason and hopefully shatter him?

My daughter died a few months ago, and I'm trying to put myself together again. For pity's sake, will you please leave me alone?

Instead I answer coolly, 'Generally speaking, I'm not. But we've all been under pressure for a while. A protracted illness in the family. I need to rest and recoup.'

Thus conveying that there is more I could say if I would, but I won't.

Only someone totally insensitive would pursue the subject after that.

He is totally insensitive.

'Joshua tells us that you are here, like ourselves, until the end of August. Presumably your husband will be spending the summer with you both? We look forward to meeting him.'

Words and sentiment are banal but he illuminates them with meaning. I guess that he is wondering whether I am here because of a marital rift. I crush that supposition immediately. 'Yes, of course you'll meet Giles. We've just come down ahead of him. He'll certainly be joining us in July.' For a few days only. But I do not say this. I am not telling a lie, just a half-truth. I pay a compliment to Giles which contains a barb for Conrad. 'My husband is that very rare commodity – an unselfish man.'

He smiles into his glass, finishes his drink, and says, 'How very fortunate for you. I wonder that you can bear to leave him.'

I congratulate myself on remaining unruffled, turning my own glass round and round in my hands, smiling across at him, talking.

'Naturally,' I say, 'I shall be glad when we're together again.'

He finishes his drink, refuses another, and makes his farewell. 'Harri will be expecting me. We eat when the girls have gone to bed. It's the only time of day we have to ourselves.'

I fumble, collecting the glasses. I have drunk a little too much, and though I didn't want him to come here I am rather sorry that he is going. For he is stimulating company, after all, and now I must spend the evening as I have spent much of the day, alone. I should like to ask him why I am a child of darkness, but will not give him the satisfaction of thinking he has either intrigued or annoyed me.

He says, on the threshold, 'Do change your mind about Sunday. The invitation still stands.' Then, looking out at the dark-gold sky, sea and sands, the burning ball of sun, delivers his exit line. 'Like the ending of the first day in the Book of Genesis, don't you think?'

And on that thought departs.

I detest vain men.

SEVEN

June–July

Joshua was evidently in love with the Gage family, but if anyone had the edge on his affections it was Conrad. My son came creeping down the stairs as soon as his new god had departed, on the pretext of needing a glass of water, and talked about Conrad for quite half an hour, in one long lightly punctuated monologue and without a single stammer.

'. . . and when I told him I couldn't swim Mr Gage – actually, he said I could call him Uncle Conrad, only it takes a bit of getting used to! – said he'd teach me, and I said actually I was frightened of the sea, and he said it took a lot of courage to admit fear, and that when he was afraid of anything he did it, just to show himself that he could, and he trains the girls, Mum – even the girls – not to be frightened, and they can all swim. And he says he's going to teach Poldy if ever he can get him away from Aunt Harriet – she said to call her Aunt Harriet! – and next Saturday Mr Gage – Uncle Conrad – and I are going off by ourselves and he's going to teach me how to swim . . .'

My throat swelled with panic. Every weekend the pressure would be put upon me to thank them, join them, pay them back for hospitality. Fortunately no one had thought about cornering either of us that Saturday.

I said insincerely, 'Josh, that's absolutely marvellous! And guess what? We're going to have a treat by ourselves tomorrow.'

Did the light leave his face? Surely not?

He said in polite protest, 'But we're sure to be doing something tomorrow with the Gages . . .'

I affected not to hear him. 'We shall get up very early, and give Webster lots of food to last him all day, and then you and I will drive wherever you want to go in Cornwall. Anywhere at all. We'll take things like lemonade and cake with us, just in case we get extra hungry, but otherwise we shall eat out. Lunch in a restaurant – I've seen some lovely places advertised in the *Helston Packet* – and hopefully our first Cornish cream tea. And we don't have to come home until late. What about that?'

Considering that I had made up the whole trip on the spur of the moment, in fear of being out-Gaged, I thought it was brilliant.

Joshua said resignedly, 'Oh, all right,' and then, mindful of the manners I had instilled in him, 'Thanks, Mum.'

I opened the road atlas.

'You choose!' I said magnanimously.

When we returned to Hendra that evening I had driven one hundred and twenty miles. I worked hard at pleasing my son that Saturday, and he responded as best he could, but it was mostly kindness and consideration on his part. There was a time when Joshua would have believed it was Christmas and birthday rolled into one if I had spent that much time and thought on him alone. Now he tolerated my company and longed to be with someone else.

To such a pass had I come. And must contend with next week, and the week after that, and find some way of circumventing Harriet's plans for Whit Monday as well.

I would not allow the Gages to organise my life as well as my son's. So I did not go to Tregonning Hill. In a fit of conscience I wrote a letter to Giles, having deprived him of our company at half-term, and said that we both missed him. In a fit of nostalgia I wrote another to Ethel, describing the stark beauty of Hendra, and saying that I must bring her here for a holiday sometime. To while away the afternoon I drove all round the Lizard to place it in my mind, and made my trip an excuse to call in on Mrs Harvey and say how comfortable Josh and I felt in the cottage.

'Come in, my dear!' she said, puzzled but hospitable. 'My 'usband's out. Always goes to see 'is mother for an hour or two on Sundays.'

My face obviously expressed my amazement that Mr Harvey still had a mother alive.

'Ninety-four!' said Mrs Harvey. 'And still do her own washing.'

I murmured admiration.

'It's the air,' said Mrs Harvey with great satisfaction.

Paradoxically, I was looking for company: company that did not threaten my inner fortress, company which simply provided a chat. And, as I can be affable when I put my mind to it, Mrs Harvey soon had the kettle on and the saffron cake out, and we sat in her kitchen this time and talked. She told me of her future designs on Hendra, involving, among other things, a petal pink bathroom suite, a stainless steel sink, and a Dralon-covered suite. Without hurting her feelings I endeavoured to persuade her to let the cottage alone.

'Dealing with houses is my job, you see,' I said,

bringing eighteen years of experience to bear on one small granite building. 'And quite apart from the tremendous amount of time and expense involved in renovating an old property – start one job and you find two more! – you would lose its character. I understand why you want to do it. We all like modern luxuries in our own homes,' indicating the shining anonymity of Shangri-La, 'but when people go on holiday they're seeking a new experience.'

She looked doubtful and I endeavoured to strike a chord. 'I expect you feel the same when you go away for a holiday, don't you?'

'Oh, my dear,' said Mrs Harvey in a hushed tone, 'I don't never go away from here. I never in my life been further than Truro. Nor want to, neither. No, no, my dear. Here I was born and here I live and here I'll be buried, and I thank the good Lord for that!'

I was at once horrified and envious. To miss the glories of the world. And yet, and yet, to be part of some patch of earth, rooted in its soil like an old tree. To know that you were home. That was something.

Then Mrs Harvey plunged into the past with the zest and memory of elderly people, and re-created her childhood which sounded hard and spare and good and true like Hendra. Once or twice she made me laugh, and once or twice I was perilously close to those terrible tears of mine, as we blackberried together in the 1910 hedgerows, and baked bread in the oven with Mother, and mended our shoes with Father. In fact, we got on famously together, and the feeling of rightness and security she had engendered stayed with me for the next hour; to be instantly dispersed when Joshua arrived home, dusty, tired, exultant, and garrulous about his day.

'And there were lots and lots of people and singing, Mum, and the Breage Silver Band played, and the new vicar preached . . .'

'Goodness!' I said sourly. 'We shall have you in Sunday School next! Now, about tomorrow. I've got a lovely trip planned, all round the Lizard. Just the two of us.'

Matters come to a head quite unexpectedly on the following Saturday morning, while Joshua and I are writing to my mother in the parlour: he briefly, on a highly coloured postcard, me at length on paper. The mantelpiece clock is chiming ten when Dagmar looms up at the front door with a note from Harriet.

I reproduce the grammar and the spelling, both of which I should have found charming under different circumstances.

Dear Marina,

Conrad must work again today and we are by ourselfs. Conrad says in joke that you do not like to picnic with him but you will like to go shopping with me by ourselfs. I am so please. Dagmar looks after all children and we shall go to Falmouth. Shall you come in my car? I treat you to lunch at Desdemona's which you shall like. It is so long that I have a civilise outing with a friend!

Harriet

I do not blame her, for she is a good and innocent woman. But I pronounce Conrad guilty, and would like to condemn him to slow death, for he has deliberately engineered this meeting to pay me out.

I say to Dagmar in stilted English, very slowly, 'Thank you. I shall come back with you to speak to Mrs Gage.'

Joshua, reading my expression, says, 'What's wrong, Mum?'

But I do not tell him, and we all walk to Trenoweth in

silence, Dagmar occupied with her usual day-dream, Joshua red and worried, and me busy composing the speech which will inform Harriet once and for all that I must be left alone.

She is busy preparing the evening meal, making everything ready so that she can leave her family without a twinge of conscience. There is something so natural and friendly and honest in the way she greets me, when I march in, that my conscience gives me an almighty twinge. But my resolve is fixed.

I open my mouth to tell her that unfortunately there seems to be some mistake, and though I don't mean to be hurtful I have already told Conrad quite definitely . . . and so on and so on.

And instead of that I sit down suddenly on a kitchen chair, unable to speak, and twin rivers of grief stream down my face.

The effect of my tears is instant and shocking. Dagmar shoots up from the fathoms of her dream world looking unexpectedly vulnerable. The three little girls are silenced, pink mouths drop slightly open in astonishment. Joshua turns his back on me and retreats to the window, pressing his head to the pane as if to distance himself and his thoughts from a mother who is making a scene. Only Poldy is unaffected, regarding this exhibition as he regards life in general: a passing show in which he plays the part of charmed spectator.

But Harriet moves swiftly, softly into action. 'Dagmar, dear, take the children away, if you please.'

The importance of the moment is emphasised when she hands her son over and says firmly in response to his protests, 'No, Poldy. Go with Dagmar! That is a good boy.'

Hoisting the child to her shoulder, Dagmar extends a fine round arm to the watchful brood and says, 'Come!' and over her shoulder, 'Come, Joshua!'

They file out after her, heads bent, and Harriet puts her arms round me as if I were one of her daughters, and says, 'Now you shall cry as long as you wish, and nobody shall disturb us.'

This was the ultimate confessional, and Harriet the perfect priest. Sometimes I just sobbed, sometimes I sobbed and talked. I told her everything: Sarah's death, Giles's emotional retreat, the reasons for coming here, even my fear of their hospitality.

She stroked my hair and listened and occasionally commented. I could imagine her expression, for I had seen her face when she comforted her children and shared their small sorrows as if they were the sorrows of the world. I knew that in my grief for loss of Sarah she grieved, too, as if my child had been one of her own. I heard myself voicing losses that I had not realised were losses, and from the deepest part of myself fears and regrets, which were in no way connected with Sarah, blinked their way out into daylight.

I relived the time when Giles and I met, and London was swinging through the sixties. How we were a refuge for each other in a city which was both enchanting and terrifying. How we entrusted each other with our future hopes and ambitions.

'We could talk about anything, then. And our backgrounds were similar in many ways. Neither of us knew our own father. They were both killed in the war. But Giles's family had more money than mine. She'd been a war widow left with a child to bring up, like my mother, but she married again and had more children.

'Both Giles and I were at odds with our backgrounds. We'd left home to find ourselves, and we found each other. We felt there was more to life than provincial poverty or suburban respectability. We wanted to live in a beautiful house, to know interesting people, to lead a life that was leavened by books and music and good food and wine and conversation. We wanted to give our children a wonderful home and education, to travel abroad, to make up to them and each other for what we had lacked in our childhoods. Giles was the teacher. I was the entrepreneur. He conducted a school of one with me, like Scott Fitzgerald. I earned the jam on the bread, and created the setting we dreamed of . . .'

I mourned the passing of youth which was prepared to do and be all manner of things.

'. . . and when I think of the risks we took and the challenges we faced, I'm appalled. And I'm also envious. I scraped up a deposit on a three-bedroomed house in Morden (one of my firm's bargains, and an absolute snip, though nothing out of the ordinary!) and took on a mortgage that seems laughable now, but was like drawing eye-teeth to pay then.

'It never seemed to occur to us that we were playing for high stakes, totally dependent on good health, full strength and no bad luck. He was a junior staff teacher and I was a junior assistant at the estate agent's office. We divided the financial responsibilities between us, straight down the middle. I had time off for a few months after the twins arrived, then I engaged a nanny, but that didn't work out either personally or financially. Then I found the wonderful Mrs Tavey, and all was well. Of course, I had to go back to work as soon as I could. I was saving up for a really lovely house. We lived at Red Queen pace, running and running to keep in the same place, and running twice as fast to get anywhere . . .'

I remembered the turning point.

'And then, quite suddenly and unexpectedly, everything clicked into place. I was promoted and put on a commission basis. Giles took the post of senior English master at a private boys' school. The house at Richmond came onto the firm's books, and I snapped it up. We were walking a highly expensive tightrope and neither of us could get down. House, child-minder, two cars, holidays, school fees. Oh, I didn't mind working. I loved my job. But the pace was killing. There was never any time.

'Then two years ago Giles and I went to the Goddards' Twelfth Night party. Sue Goddard had made a special cake, and I found a shilling in my slice. Sue said, 'You're the Queen, and anything you wish can be granted!'

'Do you know what I wished for? The opportunity to take a year off work so that I could enjoy the new house, and spend more time with Giles and the twins. And the wish *was* granted, but not in the right way.

'A month or two later Sarah became ill, and they diagnosed leukaemia. We'd just finished decorating the house and laying out the garden, and they were absolutely beautiful. But by then I couldn't enjoy them because I had to watch my child die . . . '

In the end I was washed clean, and returned to the present.

The room was full of sun and silence. Outside, the sea rushed back and forth like a favourite terrier. Harriet held me gently at arm's length and looked into my face. We smiled, sighed, and let go of each other. She went to the door and called her lieutenant.

'Dagma-a-a-r!' Then to me, 'She makes good coffee for us.'

I wiped my eyes and hands and the front of my smart white shirt blouse, which was limp and damp. I picked strands of wet hair from my wet cheeks and tucked them into place.

Harriet said practically, 'Marina, your handkerchief is not big enough for so much trouble. You should use these instead.' Offering a box of Kleenex.

Dagmar strode in with the coffee-tray, avoiding my

eyes. Whether I had embarrassed her or she feared to embarrass me I didn't know. She reported to Harriet, 'Joshua plays with Poldy. Girls are happy. Is well.' And went out again.

'Joshua is a hero to our girls,' said Harriet. 'It is nice for them – and good for him, I think,' she added gently.

'Is Sarah? Does he mention . . .? He imagines, you see, that Sarah . . . '

'Oh, yes, Sarah is with them. That is the first thing I hear about Joshua from the girls. He has an imagine . . . imagining . . . '

'Imaginary?'

'Yes. An imaginary sister. A twin sister. Bibi was so pleased because they share the same birthday, though she is a year younger. They say they are triplets, and they all play together.'

I found it eerie to think of my daughter as the living dead.

'And when did you realise that Sarah wasn't imaginary?'

'Joshua tells Conrad and me when we first meet. To protect you, Marina. He loves you very much.'

Her tone did not blame me, but did suggest that I gave him credit for his motive.

'Joshua tells us that you do not like to talk of Sarah, and so we could not speak until you did. And I tell the girls, so that they shall not hurt you with making remarks. And I tell Joshua that I, too, had an imagined friend when I was young.'

I was donning the armour of my pride. I heard my voice change, lose its tremulous quality, hone its blade. 'But that isn't quite the same thing, is it? Sarah actually existed, and now does not. People are bound to think that Joshua is behaving in a very peculiar way. Which he is.'

Harriet pointed towards the oval mirror on the

wall. 'Now look at you!' she said reproachfully. 'See what you do to yourself and your son!'

And there in the glass was a keen black hawk of a woman, angrily alert. She poked her head forward, dark brows drawn together, searching for prey, or an answer.

'How you wound yourself,' said Harriet, chiding me. 'All the time thinking of how Joshua should not do this and should do that, and what the people say of him. How should the people know what is best? It is not these people who suffer and have lost Sarah.'

I bowed my head and mumbled, 'But it isn't the same for you. You're such a normal family. There's nothing odd about your children.'

She made a short, sharp sound of amusement and disbelief.

'What dream is this? Every one of us has problems! Have you not heard Conrad say that I spoil Poldy and he is too much with me? It is true, but I am always like this with my baby. Then Bibi is jealous of Dagmar because she is the eldest and wishes to be the mother's helper. My Karin is the middle pig, neither flesh nor fish herrings. And Lisbet had so much grief when Poldy was born that Conrad made a favourite of her, and now she depends too much on him. He can be moody, you understand, and she smiles or suffers, whichever he is doing. So I run from one to the other like the sorcerer apprentice. And just as we are calm down Conrad turns us upsides again. I tell you, a large family is not easy. The Russians say, Many children, many troubles! and they are right!'

'But somehow you have found an answer to life,' I said tiredly, 'and the answer seems right.'

'How old are you, Ma-rina?'

'Thirty-five.'

'Young enough to have another child. Another two

children. A second family. I think that Joshua would like that.'

'In place of Sarah?' I asked bitterly.

'No. Sarah is never replaced. But to go forward and say yes. That is what I say to life. I say, Yes, very well. *Yes.*'

'I'm not the maternal type,' I said awkwardly, 'and Giles and I have a fairly expensive life-style which needs my income as well as his. But I know what you mean. I'll think about it. And I thank you.'

For the first time I took her hand and gave it a little shake, saying, 'Bless you, Harriet, for being good to me.'

I felt as if I had run and won a long race: exceptionally weary, quietly exultant, utterly relaxed.

We spent the rest of the afternoon with the children, who all stared shyly at me when they rejoined us.

Joshua said tentatively, 'Are you feeling better, Mum?'

I nodded and smiled at him, unable as yet to speak.

Harriet said briskly, factually to her children, 'Aunt Marina needed to cry for Sarah. If Sarah had been my daughter, and your sister, we should need to cry sometimes, do you not think so?'

They nodded in unison, and Elisabet slid from her stool and kissed me. I should not have been able to bear that normally, but I was emotionally exhausted, and so did, and kissed her back. An illustration in Hans Andersen's story of Gerda and Kay came to mind, and I wondered whether the icicle in my heart was beginning to melt.

Harriet said, clapping her hands, changing the mood, 'The tide is up and we cannot go to the beach until later. So we shall all make cakes and pies, but Marina must sit down and do nothing!'

So she organised us, and the rhythm of the household caught me up, carried me along. Joshua and the girls donned aprons for their separate tasks and followed instructions carefully. Their faces were solemn. Below the rolled shirt-sleeves their elbows were childish, tender. Poldy, once more ensconced by his mother's side, was given a piece of pastry to play with. Harriet supervised the workers and Dagmar cleaned up after them. Despite the presence of the boys it was an intensely female afternoon.

After a while I joined them of my own accord, concentrating on helping Karin the middle pig, and Elisabet the usurped baby. And when the buns and tarts were in the oven, and we paused for tea and orange juice, I took Elisabet on my lap, and nursed her while Harriet nursed Poldy.

I remembered Sarah being this age and size, and wondered whether the house in Richmond, the holidays abroad and private schools were worth the loss of countless afternoons in her short life when we could have been tranquil together.

I left before Conrad came home, needing to keep the equilibrium which Harriet had engendered, and for once Joshua chose to come back with me instead of begging to stay on until high-tea time. And proudly brought home his share of buns for our dessert.

I wanted to continue this new and satisfying feeling of being part of humanity again, but was not up to much conversation. As if he divined my mood, Joshua put himself out to be sociable, and as I cooked and he laid the table he talked to me without a single stammer. My loss of control must have shaken him, because he stayed with me after the meal instead of disappearing to talk to Sarah. And when we had washed up we went for a walk along the coast road, and Joshua told me that he had thought of collecting butterflies but Aunt Harriet said that was cruel, so he was going to collect shells instead.

At eight o'clock we both telephoned Giles, and

though his equable voice told us nothing of importance I believed that he sounded happier and more at peace with himself, as we were.

I expect that Harriet told Conrad of my emotional deluge as they sat in privacy that evening over their meal, though he never referred to it and I never accused him of provoking it. For Harriet became our peacemaker. Out of love of her we learned to be friends, and though we still enjoyed fencing with each other our blades were buttoned to render them harmless.

As well as being a remarkable person he was marvellous to and for Joshua. The improvement in my son was magical. Watching one swimming lesson, where Conrad was understanding but relentless, and Joshua terrified but determined to learn, I had to acknowledge that this stranger was doing more for the boy in their brief acquaintance than Giles and I in nine years of parenthood; that he brought out qualities which we had not believed existed; that he saw someone we had never known.

My period of playing hermit was over. Harriet and I combined forces to minimise the workload and rearranged our schedules. The two households merged into one rich and amicable whole, and accustomed as I was to organise life on a smaller and more intensive scale, I was astonished how much easier it was for three of us to deal with five children than for me to cope with Joshua alone.

We were experiencing the first promise of a fine summer and Harriet was tempted to curtail the girls' lessons, though continuing to pay their elderly teacher the full amount. Child of a northern clime, she thought it a pity if they stayed indoors when the sun shone, and decided that they should go to Miss Benney for mornings only, while we did our chores and prepared the evening meal. Conrad's working hours seemed to be extraordinarily long, and his only concession to family life during the week was to arrive home in time for a drink before dinner. So the day was our own, and we planned it to suit ourselves. One afternoon, usually a Friday, was set aside for Harriet and me to do the major shopping while Dagmar looked after the children. And one day a week Dagmar disappeared by herself and left us to cope with everything and everybody.

'But where on earth does she go?' I asked, thinking of our isolation and her lack of personal transport.

'Oh, Dagmar's ace on bus time-tables,' said Joshua unexpectedly. 'She bombs about all over the place. Falmouth. Penzance. Truro. I think she's looking for a new boyfriend. Klaus doesn't write as much as he used to. She's been to St Michael's Mount and St Ives and Land's End and heaps of places. Dagmar's ace, I tell you.'

'Then why are we idiots sticking to the same old beaches, seeing nowhere else?' I asked Harriet.

'Because we should have to set off early, and the girls are in school until twelve o'clock.'

'Then why don't we send them to Miss Benney all day on our shopping day, and on Dagmar's day off, and give them three days free? It would work out much the same.'

Harriet thought this over and said, 'That is possible, yes. But if we are going far it would be better to take our big car instead of two little cars, and I am an idiot who cannot drive it!' she replied humorously.

'I could drive it. I've driven a shooting brake before, when we went on the Continent with the Goddards.'

'But Conrad will not drive my Mini. It is too small and shabby for him. He does not like such a car.'

'Then he could borrow my Ford. That's smart enough, I should have thought. But I suppose the truth of the matter is that Conrad wouldn't care for the idea of my driving his car. Men aren't usually very happy about handing their power symbols over to women.'

Harriet thought this over for a full minute and then smiled an inscrutable smile. 'We shall see,' she said.

The result of her diplomacy was that Conrad had a wonderful evening putting me through a driving test, which I bore with remarkable good humour and even amusement, getting my own back on him by insisting that he went through the same performance in my neat green car, and having the final word by telling him that he drove too fast to be trusted with it. But we both needed transport for different reasons, and having hedged and sparred and doubted we finally decided to trust each other and swop our vehicles temporarily.

This deepened the friendship between our houses. Harriet insisted that I stay to supper that evening, while Joshua slept in Poldy's room. We laughed a lot over the meal, and Conrad and I poked fun at ourselves and each other, entertaining Harriet with an account of the driving tests. She was more of a smiling than a laughing person, but as we continued to outdo each other she laughed at the pair of us.

'But you are so alike!' she cried, throwing up her hands.

'What? Handsome, charming and exceptionally talented?' Conrad asked, catching one hand and kissing it.

'I think she means bossy, self-centred and egotistical,' I remarked.

'Which of us is right, Harri?' he asked tenderly.

In a burst of laughter she cried, 'Both of you! But both of you is right!'

She found our new freedom invaluable. Her praise of my skill, her dependence on me, made me feel more of a partner in our friendship and less of a lame duck.

The early-morning air, which had chilled us throughout May, now lost its nip. The climate became warm and even. The atmosphere lightened. Even my mother in her weekly letter wrote to tell us that her cough had improved no end in this fine weather, but Salford was stuffy.

That time, those people and those places are limned in gold on my mind.

Each day began softly with a diffused glow, as if it remembered the heat of the day before. By nine o'clock in the morning, household chores completed, food contributed, and Webster given an extra large breakfast, Joshua and I sat in Trenoweth kitchen, studying the map and the tide time-table and deciding on our itinerary, for we were in charge of these trips. Buckets, spades, swimming costumes, towels and lunch sandwiches were packed by the Gage contingent. Then we piled into the shooting brake and were off on our explorations.

By the end of June we knew every beach on the far toe of Cornwall, from Porthleven to Porthcurno, and up along the coast to Hayle. We braved the Wadebridge bottle-neck and the crowds in order to see the Royal Cornwall Show. And the children were allowed to stay up very late on Midsummer's Eve to watch an Old Cornwall Society ceremony at Predannack, where our bonfire was one of a chain of hilltop fires lighting the county from end to end.

Of course, the Gages had offered me the use of their telephone any time, but I still preferred to take a brisk walk on appointed evenings and talk to Giles from the kiosk. Our conversations were lighter, happier. We looked forward to seeing each other towards the end of July.

And on my return I called in for half an hour or so at Trenoweth where Harriet and Conrad were waiting and drank coffee with them. They welcomed me now as an extension of themselves. Sometimes Joshua stayed the night there, so that I could have supper with them. Sometimes Harriet and Conrad came over to Hendra and ate with me. And I was cooking again as I had not cooked since the onslaught of Sarah's illness, imaginatively, absorbedly, spurred on by the appetites and compliments of my two new friends. Each night I slept soundly and deeply, tired by sun and sand and children. Each morning I looked forward to what the day would bring. And as the end of term approached we were all excited – or in Conrad's case warily interested, for he did not like to share any limelight – to think of Giles joining us and making the threesome a foursome.

His school broke up earlier than most, but he had arrangements to make for the trip to Switzerland, and therefore planned to come down just for a few days, in order to see us before he went, and promised to join us for the rest of the holiday in mid-August when he returned.

So Harriet and I went shopping after lunch on the Friday, leaving Dagmar reading on the beach with the children playing round her and falling over her feet, to lay in provisions for the week. The car park was usually busy, but this afternoon we found it so full that I circled it three times before manoeuvring into a place.

'I think that everyone has the same good idea as us!' Harriet remarked.

Shops and pavements were crowded. And yet, like boulders in a current, the gossips stopped and talked, while people stepped off the narrow pavements to pass them. Cars and delivery vans were parked solidly down one side of the street, suspiciously patrolled by the traffic warden. On the other a seemingly endless single line of vehicles crawled down to the traffic lights.

We placed two staggeringly large orders with our greengrocer at the top of the town, to be boxed up and collected on the way home, and twice loaded the shooting brake with bags of food. Finally we retreated to the café with the striped blind and sat together over tea with lemon, exhausted but triumphant: bees about to return to the hive, laden with good things.

'But what a young and brown and lovely woman you look now!' said Harriet with pleasure. 'How much more happy. What a difference your husband will see in you! So cold and pale and proud you were. Shall I tell you what Conrad calls you when first we meet? The Snow Queen!'

I was suddenly and delightfully surprised, thinking of the time when I felt the icicle melting in my heart. That he and I should have hit on the same metaphor pleased me deeply. And yet I was hurt, too.

Harriet, fearing she had been rude, squeezed my hand and said quickly, soothingly, 'It is only Conrad's joke. And now the joke is not true.' Then, stirring sugar into her lemon tea, 'While your husband is here please to let Joshua stay with us, so that you have much time together.'

She was too modest and I too intensely private ever to have discussed the sexual side of marriage, though we were frank enough on its practical aspects, but I understood her meaning, and recognised it as my own. This holiday weekend was to be a new beginning for Giles and me, and Hendra the place from which we voyaged forth again. Not to replace Sarah, as Harriet had said, but to go forward and say *Yes* to life.

We left the café just before five o'clock and saw that the traffic in Meneage Street was almost at a standstill. Nose to tail they crawled now, and as they halted at the lights I saw that most of the cars belonged to holiday-makers.

Some hauled great caravans behind them. On their roof-racks they carried bicycles, surf-boards, or extra luggage. In the back seats, children of all ages lolled against each other fast asleep, or squabbled wearily, or slumped in apathy, reading comics and sucking sweets. In front, wives and mothers nursed babies or picnic baskets and orchestrated their offspring. In the warm late afternoon husbands and fathers had rolled down the windows, rolled up their shirt-sleeves. Now they leaned on the sill with one elbow and stared out. They had been travelling all day probably, leaving their box-like flats and houses, their teeming towns and suffocating cities, heading doggedly towards a Cornish dream, seeking their own Shangri-La, and they wore a jaded but exultant air.

The waitress followed us out, and hung a notice on the door saying CLOSED. And though I could remember myself, all those weeks ago, weary with distance and thirsty for tea, I no longer shared a common interest with these travellers. For by this time I felt that I was part of Cornwall, and they were outsiders. I even thought of them as tourists, not recollecting that, though my stay might be longer, I was as transient as the rest of them.

EIGHT

July

I had alternated between wishing that Joshua were not with me to meet his father, and being grateful for his presence. My fantasies had driven me to such a pitch that I felt shy of my own husband, which was ridiculous. Not only had I imagined how he would seem to me but how I would seem to him, freed from my sad city self. Perhaps he would find me young and brown and lovely, as Harriet said. I had ceased to smooth my hair into a shining coil, and tied it back with a ribbon. I wore a yellow gingham shirt, white cotton slacks and sandals.

No longer the Snow Queen, I thought. And wondered whether Giles had thought me cold and remote, as Conrad once did. Joshua, too, had changed and was no doubt expecting to astonish his father. So we were both excited when the train thundered importantly into the station, bringing with it an aura of far-away places. And we ran alongside looking for Giles's face, ready to shout and wave and make welcome. But we could not see him at any of the windows, and he was among the last to alight, by which time our first enthusiasm was spent.

He carried a briefcase as well as a small suitcase, and a light raincoat. He wore a grey suit and looked exactly what he was: a city man on a weekend in the country. As soon as he stepped onto Camborne platform I knew that I was selling myself the wrong dream. He seemed slighter and younger than I remembered, pleasant but distant, as if he were kindly disposed towards us but didn't know us very well. His brisk greeting, his friendly smile, his perfunctory hug and kiss depressed me. I could have been his sister.

'You're looking miles better, darling,' he said. 'Are those clothes new?'

'Yes, I bought them in Falmouth. Marks and Sparks.'

He patted Joshua on the shoulder. 'Hello, old chap. Good to see you.'

Joshua jumpd up and down saying, 'Daddy, Daddy! I'm learning to swim. And I'm not afraid of the sea any more.'

'Good!' said Giles heartily. 'Good.'

'Darling, was the journey too awful?' I asked lightly, willing him to communicate.

He was fussing to hand over his ticket to the collector, and did not answer me at once.

'Not in the least,' he said pleasantly. 'Very comfortable, in fact. I had lunch in the dining car and I've been working on an idea for the Christmas play at the end of next term.'

'That doesn't sound like our journey, does it, Josh?' I said, trying to spark off a reaction in someone.

Joshua said, skipping my question, 'Daddy, although I've come to meet you I'm not staying with you at Hendra. I'm having supper with the Gages and staying there instead.'

'Oh, really?' said Giles heartily. 'That sounds fun. I'm looking forward to meeting them while I'm here.'

I gave Joshua the car keys and sent him ahead. I took my husband's arm and tried again.

'Darling, don't you notice an amazing difference in Josh?'

Giles gave the sort of smile which he used for demanding parents.

'Darling, I haven't had time to orientate myself yet. Yes, Josh seems fine.'

'He's come right out of his shell. And he's far less obsessed with the Sarah business.'

'Excellent! I'm glad to hear it.'

I was rapidly turning into the Snow Queen again. We walked to the car in silence, and all the way to the Lizard I was glad Joshua was with us because he talked practically non-stop. Giles and I remained preoccupied with our own thoughts and only replied sufficiently to keep our son filling the silence between us. And yet I registered the undercurrent of Joshua's conversation and was astonished, even dismayed, to realise how deeply he had become attached to the cottage and Cornwall and the Gage family. For there was no way this holiday could go on for ever, and in September he must still return to London and his new boarding-school.

The arrival at Hendra was no better. I felt as if I were showing a reluctant client round a defective property.

'Charming little place, of course, but hopeless for everyday living,' Giles said factually. 'I'm not surprised your Mrs Harvey prefers her bungalow.'

In fact he showed more interest in Webster than in either of us, and when Joshua told him about the daily mouse offerings he laughed spontaneously. 'Good old Webster!' he said. 'I knew he couldn't be as dim as he looked!'

Our son, oblivious to his father's inadequacies, his social duties done, said, 'Can I go now, Mum? Oh, and can I take Webster with me? I promised to lend him to Aunt Harriet. There's a mouse in the pantry.'

'Yes, if you can persuade him.'

Whereupon Joshua lifted his haversack from its hook and pushed the cat into it, scratching and protesting all the way. Buckling it, so that Webster's indignant face could emerge from one side while his body was firmly held, he said, 'I'll let him come home after supper!' and strode off.

The episode lifted our spirits and we both laughed then. I took Giles's arm and we stood side by side, watching Joshua's manful step and plunging haversack, until they were out of sight. Lighter, brighter, I said, 'Darling, you must be dying for tea!' and put the kettle on.

The tray was already laid. I brought out home-made scones and clotted cream. Harriet and I had spent a glorious afternoon picking raspberries at thirty-five pence a pound at Feock, and having gorged ourselves and our families, had made jam with the surplus. 'Home-made and locally grown!' I said.

My husband sat back in the armchair which faced the window, and smiled his pleasant smile. He said, 'Ah, how lovely to be looked after again. It's been something of a bachelor existence while you've been away, Rina.'

'And you've missed me?' I asked, despising myself for asking.

'Of course I've missed you, darling!'

He was relaxing now, shaking clotted cream onto his scone, spooning jam on top of it, making himself at home. He nodded towards the window. 'What a marvellous view!' he said. And then humorously, 'Why shouldn't I miss you? It was your idea to bury yourself down here, Rina, not mine.'

I drank tea and watched him eat. I was tentatively happy again. I said, 'I've missed you, too, darling.

Particularly in the evenings. The time went so slowly. No one to talk to.' But that, I reflected, was an old truth rather than a present one. For many weeks now I had been with my friends and the days had flown. Still, the feeling was more important than the fact.

'What have you been doing in the evenings?' I asked.

'Oh, worked. Read. Fooled round with photography. Played squash. Pretty routine stuff. The Goddards asked me round to dinner a couple of times, and other friends made vague hospitable noises, but I'm not really the social type. You're the one in the family who makes things go, darling. By the way, I've got heaps of "Do come home, we're longing to see you!" messages. I wrote the names down somewhere.'

Still eating, he felt in his pocket, took out a notebook and handed it to me. He said, 'These scones are really super, Rina.'

'Don't eat too many,' I said automatically, reading. 'We've got lobster Neuberg for dinner. And the lobster was caught this morning at Cadgwith.'

'Good Lord!' said Giles, boyish, spontaneous, lovable.

I did love him at that moment, and said so.

He leaned forward, laughing, and gave me a jam and cream kiss.

So then I was sure everything would be all right. Of course it would.

But it wasn't.

We drank a bottle of champagne between us that evening, and with reminiscent tongues recalled our early days together. I felt as though one of me was floating, light of head and heart, in the air of promise. The other one stayed dumb and dour upon the ground and watched us with a sardonic eye. Did Giles feel the same way? Certainly his airy self met and flew with mine, but our bodies refused.

A man cannot hide physical failure as a woman can.

It was Giles who rolled away from me, saying,

'Darling, I'm terribly sorry. Can't think what's wrong. I must have drunk too much.'

Whereas I could answer as if I were the innocent and disappointed party, though in truth I was equally at fault. 'Don't worry. I daresay it will take a while to adjust. It's been quite a time.'

For Sarah's illness and death had robbed us of lovemaking, too.

He yawned then, a monster yawn of weariness.

'And you've been travelling all day,' I added, 'so let's get some sleep.'

Oh, I was wonderful. So understanding. A text-book response.

'You're very sweet, Rina,' he said gratefully, and was asleep in moments.

I lay awake, listening to the sea and watching the moonlight make window patterns on the wall and floor. The air smelled cool and salty, bracing. The champagne which had sent Giles to oblivion revitalised me. I slid carefully from the bed and reached for my velvet housecoat, which doubled as a dressing-gown and was a soft rich avocado green. I had bought it four years ago from an almost-new shop in the West End and still loved it. But my mother regretted the purchase on two counts: first the colour, which was unlucky, and then the fact of its being second-hand.

'I should have thought you could afford new, on your income! I've never worn folks's old clothes in all my life!'

She retracted this criticism when I told her how much the gown cost, and hinted at its stately origins, but reiterated her belief that green was unlucky. She had regretted my choice of a green car five years ago.

The housecoat was slightly shabby now but had been a friend for so long that I felt protective towards it. Like a beautiful woman growing old it still looked lovely in the right light. I crept downstairs, slid my feet into my gritty sandals, and walked to the end of the garden. Only the sea was busy.

In Trenoweth, now hushed and dark, my son slept apart from us so that we could make love and a new life. It is as difficult to relive physical delight as to recall physical pain. The experience is immediate and transitory. Words encompass only time and place, and we label the act as best we can.

'Wasn't that a heavenly weekend we spent in Dorset, in the summer of sixty-four, just when things were coming good?'

'I couldn't pass the hospital for ages after the twins were born in sixty-five. What a nightmare that was!'

Giles and I were both virgins when we met, and learned to make love together. At first we were profoundly disappointed, then Giles enjoyed himself but I didn't much. Later, patience gave us mutual pleasure, and the deliciously secret feeling that this was something we shared with each other and no one else.

But not ecstasy, I thought. I would never call it ecstasy.

We knew what ecstasy was because we experienced it in other ways. We could be moved beyond words by music, by great moments in the theatre and cinema, by beauty of every kind. Could be lifted out of and beyond ourselves, to return slightly different, loving and understanding all the world for a little while. But the joys of the flesh were secular not sacred.

I wondered why this should be, and came to the conclusion that those who knew meant something different from my interpretation of the word ecstasy, and people who did not were simply boasting. I detested and avoided the sort of woman, like Sue Goddard, who wants to exchange sexual confidences.

'My dear, I couldn't believe it. You know how close Mummy and I are? I can say anything to her. But the other day I found out that she didn't even know what an orgasm *was*! I shouldn't think the poor darling ever had one. Isn't that awful? A whole lifetime wasted.'

I like Harriet for not discussing the number and quality of her orgasms and her husband's prowess. I didn't discuss my lovemaking with Giles either. At this moment I had none to talk about.

I was walking and walking to keep pace with my thoughts, or perhaps to still them. Walking and walking through the little garden at Hendra, and down our private path to the beach. There was ecstasy here all right, in the sound and motion and the sense of eternity. A silver moon in a silver sky. A silver sea coming in on a horse-shoe of silver sand. A background of dark cliffs and rustling trees.

I felt let down and left out, but in a curiously impersonal way. To be honest with myself I had not missed Giles himself while we were apart. I had missed the adult company, which was a different thing altogether. This evening I had drunk champagne to make me feel bubbly enough to sleep with anybody, not particularly with him. And even now, when my body longed for a lover as fine as moonlight to celebrate this night, the lover would not by choice be my husband. So how could I resent his inability to be aroused by me, when I was not aroused by him? To be more truthful still I must admit that his part in this love-scheme of mine, though necessary, was a minor role. He was merely required to make me pregnant. Nor should I be surprised if, after so many years of marriage, and the mortal shocks of the last eighteen months, we were beached. There is an ebb and flow to lovemaking. Like the tide, it recedes. But then returns again. It does return.

I sat down on the sand and hugged my knees to my chest and watched the sea spreading out its lace-edged petticoats of water and drawing them away again. And so stayed mesmerised until a small chill run of water shocked my toes, and sent me shivering homewards.

The dinner-party had not been a success, even though I had produced three of Giles's favourite dishes and chosen a wine to complement each course. I wanted my friends and my husband to like each other, but Conrad and Harriet and I had created a little holiday world to which Giles was a stranger. Of this we were aware, and invited him to enter. He did not care to accept the offer. He remained stubbornly outside our magic circle, neither envious nor offended, smiling on our efforts and parrying our advances with the amiability of a schoolmaster who likes to see his pupils enjoying themselves but does not intend to join them.

We only approached the truth of each other on the importance of fatherhood, of all curious subjects. I think this arose from Conrad being amusingly provocative about Poldy's dependence on his mother. Immediately Harriet spoke up in his defence, I backed her on principle, though privately I thought the relationship too close, and Giles said tactfully that Poldy was still very young. 'But I agree that a boy should not be kept too long under petticoat government,' he continued. 'A father's influence is of immense importance in forming his character. A mother, however perceptive and broad-minded, cannot provide the necessary toughness and grit that a son needs.'

'Darling, how extraordinarily sexist of you!' I cried. 'I'm much tougher and grittier than you are with Joshua.'

He glanced at me quickly, saying, 'Darling, I'm talking objectively, not personally. I know it would have made an enormous difference to me if I had had a father at the formative age.'

I answered fairly crisply. 'Of course, it's preferable to have both parents, but many children don't. Particularly these days, with one in three marriages ending in divorce!'

Giles ignored me, bent on his hypothesis, speaking very positively. 'Something in a boy's character is lacking without the guidance of a father, and the child must of necessity find a substitute. That can be dangerous, even disastrous.'

Conrad leaned forward, eyes gleaming at the prospect of crossing swords.

'*I* had a father,' he began with relish.

And Harriet groaned softly as if she had heard this tale many times before and liked it less each time it was told. He ignored her, too.

'*I* had a father who was jealous of his sons, and ruled his household strictly. An autocratic bastard. I spent my entire youth planning how to escape from home. My choice of the theatre freed me. He cut me out of his will and forbade my mother to communicate with me. She died a few years later. When I had my first success he wrote the conciliatory letter of an old man who realises his mistakes too late. He asked if I would forgive him. I wrote back *"Go to hell"*!'

'Yes, and it was very wrong of you, Conrad!' Harriet remarked. 'And besides, you are sometimes like your father.'

He laughed, in fine good humour, and put an arm round her shoulders.

'So speaks the lady who enjoyed an idyllic childhood and had excellent parents – both of whom I hold in high esteem. We are not all so fortunate.'

It was typical of him to take the limelight. Typical of Giles to talk about masculine needs from a male point of view. I was suddenly sad for myself and tremendously angry with them both.

I said, 'At least you did *know* your father, Giles.

Even though he died when you were young, you have all sorts of memories and anecdotes . . . '

'I remember him going away from that last leave,' said Giles dreamily.

'Lucky for you!' I cried. 'I never knew mine at all, and I can't re-create him either. And it isn't only sons who need fathers, it's daughters, too. Don't you suppose *I* miss having a father, even though I *don't* bring him up as a subject for discussion?'

My words silenced everyone for a moment. Harriet looked sorry, Giles astonished, Conrad intrigued. I realised I had snipped the threads of our conversation, but before I could pick them up again Conrad came smoothly and wittily to my rescue. 'My dear Minerva, you have no need of mortal parents. I am convinced that you sprang, with a great battle cry, fully armed from the head of Jupiter!'

Which tickled Giles's sense of humour and made me laugh unwillingly, and even Harriet smiled as she chided, 'Conrad! What wicked person you are to say such things of our Marina!'

But after that brief spat of revelations our talk became conventional once more.

No one could have faulted Giles. He paid me a graceful compliment, raising his glass and calling for a toast to the creator of the feast. He was charming to Harriet, complimenting her on the health and beauty of her children and herself; and using his slight knowledge of Sweden, acquired on a school trip, talked to her about her own country.

He was judicious with Conrad, and must have done his homework before he came, for he cited plays and films which went back more than a decade. 'Of course, I'm more familiar with your work in the theatre and cinema because we don't watch much television. Tell me, which medium do you find most satisfying?'

So he encouraged everyone else to talk, and told us

nothing of himself. As we sat out in the garden, drinking coffee and liqueurs, he remarked upon the beauty of sky and landscape, and worked in a compliment to the Gages which this time contained a sour note. 'I know that Rina adores this cramped little cottage, but I should find that its charms waned very quickly. Whereas Trenoweth is a real house, full of space and character. I can't think, darling,' turning to me, 'why, with all your expertise, you didn't rent something larger and more comfortable.'

I wished that he had not voiced his complaint in public, and for once I was lost for an answer. Conrad moved deftly in to cover my silence, and to infuse the situation with humour. 'Ours not to reason why, Giles. Contrary to present feminist opinions, I have always believed that this is a woman's world, and the most sensible thing is to go along with it. As our Mr 'Arvey says in the pub, when some beleaguered husband is about to blow a gasket, "Don't you bother none, my 'andsome, just so long as she'm 'appy!" Wise man.'

He mimicked him so aptly that Harriet and I laughed. Then she too moved in on cue, to smooth any ruffled feathers. 'And we are so big a family, Giles. You would not need so big a house. For a few weeks of holiday Hendra is very good and very pretty.'

I had recovered, and remembered. I kept my tone amused. 'Giles, how on earth can you describe this cottage as cramped after some of the accommodation we've had on holiday with the twins? Lord above, think of trailing that wretched caravan all over rainy Spain, and the camping holiday in France when our tent blew over!'

Perversely, my husband refused our proffered hands. 'Oh, it doesn't matter anyway, because I'm off on Tuesday,' he said, equally lightly. Again addressing the Gages and discomforting me, he added, 'And I'm not sure when I can come down again. Quite apart from taking the boys abroad I've got a heap of things to organise in connection with the school. If Hendra suits Rina and Joshua then that's fine by me.'

I avoided looking at Harriet because I knew her expression would reflect my own feelings. His rejection of us and the cottage sat like a stone in my stomach. Giles continued to sip and smile as if nothing were wrong, while the three of us were momentarily silenced. Then I offered more coffee and liqueurs, and Conrad began to talk amusingly about filming in Spain.

On the third and last night of failure Giles sat on the side of the bed, back turned on me, and put his face in his hands. We did not speak for a long time.

Finally he said, 'I must be more tired than I thought.'

This time I could think of nothing to say, and after a while he spoke for me, using the same approach as mine on the first night. 'We'll be all right, Rina, but we've taken a battering over the last year or so. Can't expect to come out of an experience like that unscathed.'

I said, bitter for both the experience and the disappointment, 'Part of our trouble is that you won't talk about it.'

He answered angrily, 'I'm certainly not going to bare my soul and balls to a marriage guidance counsellor, if that's what you mean.'

'I wasn't thinking about our marriage,' I said, surprised. 'I mean Sarah's death. You never talk about her. Do you realise that?'

'What is there to talk about?' he said painfully. 'We went through it all together, didn't we? Wasn't that enough, for God's sake?'

I was trying to formulate what I felt, and again he answered for me. 'I deal with it the only way I can. By myself. Inside myself. You seem to think that there is a prescribed behaviour. Such as yours, for instance? Refusing to carry on with your daily life? Running away to this godforsaken neck of the woods? Let's be honest, Rina. Neither of us could cope. Not you. Not me. Death wasn't on our agenda. Given a job to do, a goal to aim for, we were fine. But thrown into a swamp without a lifeline we've made as big a mess of crawling out as anybody else would.'

I said slowly, 'I'm not making excuses for the way I chucked up London and came here. I know I behaved high-handedly. But I can give you a reason for that. I felt so isolated. You wouldn't talk about Sarah. You wouldn't discuss Joshua. You turned away from everything and concentrated on your work. You left me entirely to myself—'

He spoke warmly, angrily, now. 'I gave you *carte blanche* to do whatever you wanted. I interfered with nothing. I opposed nothing. You went off to nurse your mother soon after the funeral. Fine. I accepted that. You came back and wouldn't do anything or see anyone. I went along with that, too. Finally, you had to rent a cottage in Cornwall, and I was as helpful as I could be. You've had it all your own way, Marina. Now you're feeling much better – and I'm glad of that, grateful for that – but it doesn't mean that I can pick up the pieces and pretend nothing was dropped. I can't match up to your expectations every time.'

There was so much truth in this, though not the whole truth, that he silenced me momentarily.

I said pacifically, 'No, I understand that.' And then, 'As you say, death wasn't on our agenda. I accept that we're dealing with it as best we can, in our different ways. It's just that I wanted everything to be right between us. I'd thought that if we could talk, if we could get together . . . '

But with no communication at all, how could I discuss the possibility of another child?

After a while he said, 'It'll be all right, Rina. We'll sort ourselves out.' He made an effort to reassure me, 'Anyway, I certainly think you did the right thing in coming here, as far as you and Josh are concerned. You're both looking very brown and healthy.'

I said forlornly, 'I'm sorry you don't like Hendra. But you will come back, won't you? Even if it's only for a week with us.'

'Oh, I don't see why not,' he answered vaguely. 'It's just that I can't arrange anything now. Events in the air. Nothing fixed. You know how it is.'

'Yes. I know how it is.'

'And there's no need to worry about *us*, Rina,' he said insistently. 'We've got a damned good marriage. One of the best.'

As if he had proved something to himself, he relaxed and yawned, and on turning over said something to disturb me for the third time that evening. 'Oh, by the way, I've decided to install an answering machine. With you being here, and the house empty while I'm in Switzerland, it will act as a catch-net, socially or business-wise. Keep us in touch with people. And if I'm not around any time you ring up you can leave a message. I thought it a good idea. Don't you agree?'

At that moment I could think of no reason why it should be a bad idea. Later on, lying awake, I perceived it as yet another barrier to direct communication.

Night encourages us to be fanciful. Day is more prosaic. We were good friends over an early breakfast that morning, and some other emotion tinged our departure. Could it have been relief on both sides? Anyway, whatever it was warmed us and gave us hope. We called in at Trenoweth to say goodbye to Joshua, who was breakfasting with the Gage girls in the kitchen while Dagmar dreamed over the teapot.

He waved his cereal spoon and said, 'Hello, Dad!

Goodbye, Dad!' cheekily, which caused hysterical mirth among his young harem.

Dagmar, focusing on us, said ponderously, 'I tell *them!*' and called up the stairs in a throbbing contralto, 'Come down. Come down. Herr Mairdith now home goes!'

The children were convulsed by this announcement. Their hilarity made us, too, feel light of heart. And in a moment or so in came Harriet in a white and blue cotton housecoat, with Poldy clinging round her neck. And after her, tying the sash of his black silk dressing-gown, came Conrad: rumpled, unshaven, red-eyed, but emanating magnetism.

Giles shook his hand, kissed Harriet's cheek, and caught Poldy's soft little fist just before it contacted his jaw. Gallantly, he said, 'Your son is jealous, Harriet. And so he should be!'

Extending his gallantry to me he put one arm around my shoulders, and thanked them for their hospitality and kindness. He seemed as anxious as I to convince them that our weekend had been a success.

He said, 'You made this a memorable break for us, and we're both very grateful. When we next meet I shall bring champagne to celebrate!'

Everyone laughed, and the children joined in out of sheer high spirits. Giles hugged me to him as if we had spent three nights in an Arabian paradise instead of an Arabian desert.

I said to my friends, 'Yes, bless you both. And now it's my turn. If Dagmar can come with me, and Poldy will consent, I'll take all five children to Treen next Saturday, and give you both a day off.'

Harriet cried, 'That will be lo-o-ovely. Will it not, Conrad?'

'We accept,' he said, grinning, 'with more alacrity than is suitable in people of our advancing years!'

And he caught his wife caressingly, possessively, round the waist.

He was some years older than Giles. His face was pleasing but not particularly handsome. His hair was receding. His teeth and his waistline had once been in better condition. But his light eyes danced, and he exuded a zest for living which Giles did not comprehend, let alone possess. Despite twelve years of connubial familiarity, the Gages would make their sun run. Of that I was certain.

The hands of the kitchen clock told us it was time to depart. I put on a great show of catching my husband's hand and smiling into his face as I urged him out, and to give Giles his due he responded. But it was not quite good enough, and when I glanced back at Conrad and Harriet I saw that their smiles were fading. The Gages had not taken to my husband, and in that moment of parting I saw him for the first time through their eyes.

He seemed curiously wooden and artificial, too neat, too precise, too even-featured: like a tailor's dummy. The way that he was, and the way that he looked, now became unpleasing to me. And I saw that Conrad, recognising the difference between spontaneous emotion and mere performance, was not in the least convinced by our play of affection, and even secretly amused.

NINE

July–August

The weekend which marked a change in my marriage also heralded the beginning of the high holiday season, and changed Cornwall too.

The road below, which we had regarded almost as our own, was now noisy with traffic. Cars and motorbikes parked along the cliff top and in every available turning space. Visitors picnicked at the roadside, staring round as they ate their sandwiches and drank tea from a Thermos. The beaches were alive with shouting children, unleashed dogs and glistening sunbathers. Parents and grandparents set up temporary quarters there with the help of windbreaks, sunshades, rugs and deck chairs. Joshua and the girls, formerly monarchs of all they surveyed, now watched their territory being invaded and their rock pools fished by strangers.

The wooden hut near the shore, which since Easter had plied weekend trippers with ice-cream and pots of tea, now took on extra staff and extended its repertoire to take-away food, maps and curios. The veranda blossomed with beach balls, rubber rings, cotton sweaters, buckets and spades. It was open from eight in the morning to six o'clock at night, and sometimes later when the fine summer evenings brought out a fresh drove of pleasure-seekers. The owner and his wife still gave us a friendly nod when we bought ice-cream cornets, but we were no longer of personal interest to them, just part of a crowd of demanding customers.

Harriet and I now did our weekly shopping on a Thursday in Helston, because Friday was the day that the earliest contingent of cars and caravans arrived, filling the car parks, creeping nose to tail from top to bottom of the town. The holidaymakers who were here already strolled in a leisurely manner up and down the narrow streets, or stopped and chatted oblivious of the fact that they were blocking the way, or filled the little tea-room with smoke and talk, and stared round with mild exalted eyes.

The residents took all this in their stride. We long-term visitors, who had felt ourselves to be members of the community, did not. Indeed, when I called to pay Mrs Harvey's August rent in advance and ventured to remark on the inconvenience tourists caused, using the word tourists to describe them, she was rather firm with me in a friendly manner.

'But where should we be without the Visitors, my dear?' she asked. 'There be nothing but a bit of fishing and farming, no tin-mining to speak of, and the worst unemployment in the country. What should we do without'n?'

As if she were afraid of sounding merely mercenary she added with a hint of reproach, 'And then, my dear, think where some o' they poor souls do come from. T'wouldn't be right to begrudge them a bit o' fresh air, now would it?'

I had learned a great deal in the months we had

been here. Social niceties are observed in Cornwall by the older generation as strictly as they were in my Lancashire childhood. Mornings are for work. Afternoons are for light tasks or visiting. A Londoner's idea of country living is to wear jeans and a sweatshirt, drink tea from pottery mugs, and sit with your elbows on a scrubbed kitchen table. Here the older women change when their rough work is done, spread the parlour table with a pretty cloth, bring out their china and home-baking and prepare to make polite conversation or hot gossip, according to the company.

I had only once made the mistake of calling on Mrs Harvey in the morning and her chagrin was evident, though it took the form of a dignified apology.

'I hope you'll excuse me being in dissabell, my dear, but I don't change before two o'clock!'

I pondered on dissabell until it occurred to me that she meant *déshabille*. Thereafter, I made a point of not calling before three o'clock.

On this occasion Mrs Harvey decided I had been sufficiently reprimanded, and offered me a slice of 'eavy cake, which I accepted. Temporarily, I had lost ground with her, and I tried to redeem myself.

'It's just that I feel – we *all* feel, the Gages and Joshua and me – that there was something special in the time we've had here by ourselves. We don't feel like ordinary Visitors.' I was careful not to use the offending word. 'We feel as if we belong here. In a way. I know that we shall all come back again.'

'Well, my dear, I hope you will,' said Mrs Harvey, 'and none more welcome. But it takes more than visiting to belong here.'

She was part of the landscape and its history: a natural outcrop on the face of Cornwall. She had no need to hunt for her ancestors or their patch of earth or a meaning to life.

'Visitors,' said Mrs Harvey, 'only see one side of

us, my dear. And summer is one thing, and winter is another. You'd find Hendra some dark and lonely on they long winter nights!'

'I love Hendra,' I said, 'whatever the season.'

And felt suddenly shy, as if I had confessed to loving a person whom I had no business to love.

She looked at me with quick sharp humour, and a little kindness.

'Oh, my dear, you only know it as it be now, in the summer. But if I was to take you back to when I was a liddle maid, with six brothers and sisters, and all we sleeping in one bed, head to toe like a tin of sardines, and no running water and an earth closet outside, and the wind coming in off the sea on a stormy night, you'd find a world o' difference.'

But Hendra was my beloved, and my haven. I would not acknowledge a darker side. So I sidetracked her. 'You must have seen some changes in your time, Mrs Harvey.'

'Changes? Oh, my dear life! You wouldn't believe!'

And she threw up her hands. One of them held a little embroidered tea-napkin. My landlady was a stickler for old traditions, even if they meant hours of laundry. I took a bit of heavy cake, the reason for whose name I did not have to ask though it was undoubtedly delicious.

'No discos and television in they days,' said Mrs Harvey. 'Lucky if you 'ad a wireless, my dear. And going to the pictures was some treat. Silent, they was, at first. The first picture I ever saw was like a miracle to me. Some film stars they had then. Mary Pickford. Some sweet face. And there was one with Ronald Colman, a talking picture that I never forgot, about him going to Shangri-La. I saw it with my sister Miriam, and when we was walking home I said to her, "Miriam," I said, "when I find the 'ouse of my dreams I be going to call it Shangri-La". And so I did, my dear.'

And she looked round her modern lounge with quiet delight.

'But although you had no luxuries,' I said, anxious for Hendra to hold her best memories, 'you must have had a happy childhood. Far more natural and healthy, far more . . . satisfying than being brought up in a city?'

Why it was necessary for Mrs Harvey to have been happy in Hendra I could not have said, except that I was rootless and my world was a void and I was looking to other people and other places to fill it.

'I did love my dear mother,' said Mrs Harvey quietly, after a long pause, 'and she was a good mother, I can tell you that. And I loved my brothers and sisters, though there's only Miriam left here now. What with the boys going to Canada and Australia and America, and the other girls marrying upcountry. But my father was a hard man. We'm had many a larruping with his belt for nothing. And he drove my poor mam. Drove her to her death, he did.'

She was lost in her past now. The glories of Shangri-La gone from her.

'My mother was hardly forty when she died, my dear. She had the pneumony but my father swore it was nothing but a cold. She never had no doctor nor nothing, and she worked until she couldn't stand. We helped her all we could, us girls, and covered up for her when she ailed. But she had to take to her bed at last, and one night she died in her sleep, my dear. And when my father – may God have mercy on his soul! – woke up and saw that she was dead he shouted her name as if she'd done him an injury, and then he picked her up and shook her. Shook her like a rag doll. Because she'd gone without his leave, you see, my dear. Gone without his leave.'

I set down my cup of strong brown tea, unable to speak.

'There was seven of us living,' Mrs Harvey continued, stirring the sugar round and round in her cup, mesmerised, 'but she must have borne twice as many as that. Miscarried or died young. And I was the eldest girl, and mother to the rest of them when she were gone. I never married until I was past thirty, myself. I took my time and I chose a good 'usband.'

I wondered how I should finish that last morsel of heavy cake.

I said to myself, 'I have no trouble compared to hers.'

She came to, then, with robust common sense. 'Oh, we all have troubles, my dear,' she said, 'and our own always seem 'ardest. That's the way the good Lord made us.'

I asked a final question, no doubt goaded by the notion of a good Lord who allowed a man to work his wife to death, and then shook her for daring to die. 'Was your mother a very religious woman, Mrs Harvey?'

'Oh, 'es!' said with great surprise. 'She did trust in the Lord, my dear, and so do I. I know she's setting there now in one of His many mansions, dressed in silk, and her hands as white and soft as a lady's, waiting for us to join her.'

'And your father?' I couldn't resist asking.

She turned down her thumbs and nodded slowly and gravely.

'Best not ask, my dear. Best not ask.'

I was glad of that. At least all was fair in heaven and hell.

Then she changed the subject by saying that the Lizard air agreed with me, and I was looking better in myself. Word of Sarah's death must have trickled through the local grapevine, for though nobody mentioned it they treated me with greater sympathy. Common suffering is a great leveller.

'Folks say that if you come to live here you put

ten years on your life!' she remarked. 'And look at Mr 'Arvey's mother. Ninety-four! And still bakes cakes for the WI stall in 'Elston!'

I murmured my admiration of Mr Harvey's mother.

'Your 'usband coming back later, is he?' she asked, needing information to pass on, in exchange for what she had given.

'Oh yes, as soon as he can,' I lied. And spun a great tale of his responsibilities, and implied that Joshua and I were pampered creatures, here entirely by his love and chivalry.

'It's a good thing to have a good 'usband,' said Mrs Harvey thoughtfully. 'Mr Gage, now, would you call him a good 'usband?' And she looked at me quickly and shrewdly as if she doubted it.

'Oh, devoted,' I said. 'Absolutely devoted.'

'That's good, then,' said Mrs Harvey, though not quite satisfied with the answer. 'You sure you don't want another slice of 'eavy cake?'

I declined, but asked if I might have the recipe sometime, which pleased her. Then rose and thanked her for the tea and chat.

'You're welcome, my dear, any time,' she said, smiling.

Heavy with more than cake, I walked thoughtfully back home and stopped at Trenoweth for comfort. Dagmar and the other children were on the beach as usual, but Harriet was preparing high tea in the kitchen while Poldy played on the rag rug. Over more tea I retold Mrs Harvey's tale, since I could not bear the burden of it alone.

'No! No! No! That men should do such things!' Harriet cried, shocked, and clapped both hands to her ears.

And instantly unclapped them, to prevent Poldy from striking me with his toy truck for upsetting his mother.

'Harriet,' I said, half angry, half laughing, warding him off, 'you really must wean that child from you. Were you as besotted about the girls?'

'Not in same way. They were different. I lo-o-ved them just as much,' and she elongated the word to indicate its importance, *'but they did not demand as Poldy does. You see, this is a monster like his father.'*

'Ah, how charming!' said Conrad.

He had come in silently to surprise us. He stood grinning in the doorway, with the very devil in his eyes.

'I come home early, thinking how glad my wife will be to see me, and hear myself described as a monster who fathers another monster.'

He smote the doorpost in mock disbelief. His smile widened. The vitality contained in him seemed about to spill dangerously over. The danger was not that he might strike his wife, but that he might there and then drag her off and rape her.

Harriet shrugged one shoulder and gleamed back at him. Her voice purred, her answer was pure endearment.

'But you *kno-o-ow* you are a monster, Conrad!'

She turned to me, laughing, appealing against him.

'Oh, he is nice now, because this film he makes is what he calls the bread and butter . . . '

'It's the film of the television series,' Conrad explained, easy in himself. 'We all slip into our parts as into a row of old shoes. Family entertainment. Nothing demanding.'

' . . . and that is good for us. He is more easy to live with like that . . . '

'The only problem is the weather. Nobody was expecting a perfect summer, and they've had to alter part of the script to suit it.'

' . . . but when he plays a serious part he goes very deep. He suffers. Like giving birth. And we suffer also . . . '

'Still, the money's excellent!' said Conrad, and whistled softly and jingled the loose change in his pockets.

'Do you not make us suffer?' she asked him.

Conrad nodded, unrepentant, and she returned to her complaint.

'Always he is what he does. He can be very moody, very difficult. Even in this part which he knows so well he still looks for something more . . . '

'Because the predictable is so boring!'

'But you make it difficult for *us*. Is it not the truth, Conrad?'

He threw back his head and laughed, and padded about the room, hands in pockets. He was dressed in his usual carelessly expensive style. A cashmere sweater the colour of blood, a black silk neckerchief, slightly soiled white slacks, slightly shabby Gucci shoes. Our eyes followed him, as they were meant to do. Only Poldy looked away, pursed his lips and hummed to his shining truck. Conrad stopped in front of him, legs straddled, staring down, a Colossus. The child lifted his head and stared back for a moment or so, unblinking. Each turned away, deciding to let the other be.

'Have you a cup for me?' Conrad asked, changing the subject.

He returned to us. Touched the sides of the tea-pot.

'Tell me the news. What have you two girls been gossiping about?'

'Something I did not like to hear!' Harriet answered soberly.

He turned to me, demanding, 'Tell *me* then, Marina. Tell me what it is that Harriet didn't like to hear!'

'No, I will not listen,' she said. 'It is too terrible. I go to make fresh tea!'

He caught hold of her arm and pleaded, 'No. Stay,

darling. Stay. Stay with me and listen again,' and held her, and smiled in love and devilment.

Poldy looked up, as if to judge whether a second assault would be allowed, but thought the better of it and hummed to himself, *brm, brm, brm,* as he wheeled the truck across the bumpy terrain of the rug.

I felt stiff, self-conscious, but the tale had stirred something dark and deep in me, and for the second time I relived the horror. Harriet's forehead was furrowed, but Conrad observed and listened with total concentration. When I had concluded my story he drew a great breath through his nose, released his wife's arm and walked the room again, head in air, absorbing, savouring. Then wheeled round to face me, eyes alight.

He held up his right hand, making a circle of thumb and forefinger to emphasise his point. 'Exactly what I needed.' He turned to Harriet, who looked afraid because she knew him. 'The trouble with that final scene,' he said, 'is too much restraint.'

'Ah, Conrad, Conrad, Conrad,' she said to herself, but he paid no attention.

'When Judith dies I bend over her, say her name over and over again softly, turn her face to mine. Yes? On that we were agreed.'

He did not wait for her answer but strode up and down, up and down, possessed.

'So far so good, but not enough. And now, just before we shoot the scene, Marina has given me the answer.'

His face changed. He became what I was when Sarah died: desolate, demented, anchorless.

'I shall pick the girl up and *shake her like a rag doll.* And shout. Shout. Just once. Out of rage with fate.'

He held out his arms in crucifixion, lifted his distorted face and poured the whole of himself into one wild yell.

'Ju-dith!'

The animal howl froze us all for a moment or two. Poldy began to cry, and stumbled over to his mother.

Harriet said coldly, softly, 'I am very angry with you, Conrad. Very angry. You understand?' and comforted her son.

But I was turned to stone. His cry had echoed my loss.

Conrad registered our different responses with quiet satisfaction. Gave us a little nod of acknowledgement. Picked up one of my icy hands and kissed it.

'You told the tale so well,' he said gracefully. 'You have so many talents, Marina. I am eternally in your debt. My family also have cause to thank you. When a scene gives me problems I can be very bad-tempered. Now everyone will be happy, because of you and Mrs Harvey's father.'

He smiled on the weeping Poldy, the reproachful Harriet and my silent self.

'Shook her like a rag doll,' he repeated softly. 'Marvellous!'

And made his exit.

'You see?' said Harriet, after a pause. 'What did I tell you? A monster! Sometimes I wish he did not do this work. But acting is Conrad, and Conrad is acting, and so we must eat the thick end of the pineapples.'

The old Marina in me reared her social head.

'But theatre people are fascinating, and you must know such a lot of them. Do you entertain much in London?'

'I know no one. Sometimes when there is a special occasion I meet them. But Conrad keeps his work and his family in two compartments. He is a private person. He likes to come home and be himself.'

Unkindly, I wondered which self that might be.

'Have you no common friends, then?' I asked. 'Isn't that lonely for you?'

'Oh, yes. We have many good friends, old friends. But the work and the home he does not mix.'

She was thoughtful and silent for a while. Then she said, 'It is better that way, I think. For both of us.'

The splendid weather went on and unbelievably on, each day bright and hot, each evening balmy, each night clear and fine. Water control had been imposed in mid-June. The ban on car-washing was rather a bore but appearances here did not worry me as they would have done in London. If our cars were dirty so were those of everyone else. The ban on hose-pipes and sprinklers made no difference to us either, because these were not our gardens. Nevertheless we saved our bath-water, and felt rather proud of ourselves as we refreshed the dry shrubs: a feeling which was somewhat dashed by an acid letter in the *Helston Packet*, asking the editor why tourists' baths should take precedence over food production.

As it became evident that this was to be a wonderful summer, people pent up in stifling towns and cities became restive. On the spur of the latest forecast they would decide to get away for the weekend at least. Everywhere, bed and breakfast signs bore the notice FULL. Caravan sites were stretched to capacity. Still they came, driving through the night if necessary, weary and dusty, trailing along narrow streets which were never meant for so much traffic, seeking their place in the sun.

And as if fine weather, fresh air and change of place were not enough, a plethora of entertainments awaited them. A rash of local fêtes. Coverack Annual Regatta. Culdrose Air Day. Gooseberry Fair. A Pig Roast at Cury one week and an Ox Roast at Porthleven the next. Gweek Gala. The Lizard Regatta. A Carolaire with illuminated tableaux. And more Coffee Mornings, Afternoon Jumble Sales, Evening Barbecues, Carnivals,

Feasts, Fairs and Horticultural Shows than the most active visitor could possibly attend.

We had become adept at avoiding the worst of the crush, and were going farther afield than the toes of the peninsula now. We had whole-day adventures, ranging up to Tintagel on the north-west coast and eastwards as far as Fowey, driving inland to explore Bodmin moor, and touching on a dozen places in between, anxious to see as much of Cornwall as we could while we were here. Nut-brown and drunk with so much sun, we would return in the evening; the children tumbled up against each other, silent and satiated. And as we drove towards the Lizard we would see cars and caravans drawn up in the lay-bys, dark and quiet, while their occupants slept the sleep which follows a long journey and gives strength for the morrow.

Dreamlike as my existence had become, my former world seemed less real than this one. Giles wrote two informative letters from different parts of Switzerland, and sent a pastoral postcard to each of us, and to my mother. In her weekly letter she recounted his brief message, and said I was to tell him when I wrote back that the card was much appreciated.

Keeping in tenuous touch with my London home, I telephoned a couple of times when I knew Mrs Pettit would be there. I suppose I wanted her to reassure me that all was well, or even that she and the house existed. But each time I was answered by a slightly metallic Giles, who said he regretted that neither of us was available at the moment but if I would leave a message, and my name and telephone number, he would call me back.

I thought for a while, but decided I had nothing to say anyway. So rang off, and did not try again.

* * *

The children giggled among themselves, while we adults wore indulgent smiles. Dagmar's search for love on her afternoons off had been fruitless. She was too speechless, too large and too serious to interest the average young man. Letters from her boyfriend, Klaus, had dwindled to nothing. Harriet fretted for her a little, bestowed small gifts upon her to make up for the greatest gift of all. Then out of the blue came a sunburnt student from Berlin, rucksack on back, touring the West Country, and made Dagmar's acquaintance in Sennen Cove as she sat with the children while Harriet and I went swimming. We returned to find them chattering away in German.

Dagmar stood up as we came dripping from the sea, a flushed and victorious Valkyrie, and said, almost in triumph, 'This is Ulrich.'

He bowed and kissed our hands, and as he was alone and without positive plans Harriet invited him back for supper.

He helped Dagmar to wash up afterwards, and on being invited to stay for the night pitched his tent in the garden at Trenoweth. The night became a week. The week extended indefinitely. Using the tent as his base he was away all day, exploring Cornwall. And though Harriet's hospitality was unstinted he did not abuse it. He was the perfect guest. When he accepted an invitation to dinner he brought a bottle of wine with him. He did not disturb Dagmar at her work, but took her out every evening, and on her free day. Despite offers, he did his own cooking and washing. Simultaneously, he managed to retain his independence while courting his lady.

Dagmar was besotted with him, and Harriet strongly suspected her of visiting his tent when everyone was asleep. She worried about physical and emotional consequences, being responsible for the girl's welfare. And yet felt she must not interfere. Should she, did we think, have a talk with Dagmar?

'I shouldn't bother. She won't be a virgin. Old Klaus will have seen to that. And, anyway, she'll be on the pill,' said Conrad lazily. 'Girls know how to look after themselves these days.'

Harriet regarded him with her brows drawn together. Then I saw her aim deliberately for the heart. 'Conrad, you do not know if these things are true. You only guess. How will you feel when it is one of *your* daughters who is away from home, making love with a strange boy?'

He was swept by a sudden fury that shocked us both, though I could tell that Harriet had experienced it many times before. He raged up and down, gesticulating, shouting, pushing away what really troubled him.

'Why come to me with these domestic worries? This is your business, not mine. Do I ask you to act for me? No. Supposing Dagmar *is* a virgin and Ulrich seduces her? What of it? She must be seduced sometime, or dry up into an old maid. Which would you prefer? What do you want me to do? Sleep outside her door? Confront her lover with a shotgun? What can anyone do in a situation like this but bow to it – and pick up the pieces afterwards?'

Then he stopped in the middle of his pacing and shouting and gesticulating, drew a deep breath and sat down. He bent forward and put his head in his hands for a few moments, and when he sat up again and looked at us it was our charming Conrad. Smiling broadly. He said reproachfully, lovingly, to Harriet, 'My darling, why do you do these things to me?' And shook his head from side to side in disbelief, and walked out.

Chilled, I thought, I could not live with this man.

Harriet sat for a while without speaking, head bowed and colour high. But his rage had evidently purged her apprehensions. After a while she looked at me and shrugged as if to say, 'Very well, then, let them make love.' Aloud she said, 'If Joshua and Bibi are to have their birthday cakes then we must do much cooking!' And reached for her apron as if nothing had occurred.

TEN

The original idea of a joint birthday party was hailed with delight, but how to achieve the extraordinary when hemmed in by the ordinary was defeating Harriet and me. A week before the event we had as yet only decided against venues: too crowded to picnic in the cove, and too complicated to transport an entire birthday party further afield. And yet to hold it at Trenoweth seemed a poor answer. It was Conrad, now free from work, free to shake us out of the pleasing torpor of routine, who brought the idea alive again.

'What's all this mumbling about tea and games for the children? Why can't we carry the long kitchen table out into the garden under the trees, and have a barbecue meal for us all, starting at five o'clock and going on as long as anyone wants to?'

He jumped up and strode the kitchen, hands in pocket, head in air, smiling.

'We must have a grand barbecue in the garden,' he said, as if the Lord had personally handed down this information on a tablet. 'Yes, that is settled.'

Harriet looked at me, pursed her lips, raised her eyebrows. To him she said loudly, 'Conrad, we have no barbecue here! Our barbecue is at home.'

He stared through and beyond her. 'I shall build one out of bricks. The simplest and best form of barbecue, with a grill over it. We can leave it behind us as a present for future tenants, and for ourselves, if we come here again. I shall now go into Helston and buy the bricks and the grill.'

Ignoring us, he called on willing, milling young recruits. 'Who wants to come with Papa into Helston? Who will help me to build a barbecue?'

To be answered by a chorus of, '*We* will, *we* will!' Followed by, 'And can we have potatoes in their jackets?'

'And fish fingers?'

'And hamburgers?'

Poldy shouted, 'And sausages!'

Harriet and I looked at each other significantly, and crossed out the elegant cream tea we had planned.

'And Seven-up!' said Bibi, taking advantage of her own occasion.

'And Babycham!' cried Joshua, greatly daring. Oh, sophisticated Josh!

Which brought forth a chorus of, 'And ginger-beer and Coca-Cola.'

'And pa-per hats!' Poldy shouted. 'Pa-per hats!'

Conrad stood in the middle of the room and lifted his arms into the air, wheeling slowly round, smiling, gathering the children to him. Even Poldy scrambled off his mother's lap and embraced one of his father's legs.

'Listen. Listen, everyone! I shall be the director of this stupendous event. This extraordinary occasion. This party to end all parties!'

'Hurrah!' they shouted together, and jigged up and down. 'Hurrah!'

Conrad picked Poldy off his leg and gave him an affectionate hug. He squatted on his heels, down to child-level, keeping one arm around his son's small shoulders. He spoke confidentially, as one who bestowed news of immense importance.

'I want each of you to write down a list of the things you like best. What you want to eat and drink. What games you would like to play. How the table or the garden or yourselves should be decorated. Anything you can think of. Bibi, you will help Poldy with his list, since Poldy can speak but cannot write! Karin, you will help Lisbet, who does not write very much as yet.'

We all laughed. When our laughter had praised his wit sufficiently he clapped his hands for silence, and rose to his full height which in that moment seemed great.

'Bibi and Joshua, you will find paper and pencils. Karin, Lisbet and Poldy, you will sit at the table quietly. And when you have all finished, my friend Joshua will collect the lists and bring them to me. And then we shall go into Helston, leaving Mamma and Aunt Marina here to sort out the lists, and I'll buy ice-cream and milk-shakes for you all.'

Then he sauntered over to us, well pleased with himself, and accepted our congratulations with a flourishing bow. He had not finished yet. Harriet and I were also under orders.

'It is our party, too,' he said. 'So we must have wine. Marina will cook a special dish for the adults. Roast duck, perhaps . . . ?'

Which I cut short by saying briskly, 'Thank you, Conrad. If I'm cooking I'll choose the dish myself, and the wine to go with it, if you don't mind!'

He bowed in acknowledgement, unperturbed, and continued, 'Harriet shall make us a special pudding. And Dagmar and her lover shall be scullions.'

Harriet whispered, 'Hush, Conrad. In front of the children.'

But they were conferring together, and had not heard him.

Their lists were detailed and lengthy. The general wish was for as great a variety of food and drink as could be consumed and, I imagined, later thrown up; and for a fancy dress party with a theme in which the table and garden were transformed to match it. This was Joshua's idea, and he had written ' . . . like Robin Hood and Made Marian and the Merry Men, and the trees will be Sherwood Forrest, and we want a hornch of vennison on a spit'.

'Joshua, you shall be unlucky with the venison on the spit!' said Harriet.

That evening over our coffee, when the children were in bed and Dagmar mooned along the country lanes with Ulrich, the three of us laughed and joked together. We were more than happy. We were exalted.

It was Conrad, of course, who decided the theme, and chose the Mad Hatter's Tea Party. 'The children shall sit at the top of the table in costume, and we shall sit at the bottom wearing whatever we like – because we are adults, and it doesn't matter about us. Wonderland can only be inhabited by children or lovers or, of course, artists in their moments—'

'Ah yes, the costumes,' said Harriet coolly, interrupting his idyll. 'Tell me of these costumes, Conrad.'

Brought down to earth and finding it uncomfortable, he glided away again. 'My darling, the costumes will be no problem. No problem at all.'

'To you, no,' said Harriet grimly.

Evidently she had experienced this situation before.

'No, no, I mean it. A little crêpe paper. A little imagination . . . '

' . . . and hours and hours and hours of sewing,' I said, backing Harriet.

Conrad walked away, clapping his hands, calling the children to him, giving us further orders at second hand.

'Listen to me! We are going to have the most wonderful Mad Tea Party. Joshua shall be the Mad Hatter in a black cardboard hat, marked 10/6d. Bibi shall be Alice, with a blue hair ribbon and her white party dress and striped tights. Karin is the March Hare, with wired cloth ears and a bow tie and trousers. Poldy will be the Dormouse in grey. Grey shirt, grey shorts. Perhaps a little grey cap with pink ears. So simple. All you need to do, Poldy, is to wrinkle your nose now and again and climb into the tea-pot.'

He turned the light of his countenance full upon me.

'Ah! the tea-pot. We must make an enormous tea-pot out of cardboard, too, Marina will do that for us. I am told that Marina is very clever at making things for children's parties . . . '

Joshua turned away from my accusing eyes, stuck his hands in his pockets and whistled softly to himself.

'But what about *me*?' cried Elisabet. 'You forgot *me*, Daddy!' Her voice rose in pathetic treble. 'You *forgot* me. Who can I be at the Tea Party?'

Certainly her feelings had been hurt, but she was making the most of it. Elisabet had inherited her father's gift for histrionics.

'Oh, oh, oh,' she cried, and clapped her hands to her face in exactly his manner. 'Oh, you *forgot* me, Daddy. You don't *ca-a-a-re* . . . '

Together they played a haunting scene of sorrow and reconciliation.

But Harriet said, arms akimbo, 'I give you one guess who does the hard work to pay for this mistake!'

'My darling,' Conrad was crooning into his daughter's soft little neck, 'you shall be the very first character in the book. You shall be the White Rabbit!'

'With big white furry ears, also wired?' asked Harriet

sardonically. 'And a check jacket, and a waistcoat with a watch in the pocket? Conrad, where do I find these things? Tell me.'

Conrad, stroking his daughter's hair, said over one shoulder, 'Marina will help you, my darling. She can make anything out of nothing. A little bird told me that Marina once gave a Hansel and Gretel party, with a birthday cake like a gingerbread house, and a witch's house built out of cardboard, which was big enough for two children to sit in—'

I called out clearly, after Joshua's retreating back, 'Thank *you*, Judas!'

'Talents are meant to be employed, Marina,' said Conrad, laughing at me.

He shooed Elisabet away, consoled, and came over to me. He placed his hand on my left shoulder and shook it gently.

'Madame Meredith, you shall be our scene-setter and scene-creator.'

Then he moved away, saying idly, 'The tea-pot must be big enough for Poldy to sit in.'

I was disturbed: remembering the twins' Hansel and Gretel party, thinking how short a time we had in which to work this miracle, besieged by mixed feelings about Conrad. His arrogance, his brilliance, his impossibility, his charm, which could be used for or against you, his moods, which changed in an instant, his easy familiarity and his bloody cheek.

I thought how many hours it would take to make that tea-pot.

I said wearily, 'Harriet, you and I need a long stiff drink!'

The children were dancing round Conrad, who accepted their plaudits head thrown back, arms uplifted, as one who has just given an unparalleled performance. We left them rejoicing.

* * *

The lists had been merely the children's outward offerings, to keep us quiet and occupied. This was not a double but a triple celebration. It would have been Sarah's tenth birthday too, and by courtesy of the children she still lived. Harriet and Conrad paid no attention when they huddled together, whispering and looking over their shoulders. But I knew that Joshua and the girls had a secret. Conversation ceased when we approached their magic circle. If anyone asked what they were doing they always had an innocent answer ready. And on us, the outsiders, they turned their small closed faces and private smiles.

A kingly barbecue was built, and successfully survived a trial run on baked potatoes and sausages. Once given his own way, Conrad always behaved beautifully. He was prepared to help anyone, to drive anywhere in the interests of the event, and he kept the children usefully employed while we worked.

The tea-pot was made from a good strong packing case, round which I shaped a cardboard facsimile, covered in flowered wallpaper. I made the lid from *papier-mâché*, and tried out my creation on Poldy, who climbed in and out without difficulty, but was removed with much greater difficulty because he wanted to sleep in it. We then had a scene with Elisabet because she was too big to get in it. Such are the difficulties of trying to please children.

A good idea is like the founding fathers in the Book of Leviticus. It begets others. Conrad had asked too much of me, but not as much as I asked of myself. I took over the more intricate costumes and made paper lanterns for the trees. I planned a dinner for the adults which should be eaten at nine o'clock when the children were hopefully in bed. I chose and bought a different wine for each course. I stayed up late and woke early. I thought of nothing but the party.

A few days beforehand the weather suddenly broke, and on the eighth of August, after weeks of heatwave, we suffered a freak storm. So sudden and so violent was its onset that the Lizard peninsula was blacked out for most of the weekend and all the telephones put out of action.

Conrad and Joshua, looking like advertisements for Skipper's Sardines, dashed importantly between our houses and the village, bringing news, extra candles, and tins of paraffin for the oil lamps. The scene from my parlour window would not have shamed the onset of Noah's Flood. Thunder rumbled and cracked, lighting darted. Rain poured down into a turbulent sea. We were penned in. Bucket and spade times were over. Jigsaw puzzles, word games, hide and seek were the order of the day, and we worried lest this was the end of the summer. And yet the weather had its beneficial aspects.

Sewing costumes in the little parlour at Hendra, with Josh asleep upstairs, I was tranquil. The storm might rage outside, slapping and buffeting the granite walls like some enraged giant who would huff and would puff and would blow the house down. But it had raged in this fashion hundreds of times since Hendra was built, and still she stood. The lamplight was very soothing to work by, and its shadows were kindly. Sometimes I felt as if Sarah were with me, that I had only to turn my head and see her as she used to be, bright and dark and watchful behind me. But spirits are such shy things that I feared I might lose her if I caught her out. So I preferred to stitch away serenely, silently, while my daughter kept me ghostly company. At the heart of the storm I was at peace with myself, content.

'La-dies and gen-tlemen!' cried Conrad, beating a tattoo on Poldy's drum, 'Roll up, roll up, for the experience of a lifetime . . .'

The sun was shining as if it had never been away. In the garden at Trenoweth we adults stood beneath the trees, dressed in our finest, ready to clap as the children's procession appeared on the stroke of five o'clock. A Cinderella of a farm-kitchen table had been transformed by this fairy godmother into a crêpe festival of white and green. Two Windsor armchairs at its head waited to welcome the principal guests. Around it were grouped an assortment of lesser chairs, standing before places marked by cards. Karin, Dagmar, Ulrich and me on the left. Elisabet, Conrad, Poldy and Harriet on the right. The foot of the table had been left empty so that Harriet and I had room to bob up and down and in and out, supervising the meal.

On the long grills of the barbecue lay a crackling brown feast of hamburgers, cheeseburgers, fish fingers, chicken legs and sausages. There was not room for everything. Harriet had baked potatoes in the house oven. On a smaller table at the side a second contingent awaited incineration.

Conrad's tattoo on the drum became frantic.

'La-dies and gen-tlemen!' he cried. 'Pray give a hearty welcome to the birthday guests. Bibi Gage, who is nine years old today and Joshua Meredith who is ten! And their principal friends, Karin, Elisabet and Leopold Gage.'

We clapped as hard as we could, and from the back door came the children in full costume, hand in hand, and marched solemnly towards us on the lawn.

Bibi in white and blue, with her long ashen hair brushed away from her face, stepped forth in striped stockings and strapped shoes. Beside her, nearly a head taller, strode Joshua: a Mad Hatter in glasses. Behind them came a March Hare waggling its ears, a White Rabbit consulting her watch and saying, 'Oh, my tail and whithkerth. I'm late. I'm late,' and Poldy wrinkling his nose and demanding, 'Where's my tea-pot?'

Conrad put up one hand to halt the procession, and lifted the other to summon us to song.

'La-dies and gen-tlemen, I give you Bibi and Joshua. Joshua and Bibi. Let us welcome the birthday people!'

Something stronger than conspiracy swept over the four older children. The three girls looked at Joshua meaningfully, and Joshua spoke out clearly before we could open our mouths. 'You have to welcome Sarah, too. It's Sarah's birthday, too.'

'It's Sarah's birthday, too,' echoed the three girls with conviction.

Poldy, ignorant of the forces behind this front, added his voice. 'Sarah's birfday, too.'

For the first time I saw Conrad troubled for someone else, and momentarily at a loss. He was trained to deal with surprises as if they were normal occurrences. He should have waltzed through this one. But he hesitated because he was afraid to hurt me. He glanced at me uncertainly, waiting for guidance, I was aware of Harriet frowning in concern, and Dagmar explaining to Ulrich in German that Sarah was my *Tochter* and *tot*. But I felt neither concern nor surprise. I had not known what would happen today, but knew something would.

I nodded to Conrad emphatically.

And instantly he cried, as if there were nothing unusual about this, 'Let us wish a happy birthday to Bibi and Sarah and Joshua!'

The children smiled at each other joyfully as we sang, and Conrad ushered them to their places.

Joshua said, daring us to cross him, 'You haven't got a chair for Sarah. Couldn't you put one at the foot of the table? There's plenty of room there.'

Again Conrad looked to me for guidance, and Harriet wore her frown of concern. But I went along with the fantasy as if I had been schooled in it.

I said pleasantly, 'Why don't we bring another chair to the top of the table, and have her sit between you both? Then you'll all be together.'

The children observed me closely. Seeing that I was serious, Ulrich went indoors and found another chair.

Poldy, fixing round blue eyes on the empty place, asked, 'Who's Sarah?'

I answered, 'Sarah is Joshua's sister, but we can't see her.'

'Oh,' said Poldy, and accepted the explanation.

Harriet, daughter of a Swedish pastor, clapped her hands to bring us all to attention, heads bent, and said, 'Now let us give thanks for the good food.'

Seldom must a Christian grace have blessed such an unorthodox occasion.

Then she looked up and smiled and said, 'Now we begin!'

Conrad lifted an autocratic finger at the kitchen staff to fill everyone's glasses with either wine or fizzy drinks, and became the toastmaster.

'To Bibi and Sarah and Joshua!' he cried, and we echoed him.

The two children sat down decorously on either side of their ghostly guest.

Standing by my son with a tray of hot dogs I said, 'Is Sarah eating?'

To which he replied, 'Not really, Mum, but it would be polite to give her something, wouldn't it?'

So her frankfurter grew cold in its roll, and when we were clearing the plates I cut it up small and gave it to Webster, who was sniffing round as usual, looking for a little something extra.

Conrad and Harriet and I, busy waiting on everybody, drank a glass of wine and ate a slice of birthday cake, and said nothing of importance to each other. I think they were afraid I might break down, but there was no danger of that. I was quite content. I did not mind. I had sensed my daughter with me all week. It was fitting that she should attend her birthday party, and there she remained from start to finish. Conrad was in his element, sustaining the fantasy with gusto. When the children included her in their games, he made sure that she won two of them.

The heat of late afternoon softened into early evening. Excitement and exhaustion began to take their toll. At seven o'clock Poldy threw a tantrum and was put to bed. At eight o'clock Elisabet quarrelled with Karin, and they pulled each other's furry ears off and cried, and were put to bed also. But Joshua and Bibi seemed tireless.

It had been a long hard day for the adults. We needed to be by ourselves, to relax, to eat the dinner I had prepared. In return for our privacy we granted the birthday-children unlimited play-time within the territory of Trenoweth and Hendra.

'Even until ten o'clock?' Bibi asked incredulously.

'Yes, if you can stay awake that long!'

'Oh, thanks!' they said in chorus. 'Please can we play with the tea-pot?'

'Yes, but take care of it.'

'We will, oh, we will.'

I tried to think of any possible mischief that they might get up to, and came up rather feebly with, 'Don't put Webster in it.'

The shook their heads solemnly.

We had been taking photographs of the party during its progress. On an impulse I pick up the camera and capture Alice and the Mad Hatter walking away from us, along the path between the trees, carrying the vast flowered tea-pot by its spout and handle. On his hat, cocked at a rakish angle, is printed 'Latest Style. 10/6d'. A blue ribbon restrains her long pale silver hair. The leaves nearest them are transparent with evening light. I have the snapshot still. There is fantasy in it, and mystery, and terror. Or do I see the terror only in retrospect?

We have dined royally and are all slightly drunk. We smile at each other for no particular reason and conversation ceases. Dagmar and Ulrich sit in amorous silence: heads together, hands entwined. Harriet's blue-grey eyes are pleasantly dazed. But Conrad is rising from his chair to give yet another toast. As he lifts his glass it sparkles against the light. His wine is the colour of blood, the colour of the flowers splashed over my black cotton dress.

He pauses until even our wandering attention is focused on him, and when he speaks his voice is as mellow as the summer evening.

'To Ma-ri-na! Creator of the largest tea-pot in the world – and this most exquisite feast!'

He allows them to applaud and sip, then raises his hand for silence. The words come tenderly, beautifully.

'"Age cannot wither her, nor custom stale her infinite variety . . . "'

He gestures at the crumpled table-cloth and smeared napkins, the wild flowers drooping in their jam-pot vases, and dregs and crumbs of a banquet.

'"Other women cloy the appetites they feed . . . "'

He is looking directly at me as he speaks, and I stare back hypnotised, hoping that Harriet is really as sleepy as she seems.

'" . . . but she makes hungry where most she satisfies."'

My legs begin to tremble and I stiffen myself against the tide of his feeling and meaning. I smile as if I am flattered by his deliberate flattery, and pray that everyone else is taking it that way.

He smiles too, in triumph at the effect he is having on me, in wry humour because in order to trap me he must also trap himself.

Dagmar and Ulrich are not listening. Harriet's eyes are closing.

Conrad leans forward so that only I can hear him, and says softly, '"Let's have one other gaudy night."'

Alice is running, running through the tulgy wood, pale hair flying behind her. Is the dreaded Jabberwock in pursuit? Are the Lion and the Unicorn about to engage in furious battle? No, she has changed roles and become the King's Messenger.

'Oh, come quickly! Oh, come quick!' she cries. 'Joshua tried to climb the cliff and he's stuck half-way and can't get down!'

We are all instantly sober and on our feet. Conrad takes charge of the situation as by right, though with consideration for my feelings.

'Marina, you will want to come with me. And Harriet also? Dagmar, stay here with the other children, please. Ulrich, I shall need you.'

Alice flies ahead of us and we stumble after her, pell-mell down the path and over the road, which still holds its complement of evening cars. A little crowd of watchers is huddled at the edge of the sea, staring upwards. As we push our way through their words catch us distractedly.

'They were playing on the sand one minute, and the next minute he was up there climbing . . . '

' . . . always the same in the holiday season. Two girls trapped on a cliff near the Lizard last month . . . '

' . . . two lads blown out to sea in a dinghy at Kennack Sands . . . '

' . . . just come down to exercise our dog, and then we see that boy up there, and the liddle maid with the tea-pot . . . '

The centrepiece of our Mad Tea Party is parked on a flat-topped rock some yards away: a flowered and sinister fantasy in the evening light. With one part of my mind I see the perils of its situation, but then my son is at greater risk and I forget my cardboard creation in favour of my human one.

' . . . doing a bit of evening fishing, you see. Didn't notice at first . . . '

' . . . and we wasn't near enough, or we'd have stopped him . . . '

Conrad cuts through the noise of the extras, crying importantly, 'The boy belongs to us. Let us through, please. Let us through!'

'It's the boy's parents!' they tell each other. 'Let them through!'

We find ourselves suddenly propelled to the front row.

'There!' says Bibi, pointing, and bursts into tears.

The party to end all parties and the accepted presence of Sarah has been too heady a potion for Joshua. A temporary Lord of Misrule, he has left the safety of home ground to seek further adventure and excitement, and found himself unaccountably imperilled.

The Mad Hatter is standing on a ledge, clinging to the face of the rock, still wearing his top hat. High spirits and general elation have tempted him up this steep pitch, and he has scrambled nimbly enough until, Alice tells us, a crumbling hold gave way and stranded him. He is now immobilised: afraid to go on and unable to come back. In the flurry his glasses fell off. She points to a boulder just ahead of us. The evening sun winks off his crazed spectacles like a portent of what is to come.

'Marina,' says Conrad, 'will you allow me to deal with this?'

I nod, because I cannot speak and would not know what to say if I found my voice. Harriet puts one arm round me and the other round Bibi.

Conrad's voice is light and genial and carries splendidly. We all listen, mesmerised. Someone whispers,

'That's Conrad Gage. He's been making a film on the Lizard.'

'Joshua, my old friend, I am here. Don't worry. We'll get you down but it may take a little while. Just hold on.'

The Hatter's voice is light and frail.

'I am – holding on – but, please – don't be – very long.'

The watchers offer us information and advice.

'Call the fire brigade. They'll bring one of they ladders!'

But the sea is coming in fast, and the sand is treacherously soft.

'Throw a rope from the top and pull the boy up!'

But a notice warns that the edge of the cliff is unstable and people should stay well away from it.

Ulrich then proposes to climb up and guide Joshua down, but a fine rain of earth, a soft patter of stones beneath his plimsolls, tells him that the cliff face is not particularly stable either.

An elderly Cornish couple, whose dog trots hither and thither busy with its own concerns, speak in tones of doom. ' . . . some speed that tide's coming in!' Slyly it rushes up, wets the heels of Ulrich's plimsolls, and coyly recedes. ' . . . and if the boy be marooned then I don't know what!'

Keeping his eyes on my son, Conrad says to Bibi urgently, affectionately, 'Run like the wind, my darling. Ring 999. Tell them what's happening and ask for help. Quickly. As quickly as possible.'

Harriet says hurriedly, 'I will go with her. She is only a child, to give and take such important messages.'

'Is – Mamma – there?' Joshua asks.

Only fear or desperation could have forced out his baby name for me. I find my voice and say, 'Yes, darling. Hold on. Hold on.'

Conrad grasps my arm firmly to give me comfort

but his attention is concentrated on my son. He is summoning all his knowledge and his personal magnetism to hold Joshua where he is. The watchers gather round us, hushed and horribly fascinated.

'Joshua,' Conrad says lightly but firmly, 'keep facing the rock. Don't try to look round. Don't talk if you don't want to.'

A little silence. Joshua is nodding, and probably swallowing his terror in order to speak. Now Conrad's voice changes, and becomes so friendly and intimate that they might be talking alone together.

'I didn't know you could climb so well. Have you been climbing long?'

My son, endeavouring to adopt the same tone, sounds strained and near to tears, and his breath comes short and fast, punctuating his sentences. 'Only – trees – but the rocks – looked – pretty easy – and they were – at first. Then I – looked down – and I'd come – further up than I – meant to – and I felt – scared – and I wanted – to come down – but then I thought – I'd better – go on – because you said – never to give in – to fear . . . '

If I could move my stone fingers I would turn on Conrad then and rend him to pieces. He knows that and does not blame me, tightens his grip on my arm and says, 'Sorry, sorry, sorry!' under his breath. Then focuses again on Joshua.

'That was very brave,' he says. 'I'm rather old to start climbing but I'm pretty good at walking. You and I must do some walking together. Perhaps Ulrich will take us hill-walking. Ulrich is a great walker.'

'I kn-know,' Joshua stammers. Then he too makes an effort and repeats firmly, 'I know. He told me.'

Ulrich speaks better English and has a better grasp of the situation than Dagmar would. Picking up his cue from Conrad, he joins in the bid to occupy Joshua's mind with matters other than his imminent downfall.

'Next year I plan to walk in Swiss mountains. Perhaps, Joshua, you come and stay with me, and we walk much together?'

Joshua's voice floats down to us, disembodied, hollow, but doing its best to sound interested.

'I-I'd like to climb the M-M-Matterhorn some d-day!'

I begin to sob quietly under my breath. 'Oh, Josh, Josh . . . '

Bibi is back, running, running, followed by Harriet.

For years afterwards, whenever I thought of Bibi it was in her guise that late summer evening as Alice: running, running, pale hair flying behind her, eyes serious, mouth intent.

Her message, jerked out as she runs, is picked up and carried towards us by our ever-attentive audience.

'They're sending a helicopter . . . '

'Sending a helicopter . . . '

'From Culdrose . . . '

'Culdrose . . . '

And everyone heaves a great sigh of relief and delight, for the rescue will be as thrilling as the escapade.

An onlooker forms his hands over his mouth in the shape of a megaphone, in order to convey the news to Joshua, but Conrad rightly regards this as his prerogative and refuses to be upstaged. Before the man can speak he pitches his voice so that message rides magnificently over us all.

'Joshua, they are sending a helicopter from Culdrose! It will be here any minute now!'

And this is good because the tide has driven us up the beach and is swirling round the foot of Joshua's cliff and the light is fading fast.

Between them Ulrich and Conrad write a scenario of walking and climbing summers to come, but my son is silent now. Someone thrusts a pair of binoculars in my hand. I focus them and see him, face pressed against the rock, eyes closed, tears trickling slowly down his cheeks, and water trickling down one leg. He has reached his pitch of terror. We are all silent then: watching and waiting and praying. Yes, I am praying to You. Giving You one more chance. Where were You when my remaining chick took it into his Mad Hatter head to climb a dangerous cliff?

Presently, heralded by the thrum of its propellers, a black spot against the dark gold sky swells larger and larger until it becomes a Sea King helicopter, hovering overhead to assess the situation. Joshua neither looks nor turns, immobilised against the grey rock. The helicopter judges its distance nicely, and presently lets down a man on a line, who finds a ledge a few yards to one side of the boy and makes his way across crabwise.

I am dreaming now, no longer angry or afraid. I lean humbly on Conrad and he puts his arm round my waist and holds me fast. I watch my son being persuaded to part from his refuge. This takes time and is difficult because his fingers are welded to the rock which is his safety, but at length it is done. He is caught up, caught fast, by his rescuer, who signals the helicopter to draw them both up. I watch that small body swinging out into space like a mouse in an eagle's claws. The Mad Hatter's hat is falling and turning, turning and falling, onto the crawling gold of the sea, and my heart turns and falls with it. Down, down, down.

No one makes a sound. No one moves. We all stand with our mouths open and our faces lifted to the sky. Joshua is being drawn up little by little to safety. We hold our breath until we see the soles of his Clark's sandals disappear into the belly of the helicopter. Then pandemonium breaks loose, and we cheer wildly and clap and stamp and shout, for this has been a breathtaking performance. For some moments we stand in silence, all emotion spent, and then smile at each other. Some onlookers shake my hand or pat Conrad's shoulder. All of them wish us well, and hope that the boy will be none the worse for his experience. An onlooker has rescued Joshua's broken spectacles and gives them to me with a bow and a courteous apology.

'Thank you, but it's all right,' I reassure him. 'We always carry a second pair, just in case of accidents.'

We start to walk away to lead our ordinary lives. But there is to be an encore.

Bibi cries in anguish, 'We forgot the tea-pot! Oh, can't we save the tea-pot?'

And everyone stops and stares as the tide, which has been rushing round the flat rock, lifts my creation, bobs it towards us as if to say, 'Look what I've got!' and immediately carries it beyond our reach.

Conrad answers for us all. 'No, no. It's too far out. Too late. Too dangerous. Too dark.'

Someone says, 'It's following that top hat.'

Only the white ticket is clearly discernible in the twilight, rocking to and fro as if waiting for its companion. 10/6d. 10/6d. 10/6d. 10/6d. 10/6d. The tea-pot, now well under way, floats after it in stately fashion.

We stop and stand and watch as the final curtain falls on that curious day, and the props set sail for another Wonderland.

They took Joshua to Treliske hospital and treated him for shock. I think Conrad drove me there, and brought us both home, but I don't know when. I didn't connect things for a day or so. I know I relied completely on Conrad because I couldn't get in touch with Giles. When they gave my son back to me at last, I held the boy very tight and cried, not caring that I was making a fool and a mess of myself and shaming him into the bargain.

Back in the land of the living, Joshua apologised handsomely to everyone, and wrote a letter to Culdrose to thank them, as I had done. He took full responsibility for the incident, and with chivalrous care he exonerated Bibi who had endeavoured to dissuade him. But when I asked what on earth possessed him to climb an unstable cliff at that time of the evening, with the light failing and the tide coming in, he shook his head and remained as puzzled as the rest of us.

Something had been abroad that birthday night, something strange and perilous, which had subtly altered our relationships. Now I felt Sarah's presence so palpably that I would turn round expecting to perceive her bright spirit. Yet I noticed that she no longer played a central part in the children's games, and Joshua was closer to me than to his twin.

Harriet seemed preoccupied, though as kind and caring as ever. Between Conrad and me lay something we could not acknowledge. We kept up a cordial mocking discourse, but I was locked in a fantasy world to which he held the key. Occasionally a covert gleam from him acknowledged that we were fellow prisoners. And all of us continued our brief summer lives together.

ELEVEN

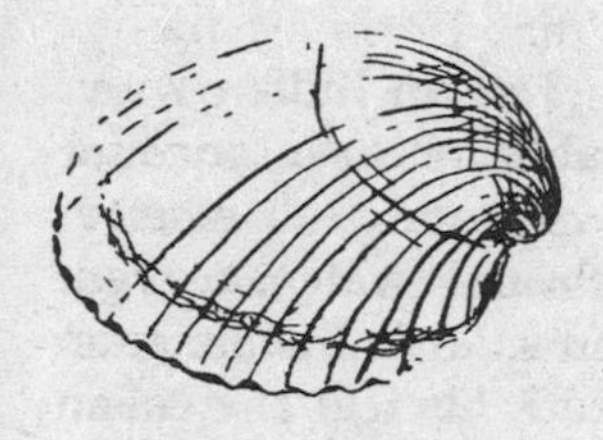

What a holiday Webster was having. The Gage girls adored him. I am sure he would have preferred to be left alone, but public adulation makes idiots of us all and he was no exception. In homage to his admirers, he had extended his territory to include Trenoweth as well as Hendra, and made it his hunting ground. Now and then he caught a mouse in Harriet's pantry, but only under protest, in spite of the choice morsels offered as reward, because he was a busy fellow who led a double life.

Though Webster had been neutered this did not prevent him from snuffing and leering at female cats. In London his long-standing and unconsummated love was for a spayed Persian of noble pedigree who lived next door. Her proximity apparently gave rise to pleasant frissons but no discontent. He seemed happy to sit for hours, winking and washing his whiskers, keeping a chivalrous distance, while she sat in her blue-grey bower of fur and fixed him with relentless amber eyes. Here in Cornwall he should have remained in a state of innocence, for there were no domestic cats within half a mile of us. Then, soon after our arrival, a wild Delilah wandered into his territory: unspayed, untamed, and very pregnant.

From the beginning he had allowed her – or perhaps could not prevent her from stealing his food. When her progeny arrived, his offerings were laid at her feet instead of ours. He became the involuntary, unthanked, unrewarded father of a family which was not his own.

According to Joshua, soft-footed as an Indian when his curiosity was aroused, Delilah concealed her four kittens in the hollow of a ruined stone wall nearby. He had crouched in the bushes and watched them playing while their mother stood guard. But as soon as she heard a twig crackle beneath his feet she called them, and they vanished into their sanctuary.

We felt rather sorry for Webster, whose days of careless love were over. As the kittens were weaned from mother's milk to fresh-caught meat his responsibilities became greater still and he wore quite a harassed air. Out of compassion for his plight I put saucers of food for Delilah and her brood down at the bottom of the garden. Still Webster remained her slave: overworked, undervalued, and unrewarded.

During the month that changed all our lives Delilah came into heat. At once his humble domestic Eden became a jungle invaded by wauling toms, and he himself must have been besieged by longings he could neither understand nor satisfy. He redoubled his attentions to Delilah, but they were not the ones she wanted. We saw him in his few free moments sitting thinking, trying to puzzle the situation out. And, of course, being Webster, he came up with the wrong solution. He decided that his lady was innocent and he must defend her virtue.

Joshua and the girls were delighted. The call of

'Webster's fighting again!' would fetch them from anywhere. Occupying vantage points from which they could watch the gladiators, the children cheered their champion on and reported his exploits afterwards. And he who had been such a coward in London, staring the other way when our garden was trespassed, now took on all comers, however huge, gnarled, ugly and experienced, and finally chased them off his territory. Such exploits of tooth and claw were new to the children, and Conrad aroused their greater interest by explaining the sexual and reproductive life of cats. Meanwhile Josh and I had a regular task at the end of each day, bathing Webster's wounds with diluted Dettol while he howled mournfully and scratched us for helping him.

The children took him everywhere with them on our private ground, but I had always refused to let him be carried to the beach, because a road lay between there and home. And the animal himself showed plenty of common sense, for when his admirers stood under the wall outside and called seductively up to him, 'Web-Web-Webbie!' he would poke his flat head through a thin part of the hedge and look down, as if to say, 'You won't persuade *me* to go out there!' and then withdrew, leaving them to come to him or stay away as they chose. But when the hunt is up, the hounds running, the blood coursing, and the wild horns blowing, only the moment counts.

'Mummy! Mummy! Mummy! Something awful's happened!'

It is Joshua, streaked with dirt and tears, breathless with grief, who flings himself into my arms and bursts out sobbing. 'Oh, Mum, it's Webster. Poor old Webster. He chased a tom-cat right down the lane. We were following, Mum, and egging him on. A great big tom-cat, about a hundred times as big as old Webbie.

And it shot across the road. And Webbie shot after it, and there was a car coming round the corner. The tom-cat got away, but Webster's dead, Mum. The car spun him up in the air. And it never stopped, Mum. Never even stopped.'

'So we looked both ways, and when the road was clear we went over and picked him up. Bibi said she wasn't sure he was dead, but he looked very flat and he had a funny grin on his face, and he felt wobbly. So we took him to Trenoweth, and Aunt Harriet said, yes, he was, and she wrapped him in a tea-towel. And all the girls are crying, and Poldy's crying, and Aunt Harriet. Uncle Conrad isn't crying, but he's very sorry, and he says he'll bury him if you like. But I said I must tell you first. I must go and tell you that Webster's dead.'

And he sobbed aloud.

'Oh, my dear child,' I said helplessly, more concerned for boy than cat.

I would have put my arms round him, but he held me away.

'And that's not all. It's not all. Mum, I didn't believe about Sarah being dead. I knew she was, but I didn't believe it. D'you know what I mean?'

'Yes, I know. I know.'

'But when I looked at Webster I *knew* he was dead. And at the same time I knew *Sarah* was dead. And now I've lost both of them. Both at once, Mum.'

I had no words with which to comfort him, but he let me hold him to me and I pressed my lips to his head, and stroked his dark and silky hair. My fingers perceived the bones of the skull beneath, reminder of mortality. The force of his sobs shook an answering sob from me. His sorrow re-created my sorrow. And we cried together for both Sarah and Webster. I had not realised until then how fond I was of that contrary animal.

If Harriet had been comforting Joshua she would

have spoken of the glories of heaven, for Harriet had faith. But I had not, and could not. Still, the spirit lived on. That much I knew from Sarah's presence. For I sensed her behind us at that moment, standing in the doorway watching us.

So I was able to say, 'Yes, they're both dead, Josh. But they'll be alive in our minds for as long as we live. And Webster will be all right because Sarah will look after him now.'

I felt his nod beneath my cheek, and spoke into his silky bony head. 'He'd had such a wonderful summer here and he went down fighting,' I said, 'and his death was very quick. He couldn't have known.'

Another nod, and a snuffle.

'He need never leave Hendra now,' I said more cheerfully. 'He can be buried here. Webster's happy hunting ground! You must admit that he wouldn't have cared much for life in London after all these adventures.'

A bubble of laughter interrupted Joshua's sob. He lifted his face to smile on me, took off his glasses and wiped his eyes, wiped his glasses, blew his nose.

'I'll bet the mice will be glad!' he said.

I rubbed his head and stood up. 'What about a glass of lemonade?' I asked.

'Yes, please. Oh, and, Mum, Aunt Harriet said they'd all follow me in about a quarter of an hour. But they're in trouble themselves, Mum. Ulrich packed up his tent this morning and left, and Dagmar's having hysterics.'

'You mean they've quarrelled?'

He gulped at his lemonade and said gratefully, 'Thanks, Mum.' Then, 'Nope. Ulrich just said he must be moving on. And he seemed to think it had been jolly meeting her, but that was that, sort of thing. And Bibi said that Dagmar ran into the kitchen in her shortie nightie, straight from Ulrich's tent, and told them. Bibi said she screamed and threw herself down on the floor and beat it with her fists. And Aunt Harriet put her to bed. And Ulrich came to say goodbye to them and he sort of apologised for upsetting her but he went just the same.'

'Dear God!' I said, sympathetic and yet, I must admit, slightly amused.

'She'll get over it,' said Joshua, downing his lemonade.

This was the voice of the male, and I surveyed my son with some irony. 'You rotten blighter!' I said lightly.

He looked up at me, a rim of lemonade on his mouth, and said quite seriously, 'I'm sorry about Dagmar, but she *is* alive, Mum!'

A little procession of Gages was coming through the garden gate, headed by Conrad with a spade over his shoulder. Harriet held Poldy by one hand and Elisabet by the other. Bibi and Karin solemnly carried a tray before them on which lay the body of Webster, wrapped in a clean tea-towel.

'Madame,' said Conrad, his tone in keeping with the formality of the occasion, 'your word is my command. How do you wish me to dispose of this noble animal, who died in pursuit of the enemy and in the cause of chivalry, upholding the honour of his lady?'

I answered him, but spoke to the children. 'I think we should give him a lovely funeral. Not the usual dismal kind. A joyful funeral. A celebration for Webster. Shall we?'

The children's faces brightened.

Conrad answered, 'It shall be done!' and presented arms with his spade.

As with the birthday party, everyone had their own idea how the ceremony should be conducted, so Webster's burial was both rich and strange.

Conrad cast himself as both pagan priest and sexton, extolling the glories of love and battle, and gave Horatio's final speech from Hamlet, which made everybody cry again. Joshua laid him to rest in the dark Cornish earth, surrounded by his few possessions: cat dishes, flea-comb and brush, and a tin of Jellymeat Whiskas as provision for the journey. Harriet made a cross out of two sticks of firewood and etched his name on it with a black biro. The girls filled an empty Rose's Lime Marmalade jar with wild flowers, and set it there in tribute to him. And Poldy beat a final tattoo on his drum.

So we made an event of farewell. The day became hot and bright but our general mood was quiet and contemplative. The Gages went home to deal with their own casualty.

Left to ourselves, Joshua and I spoke of Webster as I had longed to speak with Giles of Sarah. We remembered him, which is all that is required. For the living cannot relinquish the dead at once, but must let them go gradually. We should not cling too hard nor too long, nor try to raise them, but we have need to speak of them and to relive the times we shared with them.

We talked of his obstinacies, his ingratitude and his independence. We marvelled at his final three months, in which life was lived to the hilt, and spoke of his end, which was in its way glorious. And when we had finished, and washed our eyes and hearts clean, we went for a stroll along the beach and collected some more shells.

Late that evening, when Joshua was fast asleep, I walked over to Trenoweth to see how their own crisis was faring, and met Dagmar in the hall, carrying a supper tray upstairs to the privacy of her room. She was wearing a black and white caftan and bright pink carpet slippers. Her hair hung down her back, long and loose and slightly damp, as if she had recently taken a bath. She looked very young, laid bare by sorrow.

For the first time I saw her as a human being rather than an object of fun, and asked her if she was feeling a little better.

She nodded, wordless, and seemed about to cry again, which I had not intended. Quickly, I diverted her attention from her heart to her stomach.

'Oh, doesn't that look and smell delicious?' I remarked, of the buttered eggs and hot coffee, the ripe peach on a blue plate.

Her face was swollen with the day's grief, but she did her best to answer. 'Harriet does this,' said Dagmar. 'Harriet is good to me always.'

The tray had been set with care, tempting both eyes and appetite. Only one touch of artistry was missing.

I took a red rose from the vase on the hall table, and placed it on the tray. 'To a new love!' I said gently.

Joshua dashed in, delivering messages in short bursts, 'The tide's coming in and Dagmar's taking us swimming. Where are my trunks and snorkel? And Uncle Conrad's here with the millionth invitation this summer.'

I put Marina Meredith forward to answer with her usual composure while my inner self shivered.

'Your trunks and snorkel are on the bathroom floor, where you dropped them this morning. What time will you be back? Hello, Conrad. Just let me deal with this whirlwind and we'll have an early-evening drink.'

Conrad looked as if he had been sailing, but though his clothes so cleverly played the part I knew very well he had not. A chameleon, he took colour and tone from the place in which he found himself, and had decided on this role.

'You didn't tell me you owned a yacht!' I remarked unkindly.

He sat down smiling, saying, 'Why do I prefer to be snubbed by Marina rather than be praised by anyone else?'

Like Jesting Pilate he did not stay for an answer but went on, 'Dagmar is writing to Ulrich – who had been careful not to give her an address but unfortunately let slip the name of his university. And also to the long-silent Klaus. Very much against my advice, I can tell you. It's obvious that neither of them is interested. Leave hunting to the men! I said. But she wouldn't listen to me—'

'Mum, where are the beach towels?'

'Poor old Dagmar,' I said automatically, and in a louder voice, over my shoulder, 'In the top drawer!'

Conrad settled his head back, crossed his legs, swung his foot to and fro. 'Meanwhile she has returned to reading romantic German novels, of which she brought a haversackful. Inflaming an appetite which cannot be satisfied. "Read English trash instead," I tell her. "That way you'll learn the language!" But she pays no attention. She is incapable of learning anything.'

An apparition in a snorkel, with a bundle under its arm, snuffled at us 'See you later, then!' and shot out.

Afraid to look at Conrad I walked over to the corner cupboard, saying, 'What would you like to drink? Scotch on the rocks? Scotch and soda?'

I was so aware of his presence that my flesh cringed. And I was counting in my head because I could judge his timing. The slower he was in replying the more devastating the effect.

One, two . . .

Would his answer be prosaic? *I'll have whatever you're having*.

Three, four . . .

Poetic fantasy to throw me off-balance? *Lady, three white leopards sat under a juniper tree . . .*

Five, six . . . here we go!

He said very simply, 'I love you'.

As no one had ever said it before.

I dropped the bottle, and as if we had rehearsed this scene a thousand times he stepped over the broken glass and put his arms round me.

I endeavour to think of sensible matters such as a floor-cloth and a dustpan and brush. I see his face coming so close that it blurs away. I hear my breathing and his. I smell the fumes of spilled whisky. I feel the strength of his embrace. My own arms come tentatively round his neck and then my fingers grip his shoulders. And the flesh shouts for joy.

Who gave me my first kiss? Whoever he was his kissing is forgotten. But Conrad kisses with ferocity and gentleness, and as I cannot dissemble I kiss him back with an abandon I should have found deplorable at any other time. We kiss as we might eat: we savour, we sip, we are greedy for more and still more. At that moment he could have taken me on Mrs Harvey's carpet without protest, and had anyone walked into Hendra's prim parlour I should neither have noticed, cared, nor called a halt. I was prepared to frighten every horse in Cornwall if need be.

But timing is one of Conrad's fortes. He gives me a taste of what could be, and then draws back to assess the effect, while I hold on to him lest I fall.

He laughs then, at himself as well as me, and says, 'My God, how I lust for you, Marina!'

I find nothing to say. We come apart somehow and mop up the mess. I have no more whisky but both of us need a strong drink, so we dash a little tonic into a large vodka, and clink glasses ceremoniously. I am glad to sit down and let the alcohol take over, and I wonder how my voice will sound when eventually I use it.

Conrad has banished the devil from his eyes and the seducer from his voice. He looks at me seriously, tenderly. His tone is pure courtesy.

'Marina, you are an astonishing and beautiful woman, and I care for you very much and I want you very badly. But what I feel for you makes no difference to my love for Harriet, and I would never want to hurt my wife or to harm our marriage.'

I have the feeling that a door has been opened, only to shut in my face, but what else had I expected him to say? He is talking common sense and cold truth. I don't want to hurt Harriet either, and I have a marriage of my own to consider. I am a modern woman and I know the score even though I have never played the game. Yet if he had begun like this I should have rejected his advances, however badly I wanted him, out of pride. But he was too clever. He caught me off guard with a simple and open declaration of love. So apparently I still equate love with the end of a search, the beginning of eternal bliss with one person to the exclusion of all others.

More fool me!

Conrad takes my hand, lifts it to his lips, and says, 'Marina, I love you for having no illusions about me. You know I'm a scoundrel.'

I answer with sweet-sour honesty. 'Oh, I wouldn't have said that, Conrad. Just exceptionally selfish.'

The answer pleases me and amuses him, and we both laugh. He pats my knee: part-comrade, part-lover. 'We have so much in common,' he says slyly.

His eyes are mischievous, his smile provocative. I am astonished that half of me can observe him with detachment while the other kneels in worship.

'Understanding the situation and each other, as we

do,' he continues, playing with my fingers, holding my gaze, 'shall we meet in London?'

His smile widens as I hesitate, and he says with silky malice, 'Or are you going to follow the rules of a lifetime and play safe?'

In cold anger I reply, 'I think you're confusing safety with consideration for others – something you conspicuously lack.'

Still smiling, still holding my eyes and stroking my fingers, he remarks, 'How you clutch the chains that bind you, Marina.'

I grow more angry because I cannot anger him.

As coolly as I can, I say, 'And I find something rather sordid in the idea of deceiving people, but I suppose you don't mind a little deception. Fidelity is hardly one of your virtues, is it?'

He laughs in genuine amusement and says, 'Not only clutch them but forge them as well!'

I push him away and stand up. Stand at a safe distance from him. Aim to wound him. 'And all those clichés,' I cry, breathless with hatred and desire, 'all those well-worn lines about your wife and your marriage, which have probably been trotted out again and again as the situation served, are nothing more than lip-service. You wouldn't give up a single pleasure to save Harriet pain. I shouldn't be surprised to know that you find even the risk to your marriage exciting. I wonder if you care anything for anyone, including yourself. That is, if you yourself exist. Which I doubt.'

The heat of rage balances the heat of love. The temperature of both registers high fever.

Conrad is still smiling, but the smile has lost its authority, his eyes are wary. I have hit a nerve or two.

He says lightly, 'Then continue to live within the walls of your cell, Marina. And some day, when you are old, I promise that you will look out of its single narrow window and wonder where your life has gone.'

Am I as pale as he beneath my holiday tan? As we stand apart, he in the doorway and I by the fireplace, the emotion between us is almost tangible.

I want to cry, 'It's the truth about both of us, but I'm sorry we said it.'

He may know me well enough to guess that, or to read my face. Now he speaks honestly, plainly, and I think the lines are his own.

'We shall be here until the end of the month. If you change your mind before then, will you let me know? Marina?'

As I do not, cannot, answer, he adds quietly, 'I wish you would.'

And lifts one hand in salute, and is gone.

TWELVE

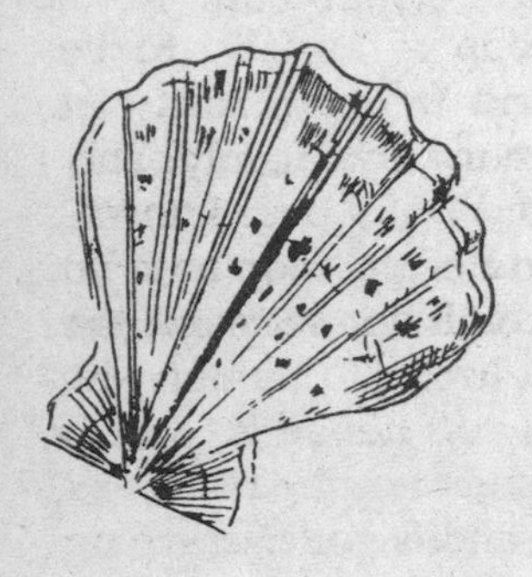

Giles was expected back the following weekend. I telephoned hopefully but not expectantly on Saturday evening; confidently on Sunday morning; worriedly on Sunday night. Each time his taped message regretted that we were both out, and each time I left my name and asked him to ring me at Trenoweth.

Monday was one of the worst days of my life, waiting. At six o'clock in the evening I tried to contact him for the fourth time, and put the receiver down when the answering machine blocked me. The hot kiosk was claustrophobic, stinking of stale smoke. Visitors had been here, too, leaving their initials on the walls, scrawling a number in lipstick on the mirror, spitting on the floor, stamping out their cigarette ends, leaving a fish-and-chips paper, which stank of vinegar, screwed up in one corner.

As I walked down the dusty lane, I could have shrieked aloud with terror and frustration. Pursued by Conrad, evaded by Giles, uncertain of myself, I sought to resolve the situation by escape. I must get out of the mess I was in by going away. Reaching this decision, I turned resolutely into Trenoweth. I had been avoiding Conrad but he was usually absent at this hour, leaving Harriet and Dagmar to deal with the children, and turning up in time for the evening meal, exuding charm, bearing a bottle of wine.

It was difficult to ask a favour of Harriet, to be trespassing on her marriage and her generosity at the same time, because she was my friend, probably the closest and best woman friend I had ever known, and I loved her. But she was also the only person who could help me at the moment, and if I achieved the result I hoped for it would help her, too, though she would not know that.

Drawing her apart from the general mêlée I said, all in a burst, 'Harriet, you'll have realised that everything wasn't right between Giles and me?'

The slightest of nods acknowledged this. Her eyes were clear and watchful.

'I know that he's home by now. His last postcard said he would arrive sometime on Saturday. He's said nothing at all about coming down here, and I've rung four times, and left messages, but he hasn't contacted me and I feel so out of touch, so helpless. I've got a hunch that if I dash up to London and surprise him . . . if we could have a couple of days together by ourselves . . . talk things over . . . he didn't care for Cornwall and Hendra, you see, but I feel that if we were at home together it would be different. Our own atmosphere. D'you know what I mean? Only . . . can you help me out, Harriet?'

'You wish me to have Joshua while you are away?' she asked gravely. 'But of course I will, Marina. Of course. When do you go? Tomorrow?'

I had not dared to ask so much so soon.

'Would that be taking advantage of you?' I said humbly.

'No. It would be sensible. And do not come back before Sunday. Then you have four days, and you miss holiday traffic.'

'Are you absolutely sure?'

'I am sure,' said Harriet, and nodded emphatically.

I tried to think of something adequate in the way of thanks. 'Our roses should be at their best by now. I'll bring you an armful of roses from the garden, Harriet. The finest and most beautiful roses we grow.'

She answered, smiling, 'That will be good.'

Spontaneously we hugged each other, relieved and pleased, she to give and me to accept. And I swore within myself that I could not, would not hurt her, that I would direct this errant and potentially destructive emotion into the right channel. I would change it into a positive and creative force, to save my marriage and spare her grief.

I said, 'You've been so kind to me, Harriet. I'll never forget that, or you.'

When we drew back we both had tears in our eyes, and first smiled and then laughed ruefully as we had when first we became friends.

Harriet said, 'You would think we say goodbye for ever, but it is only for a few days. Marina, you are to stay with Giles as long as you like, as long as you must, to make things well between you. Let us have Joshua tonight, and then you make an early start tomorrow.'

We were planning my escape as we had planned scores of picnics.

I said, 'I'd like to leave Hendra's keys with you. I'll pop them through your letterbox on my way out, and pick them up on my way back. And I'll phone you tomorrow night tc say I've arrived safely. Oh, and Josh and I will have supper together by ourselves at Hendra tonight.'

'No, no, you must eat here. You have much to do.'

I dreaded having a meal with Conrad. 'Not as

much as all that. And I must make a fuss of Josh. I don't want him to think I'm just walking off and leaving him.'

Harriet understood that, and turned her attention to Giles and me. 'Listen, Marina, I do not say this before, but I wish to help you.' It was a labour for her to be disloyal. She spoke slowly, painfully. 'Conrad and I have many times said, "This is the end of us!" But it is never the end. You know he goes away for weeks, for months? It is not only his work that takes him. Sometimes it is other women. Once, twice, I think he will not come back. More than once, twice, I come to the end of my string and say, "Now go! Go for always!" But always he comes back. I come back. We come back to the marriage and the children because we are all part of each other. The marriage, the children, Conrad and me are one whole thing. Conrad says we are the bread of life to him. That is beautiful, is it not?'

Even fighting for survival in a sea of emotion and desire I smelled theatre in that line. And I was jealous, too. God help me. Jealous.

'But then, Conrad is Conrad,' she said, and shrugged as if the burden were a load of feathers. 'There is no other man.'

Her command of English was not sufficient to explain whether she meant there could be no other man for her, or that Conrad was beyond comparison with other men. Possibly both. But though I realised that their relationship kept her in bondage I wished, oh, how I wished, that I could feel the same way about Giles.

So much a part of the Gage family, Joshua accepted the suddenness of my decision and my coming absence with remarkable equanimity. He did not even enquire the reason for going. Conscience-stricken, I asked what he would like to eat. Sensing that he was in a position to push favours he chose sausage and chips, shop apple pie and Bird's custard, with lemonade to wash it down. 'Unless,' he said courteously, 'you can't face cooking in the heat.'

'I don't mind cooking, Josh, but I won't join you. I'll make myself a cheese salad instead.'

He laid the table carefully, festively, and filled an empty fish-paste pot with small wild flowers. He stood by my elbow, eating a bag of crisps, as I fried up. He knew I was guilty and conciliatory. He made the most of it.

'I suppose it's not possible to move from London and live here for good, is it?' he asked, so seriously that I had to consider the question.

I said, 'Not as long as Daddy and I have to earn a living.'

He had thought out his argument. 'People earn livings down here, too. And they've got good schools and big estate agents' offices in Cornwall. I should have thought they'd be glad to have important people like you and Daddy working for them. And you'd get a lot more money for our house in London than you'd pay for one here.'

'It's not as simple as that, Josh.'

'But it could be,' he persisted. 'If you really wanted to, it could be.' He pressed his advantage. 'And *you* like it here, don't you?'

'Yes. Very much. But I don't know whether I'd like it all the time. Mrs Harvey says we've got to winter it as well as summer it.'

He seemed to consider this more of a challenge than an obstacle.

He said, with the piercing truthfulness of a child, 'Anyway, Mum, you're a lot nicer down here than you are in London. I didn't know how nice you were until we came here.'

This set me back on my heels. I dished up his meal

and brought mine from the refrigerator in silence.

As he stuck his fork into the first sausage I asked uncertainly, 'Am I not very nice in London?'

He chewed and thought, and swallowed. 'I don't mean that you're nasty ' he said fairly, 'but you're a lot harder to get on with. Besides, we didn't see much of you.'

I neglected my cheese salad while he dabbled his chips round in tomato sauce, and cried out in self-defence, 'I know I was working all day, but you had Auntie Tavey, and even when you and Sarah were very young I always got home in time to bath you both and read you a story at bedtime. And later on, when you were older, we all had supper together in the evenings, and weekends were always family times.'

I spoke to them both, sensing Sarah there with him, making a joint complaint of neglect.

He looked up, startled, solemn, crestfallen at the anguish in my tone. 'I kn-know, I kn-know,' he said quickly, forestalling trouble.

His tongue tripped over the words. Three vermilion chips trembled on his fork. Then, as if he felt himself to be on the brink of an old abyss, he visibly drew back, restored himself. Shoved his glasses back on to the bridge of his snub nose. Faced me.

'But you never had enough time, Mum,' he said factually. 'You were always watching the clock and saying, "Oh, Lord, look at the enemy!" Whereas,' he went on, in a louder voice, to prevent my answering him before he had finished his statement, 'down here you don't bother a bit, and there's plenty of time to do nothing much. And you're always around. And I like that.'

I was being judged by my child. My defence sounded a little shrill. 'We had the summer holidays together. Four whole weeks every year. Lovely holidays. Going off together to different countries.'

He helped himself to more tomato sauce while I spoke. He would not be deterred. 'Yes, but we never had a proper holiday like this, where things didn't matter. We always seemed to be going to places the Goddards said we ought to go to, and going with them and meeting other people there, and you were always giving blooming old parties.'

He was too young to formulate his ideas into words, to say, 'You could never relax. You always had to be in the social swim, to put on a show.'

Puzzled how to explain what I knew he meant, he said finally and most damningly, 'It was just like being at home on a Saturday evening, with people coming to dinner.'

I said, deflated, 'I didn't know. I'm sorry you didn't enjoy yourselves.'

He unwrapped his individual apple pie and helped himself to custard. 'Oh, it was all right. But it wasn't as good as you coming down to the beach when we're playing, and bringing lemonade and buns, and talking about the sandcastle, and having walks together and collecting shells. And I like us mucking in with the Gages, and going off all day for picnics.'

I reflected that my daughter had not known how nice I could be, and now never would. 'Did Sarah feel the same way as you do, Josh?'

He grinned at me, all crumbs and custard. 'I don't think so. She never said so, anyway. She was more like you than I am. If she'd grown up she'd have given lots of parties and been like you.'

Perhaps he felt that this assessment sounded a trifle harsh, for he smiled at me openly and sweetly, and said, 'It's just that I do like us being here, and I don't want to go back to London ever.'

There was yet another favour to ask, but he waited until I was drinking coffee and wishing I could smoke a cigarette.

'Mum, do I have to go to that boarding-school in September?'

'Well, yes, you do rather. It's all arranged.'

His head drooped. 'I was hoping you might ask Daddy if I could go to a day school, and then I could be near home.'

I thought this one over, but could see no way out but onwards. 'I think we must accept that Daddy knows a great deal more about educating boys than we do. He has a high opinion of Jefferson's, and he believes that you need more independence from home, not less. It's a really informal and friendly school and very progressive. You can ring us up whenever you like, and they have nice long holidays. Do give it a try.'

He said persistently, 'But Dad would listen to *you*. He does what *you* want. If *you* asked him I know he'd change his mind.'

Again disquieted, I answered, 'That's not the case, Josh. We *both* decided that Jefferson's was a good idea.'

I thought, Now is that the truth or isn't it? And either way there's something wrong with it.

Joshua gave a long sigh and capitulated.

'J-j-j-just — '

He stopped, visibly pulled himself together, and said nonchalantly, 'Just thought I'd ask. Better be off to Trenoweth now.'

Our sense of companionship had vanished. We packed his rucksack and I helped him to shoulder it. Once again he was the victim and I the tyrant. Once again I had let him down. But he was not so ready to go under as he had been.

'It's a good thing, in a way, that we don't have to cope with Webster,' said Joshua stoically. 'If I took him to Trenoweth he'd run off, and if we left him in Hendra he'd make messes on the carpets. Poor old Webs. He always got it wrong.'

He looked round his bedroom to make sure he had forgotten nothing.

'I'll leave the bears here,' he said. 'They can keep each other company.'

Downstairs, he said, 'Give my love to Daddy.' And then, anxiously, 'When are you coming back?'

I had long since been forbidden to kiss him, so kept my farewell casual. 'Sunday, Josh. About tea-time, probably. Now take care of yourself, and have a good time at Trenoweth.'

He nodded, face averted. But on the threshold he turned and said authoritatively, 'Don't drive more than two hours without a break, Mum. And remember that you turn off for the Redruth bypass at the second lot of traffic lights, not the first.'

Then he set off at a run, rucksack jogging rhythmically. I watched him until he disappeared round the bend in the lane, and went indoors on leaden feet with a leaden heart.

I slept uneasily, and dreamed I was wandering alone in a city which had once been familiar but was now strange. Squares and streets were empty and silent, their names blotted out. I had neither map, money nor transport and no one to direct me. I did not know why I was there nor what I was supposed to do, although I felt that something or someone was watching, weighing, judging my reactions.

All night I walked and sought and did not find, and woke at first light, surfacing with the sea and the cry of gulls, unrefreshed and full of apprehension. Superstitiously, I did not pull the coverlet up over my bed but left the sheet turned down to welcome my return. And touched the doorpost on my way out and told Hendra I should be back.

The occupants of Trenoweth still slept behind curtained windows. I slid the keys into the letterbox and was on the road soon after six o'clock, and driving across the Tamar bridge by eight. Here I had to pay toll, as if the county which welcomed you in for nothing exacted a penalty for leaving, and so crossed over into Devon, and stopped for breakfast at the first place I found open.

It was a transport café. Undaunted, I left the Ford parked between two pantechnicons so huge that their tyres looked as large as the car.

'Don't talk to either of them while I'm away!' I said facetiously, and walked into the café as if such places were habitual to me.

Apart from the fact that I was left strictly to myself at an oil-clothed table, no one took any notice of me. Uncharacteristically, filled with a sense of adventure, of unreality, I ate a very good hot breakfast and drank two cups of strong tea. The bill was extremely reasonable and I gave the owner a generous tip.

Morning traffic was at its height for the next hour, and did not show signs of flagging until I reached Exeter. Pacing myself for time and distance, I had coffee at Yeovil and stopped for lunch at Salisbury. I was calming down mile by mile, and my mood was changing. The further I drove from Cornwall the more self-contained I became. It was as if the persuasive charm of the county had tricked me into baring my heart and soul, and behaving in a manner which now appeared at best to be self-indulgent and at worst downright disgraceful.

The facts, when faced, were as follows. Giles had been home not quite three days, needed time to recover from a fortnight with a group of fourteen-year-old boys, and happened to be out when I telephoned him. Seen from this angle my anxiety was absurd, unfounded. What on earth would he think when I raced home in such a hysterical fashion? And what would be the effect of a plea for reconciliation, when there was nothing to reconcile but the difference between my expectations and his reactions?

I wondered what had become of my cool nerve and quiet competence. Until the appalling business with Sarah I had been moderate in all things. Had deplored emotional extravagance in other women, easy tears, shrill demands, wild suspicions, and the insistent constant clamour for love, love, love. Now, because my husband had failed to clutch me to his manly breast and, mad with passion, make me pregnant, I had fallen in lust with a middle-aged over-sexed actor who was someone else's husband. I was, in truth, skittering round like a hen with her head cut off.

Ashamed, I sat in Salisbury cathedral for half an hour to draw strength from the beauty and serenity of the building. Then I rethought my attitude and my plan of campaign. This encounter wouldn't be a plea for understanding by a wife in desperate straits, but a fun visit on a special occasion.

I try out scenarios in my head.

The house is quiet in the late afternoon sun. His car is not outside. I park further up the road so that he shall not know I am here. I let myself in, quickly, secretly, with delight, removing all traces of my presence. Handbag, overnight bag, scarf, car keys. When he comes home I shall have cooked dinner for us both, laid the table in the dining-room, dressed beautifully, ready to welcome him.

The scenario accommodates itself to the other possibility.

The house is quiet in the late afternoon sun. His car is outside, but I don't ring the bell. I let myself in, full of secret delight, and saunter nonchalantly down the hall, calling, 'Giles! Are you there?'

And when he opens the kitchen or sitting-room door I am outside, relaxed and smiling, full of secret delight.

'Darling, it's me! I've driven three hundred bloody miles just to say hello! Pour me a good strong old-fashioned, will you?'

He has been startled. Now he is amused. We begin to laugh.

'Darling, you're mad!' he says, putting his arms round me. 'Utterly and gloriously mad.'

I do not withhold myself. I return his embrace warmly, lightly, but do not melt into it. My body must promise subtly, not collapse in gratitude. It must make no demands. I have forgotten past disappointments and am expecting nothing. We are old friends, good friends, long married. Marvels can happen, but need not.

Yes, that is the right approach.

I shop for the evening meal thoughtfully, exquisitely: food that I can cook quickly, with the minimum effort, the maximum effect. Everything of the best. Crisp red radishes to be eaten with a little salt, French-style, as a starter. Fillet steaks, new potatoes whose skins will slough off, a green salad with amusing kinds of lettuce. Soft ripe raspberries and Wiltshire cream. A bottle of Moûton Cadet, coffee beans (in case he has none in the house) and his favourite orange-bitter chocolates.

Time slips slyly by. I begin the last lap of the journey in mid-afternoon and finish it in the rush-hour along roads which shimmer with heat.

London is daunting in high summer. Miles of industrial buildings and terraced houses, hard pavements lined with dusty trees, office blocks glittering up into a parched sky. The sun flashes off windows and car roofs into tired eyes. In a nose-to-tail queue I wind down the window, lean one arm on the sill, watching and waiting stoically with the rest of them. The pulse of the city beats like a soft interminable drum, calling all its citizens to arms. We are here to win the battle of life! it says. To succeed. To achieve. To be known by, and to know, the right people. To go to the right places and wear the right clothes. To become somebody. Are you rich? Are you influential? Have you arrived? Hurry! Hurry! Hurry! Let no one sleep. People are awake all night here, and time is passing.

My own pulse quickens in response. I am far from Cornwall now, restored to a familiar self. Apart from my tan and physical well-being I might never have been away.

The house is quiet in the late-afternoon sun. His car is outside, but I don't ring the bell. I let myself in, full of secret delight, put down my overnight bag and walk through the hall, calling, 'Giles! Are you there?'

No reply. I open all the doors, make sure that he is not in the garden, where roses bloom in splendour, and come back to the foot of the stairs.

When I stop and listen I can hear the faint sound of rushing water. My husband is in the shower which opens off our bedroom, washing away the toils of the day, as I should like to do. As, in fact, I intend to do when he has finished.

Without difficulty I change my scenario and my costume. The evening will begin in a really relaxed manner, each of us freshly bathed, smiling over drinks, in matching plum-blossom kimonos.

I mix a couple of strong old-fashioneds, set them out on a little silver tray, slip off my shoes, and mount the stairs with something approaching exaltation. I stop outside our bedroom door and take a deep breath, preparatory to delivering my opening line.

Giles must have heard me. He has left the shower, which hisses on without him, and come out into the room to speak to me. I cannot grasp what it is he is saying, so light and rapid, but his tone is caressing. He is glad to see me, and I am filled with an exaltation which is perilously near tears. I had not realised how much I was depending on his reaction. I move my tray into one hand like a waiter, open the door with a flourish and stand there smiling. I know from the mirror in the hall that I am looking good. Tall and brown and splendid.

I say, 'Giles, darling! It's me!'

And stop.

Giles is reclining on our bed nearly naked. A small towel covers his loins. In his hand is a large old-fashioned, and he is talking lovingly, intimately, to someone in the shower. The scenario is perfect. Except that, unaccountably, it has left out a part for me.

The moment when we both grasp the situation is very long, as if time had snapped us and was studying the still at leisure before moving on. This glorious summer is suiting Giles, too. He is bronzed and lithe and his spurious air of youth sits well upon him. He is experiencing a renaissance. No, not a renaissance, for he was never like this. He has come alive. With the help of someone else. And though he is growing pale and mottled under his tan, and his shocked face has fallen, he is still alive. And not for me.

How do I look? I wonder. My script says a mature and handsome woman, dressed with casual elegance, amusing, understanding, possessed of hidden powers and depths. But I have burst in on the wrong scene and spoken the wrong lines. Worse than humiliation is the knowledge of the disaster to come. Since I have wrecked Giles's script and misread mine, the coming scene must be played by ear.

In slow motion, I put the little silver salver down on my dressing-table and sink on to the stool facing him. When we speak our words sound numb and we do not use each other's names. Names are a sign of intimacy and we are suddenly too far apart.

I say, 'I brought you a drink, but I see you have one already.'

And pick up my glass and sip it. Waiting.

Giles has slopped his drink on the coverlet and mops the spilled liquor distractedly with a Kleenex.

He says, not looking at me, 'Is Josh with you?'

'No. I came up by myself. You were out whenever I telephoned. This was the only way I could reach you.'

'There's nothing wrong, is there?' he asks, alarmed.

I recover sufficiently to answer with some acerbity, 'That's up to you to say, isn't it?'

He swings his legs off the bed, clutching the towel to his genitals as if we have never met before. Perhaps we haven't. He reaches for his kimono and slippers, and obviously feels much better when he is clothed against me. I sip and wait. The shower has been turned off and a dreadful hush ensues. She is in there, listening, wondering. Whoever she may be.

In an agony which astonishes me, I say, 'Is that woman one of my friends? Is it Sue Goddard?'

Unfaithfulness is cruel enough. Coupled to personal treachery it is unbearable. And yet must be borne.

Giles speaks loudly, urgently, to his invisible lover, 'Hang on a minute there, will you?'

To me he says hurriedly, intimately, 'Rina, I never intended you to be involved in this.'

Fury releases my tongue. 'But how could I fail to be involved? We've been living side by side like hotel guests for months. I thought it was Sarah's illness that altered the way you felt towards me. I didn't know it was another woman.'

He stands looking down at me, hands in pockets, perplexed and sorry.

He says, 'Sarah's illness simply brought the situation to a head. And this is a recent development. It can't be explained easily.'

Then his tone changes. For my sake he tries to keep it factual, and yet I hear the authentic voice of love as he opens the door of our bathroom and says,

'You'd better wrap a towel round you, and come and meet my wife.'

My throat is dry in spite of the whisky I have been imbibing. I wait to see the embodiment of Giles's desire, which I have evidently never been, and wonder momentarily whether I could change myself to suit him. Then I despise myself for the thought, because although I am self-made I did create a person not a chameleon.

A golden fleece of damp bright hair. A dimple in the chin. Very blue eyes, with incredible lashes. An air of studied nonchalance. One of my best scarlet bath towels wound round a slim athletic body.

Giles's lover is a young man.

He is the young man who stood under the trees at Sarah's funeral.

THIRTEEN

My first impulse is to scream, to throw my drink into Giles's face, to follow it with his drink, to hit him until my arm loses its power, and then to drive away dangerously fast.

Years of self-control come to the rescue and immobilise me.

Giles says, 'Marina, this is my friend Timothy Mungus.'

I cannot speak. Nor can he. We incline our heads.

I pick up my drink and walk out, finish it downstairs and pour myself another. Some time later both men join me, fully clothed, endeavouring to seem at ease. I do not help them, but stand there waiting for Timothy Mungus to go. He knows this, and takes a subdued leave of us both. Departs, as presumably he entered, by the back garden gate, and strides away. Seen from behind, now dressed in blue jeans and a Miami beach shirt, the fleece of hair curling on his neck, slender feet thrust into Italian sandals, he could belong to either sex.

Among our friends' marriages there were many casualties, some fatal, some mended. Though Giles had always seemed the most faithful and undemanding of husbands, I had long since worked out my own reaction to passing infidelity. I would take a long-term view; believe in the excellencies of our partnership, the strength and length of its bonds; and recognise that our marriage need not be permanently threatened by a temporary aberration. Together we would achieve a greater level of understanding, learn from the experience, and use its lesson to move on.

In what I now see was both ignorance and arrogance, I had reckoned I could cope with the situation, but this affair thrusts me into chaos. As a wife of many years, facing the challenge of a momentary mistress, I would have had time and status on my side. But as my husband prefers men then I am redundant and have nothing to offer. Timothy Mungus has rendered my marriage null and void twice over.

Midnight, and the two of us are still talking. A dialogue between strangers.

We have not been able to let each other out of sight for a moment. On our third whisky apiece we decided we were famished. Giles laid the kitchen table and mixed two more old-fashioneds, so that we could talk while I cooked. We drank my bottle of wine over dinner, eating hugely, mechanically, ravenously. Giles made Irish coffee afterwards and we wolfed the chocolate. Now we brew China tea and open a box of Italian macaroons. All the time our mouths are compulsively sipping, chewing or debating. It is as if we cannot stop talking and eating. We consume each other.

I am living at a furious high, as I have not done since I left London three months ago. I have walked into a feverish situation and picked up the city's feverish pace at the same time. At Hendra an evening freshness will come in from the sea. The summer night here is heavy with the day's heat.

Giles's voice and face are troubled. He is full of pain. He labours to explain the inexplicable. I do not help him to come to terms with himself. My task is to bring out the truth, at whatever cost to him or to me. That is the difference between us. Even now he would like to hide it.

There is another difference. When we speak of Giles's lover Giles refers to him by name. I do not. He is he, and that is enough.

'Who is this young man, anyway? What does he do for a living? Or isn't he employed?'

'Tim? He works in his father's firm in the city. Plenty of money, both earned and inherited. He's not sponging on me, and he's not a male prostitute if that's what you're worried about.'

This last sentence is delivered in an injured tone, but Giles is not the injured party and he knows it. He throws a sop to my understanding. 'Rina, I understand how you must feel, but Tim's a lovely person. Caring. Cultured. Intelligent. Under different circumstances I'm sure you'd—'

There are no other circumstances. Only these. I cut him short. 'Is this is your first affair?'

He nods his head and gives a quick hard sigh, and says, 'Oh, yes, Rina. Yes. Indeed it is.'

'How long have you known him?' Detective-like, I warn him not to lie to me. 'We saw him at the cemetery, if you remember. And you said you didn't know him then. You said he was just a nutter who liked attending funerals.'

'I was lying,' says Giles frankly. 'It was the best excuse I could think up at the time. I did know him. Reluctantly. I'd been trying to avoid him. I didn't notice he was there that day, until you pointed him out to me. I was scared stiff. And it bowled me over when I realised

Tim had come to – well, to mourn with me, if you like. I thanked him, of course. But I did ask him to go, to leave me alone.'

'Where did you first meet?'

'At the squash club, about nine months ago . . . '

In the final stages of Sarah's illness. During the time we had tried to keep each other healthy and reasonably normal. Your turn for an evening out, my turn to sit with Sarah.

' . . . and we started talking. Tim was a sympathetic listener. We had a couple of drinks together afterwards. I told you about it at the time. How understanding he had been, even though he was young and had no ties or responsibilities. I told you at the time.'

'I don't remember.' I amend this statement. 'I don't mean that I don't believe you, Giles, just that I honestly don't remember. A lot of people were being sympathetic then.'

This statement consoles him.

'Exactly. And that's how I read it. Just another sympathetic person. And it was true as far as it went, but there was more to it than that. We got into the habit of having a couple of drinks together after the game, and talking. After a while I realised that he had a – particular – interest in me. As soon as I realised that, I wouldn't have anything to do with him – or with it – with homosexuality. I was thinking of the implications. At home, I had a son of my own. At school, I was in charge of the education and the moral welfare of adolescent boys. And it was not only what other people, my family and relatives and friends, would think of *me*, it was what I would think of *myself*. How I would feel about myself. I didn't know, didn't *want* to know, what I was.' He corrects himself stoically, 'What I *am*.'

I think, I didn't know you either.

And then I think again. Why, yes, I did. And

must have done. It's like slotting a peculiarly elusive piece of jigsaw into the puzzle, the sort that has no outstanding shape or pattern to it, but once fitted is a key to much of the rest. His tentative, tepid, and finally book-learned and earnest love-making. His puritanical rejection of homosexuals, in contrast to my easy acceptance of them. His refusal to entertain a gay colleague of mine, of whom I was very fond. How my female vanity had fluffed up its feathers, believing the refusal to be a mistaken case of jealousy. Oh, I am Fortune's fool.

A maiden all forlorn, Giles is saying ruefully, 'But Tim – persisted. He wouldn't accept that this was just a friendship. He *did* know what I was, you see. He knew *me*. And in the end I had to admit that I – felt as he did.'

I sound as I feel. Ironical. 'So when did you decide he was right about you, after all?'

'He came round one evening, soon after you'd gone to Cornwall.'

He looks directly at me, with that soft dark look which used to work like a charm. Oh, my darling Giles, I used to think. Neither mine nor darling now.

'I'm not blaming you for dashing off and leaving me, Rina. We were both suffering from shock. I know I wasn't any help to you. To tell you the truth I couldn't even help myself. I'd reached the end of the road. I don't mean that I stopped loving you, that I wasn't devastated by Sarah's death. But by that time I felt as though it was all happening to someone else. I felt so inadequate that I didn't want anything more to do with family life. I was telling myself, without knowing it, that I wasn't cut out to be a husband and father. Never had been. Never would be. And I couldn't deal with any more traumas. I did love you and Josh in my own way, and as long as you were around I was safe. Safe from myself. That's why

I wanted you to go to Brighton. You were within reach, you see.'

My fury spouts to the ceiling. 'Then why the hell didn't you say so at the time?'

'How could I?' he cries defensively.

He even shrinks a little at the tone of my voice. Then recovers both humour and dignity and speaks up. 'What should I have said, Rina? Save me from Sir Jasper's wicked wiles? You were teetering on the edge of a severe breakdown already. That would really have pushed you over.'

I am reminded of Joshua stuttering under one of my attacks, and then pulling himself together, facing me. Am I as terrifying as that? Have I emasculated the pair of them?

I soften my tone and answer reasonably. 'No,' I say, 'you couldn't have told me. I *was* half mad. I couldn't have dealt with any more trouble. Circumstances were against the pair of us.'

The atmosphere has become less charged. We stack the dishwasher in companionable silence. An old yearning possesses me. I say, 'I'm sure I've got a packet of cigarettes somewhere.'

'Oh, don't start smoking again, Rina. You've done so well, so far.'

I take no notice. What has he to do with me? I hunt down the unopened packet and shake one out.

Always the gentleman, Giles lights it for me.

'Oh, God!' Why do I bring Him into every flaming crisis? I wonder. 'Oh, God, it tastes like old hay!'

'Then put the damned thing out,' says Giles, and actually takes it from my lips, douses it in the sink and throws it into the pedal-bin.

'Let's have a nightcap instead,' he says.

And finds that we finished the whisky during the opening rounds.

We stand in front of the drinks cupboard deciding

what to shrivel our livers with next, and settle for a long gin, lime and soda.

Almost amicably, I say, 'But, Giles, how could you *not* know?'

He is fussing with lemon slices and ice cubes. He shakes his head. 'I suppose I wouldn't face the truth. There were a couple of mildly sexual incidents at boarding-school when I was in my teens, but then that's a phase boys go through, particularly when they're thrown together. It doesn't last. With ordinary men, that is.'

'But you must have realised that you found men attractive?'

'Only in an aesthetic sense. At any rate, that's what I told myself. But, then, you admiré beauty in women. It doesn't necessarily mean you want to have sexual relations with them.'

'There's no *necessarily* about it,' I cried. Up in arms. 'I don't.'

He shrugged apologetically, but he was not interested in his apology, nor in me any longer. In his trouble and his awakening, he looked younger than ever. Giles was the sort of man who would remain young, at first glance, for a long time. And afterwards still boyish, in a slightly worn sort of way.

It is two o'clock in the morning. Twenty hours since I left Cornwall. In that time I have driven three hundred miles, sustained a major shock, drunk an extraordinary amount of alcohol, and am still wide awake and looking all round the problem.

Giles, on the other hand, is beginning to run down. He swirls the ice cubes round his glass and sips. He grows philosophical.

'I suppose that's why I've always preferred women of character rather than bits of fluff,' he says. 'A strong sort of beauty.' He gives me his mild, sweet look. 'Like yours, Rina.'

Then his face changes. He has realised that the two of us as a couple are yesterday. All over. Finished. Kaput.

'Oh, Christ,' he says, and sets down his drink and buries his head in his hands. 'Why did this have to happen to us?'

My reply is crisp and to the point.

'Look, Giles, I'm not prepared to be maudlin with you, so let's leave the regrets and the compliments out of it. What do you propose to *do*? What are *we* going to do about this situation?'

My asperity has its uses. He collects himself together again, and thinks.

'I can't give Tim up,' he says finally. 'I simply can't. I suppose you'd call it infatuation—'

'Let's say passion.'

He looks at me gratefully. No one wants to be infatuated, which implies idiocy. Few mind being called passionate, which means intensity.

Encouraged, he says, 'I know passion doesn't last, and there may be nothing left for Tim or me when it goes. But while it lasts I must live it, because this is the first time I've ever felt fully alive. And who knows, we have a lot in common. It could deepen, could become something more.'

I remember Ethel talking about the Manchester blitz. 'Crouched in the cupboard under the stairs for eight hours, with an old woman and a new baby, wondering whether the next bomb had our number on it. Afterwards they said, "Britain can take it!" As if we were heroes! There was nothing to do but take it. We had no choice. Just sit in the shelter and take it and wonder if we were going mad along with the rest of the world.'

I suppose this is my blitz, and I am taking it now. I have no experience on which to draw for a situation which is not only new to me but unimagined.

Giles says pleadingly, 'Say something, Rina.'

I am still his drogue anchor, apparently. I bring him to a stop. 'Have you thought what it will cost you if anyone finds out? Your job, for one thing. Your prospects. Your entire future.'

He nods, and then says hurriedly, 'But we've been careful. It wouldn't do Tim any good to be labelled either. His parents. The firm.'

I am relentless now. 'And how much will your secret cost us to keep? Hiding it from Joshua, from our friends and relatives and acquaintances. Both of us leading your double life, with me pretending that everything is normal, and covering up your absences as if I were an accomplice.'

He lowers his head, not in defeat but in acceptance of that cost.

I say more sharply still, 'And what will *my* position be in five, ten, twenty years' time?'

His head jerks up.

'What sort of future can I expect with you? Must I, if this affair passes, put up with a series of your boyfriends? Or if the feelings between you do deepen and become something more – as you put it – are you planning to move out and set up house with him instead of me?'

Giles stares at me in dumb misery.

I say savagely, 'I realise that as a woman I shall be ignored, but am I also to be discarded? Because if so we'd do better to split up now, while I'm still young enough to make another life for myself.'

He stumbles badly over this proposition. He has not thought the matter through. Perhaps Tim should also be here to discuss his future plans, if any.

Giles pleads, 'You and I have got a good working relationship, Rina. Don't throw that away.'

'I've got good relationships at work. At home I'd a damned sight rather have a good marriage.'

He says in desperation, 'Rina, I need you. Just give me time. At the moment I don't know where I am. I don't know what's happening, or what will happen. How can I? We've got Josh to think of, and our home and the life we've made together. For God's sake, what do you want to do? Divorce me? Disgrace me?'

Our marriage has gone with a bang. I don't propose to let my future fade away in a whimper. I am implacable.

'I shouldn't dream of disgracing you. We could divorce on grounds of incompatibility, or simply live apart for a few years and then divorce.'

He is panic-stricken at the thought. 'But what have I said to give you the impression that I want to leave you? I don't. When I said my feeling for Tim might deepen I wasn't intending to live with him.'

'Suppose,' I say unkindly, '*he* wants *you* to live with him? Suppose the relationship becomes important enough to warrant that?'

'How could I? I'd lose my job.'

'There are other jobs. You're well qualified. And this is a broad-minded age. I don't doubt that you'd find something else.'

'I don't want anything else. I want you and I to go on the way we are. Only with the knowledge we both have about me and Tim.'

He seeks to placate me. 'I shall be discreet in every way. I'll never mention Tim again.' He recovers some dignity. 'I never intended you to know. To be fair to me, if you hadn't taken it into your head to dash up here, you never would have known.'

I say, with considerable asperity, 'I certainly shan't want to chat about him, but what about *my* personal life? I take it you don't object if I have an affair, or affairs, too?'

Giles has not thought about this either, and doesn't care for the idea, but there is no choice. He first shakes and then nods his head. I move on to the final question. 'And suppose I meet someone else and the affair turns into something more serious, and *I* want to marry again?'

Stiffly, face averted, Giles says, 'I must give you your freedom, naturally. But for the time being, Rina, can't we leave things as they are? For Josh's sake, if for no one else's.'

Reluctantly, I agree to that.

He relaxes. He yawns. He stretches. The discussion is over. Our son is safeguarded while we adjust to this new life together.

'Nearly three o'clock!' says Giles in disbelief. 'You must be whacked, Rina. I know I am. Shall we go to bed?' He anticipates me. 'You must have our room. I'll sleep in the guest room.'

The flesh is possessive as well as demanding. Jealousy revitalises me. 'I'm not sleeping in our bed if *he's* been in it.'

'Of course he hasn't. I wouldn't do that to you.'

'He was using our shower.'

'Only because the other shower wasn't working. The plumber's coming tomorrow to look at it.'

As I continue to look belligerent he says, soothing me, 'Tim and I have been in the guest room and used that bathroom.'

Reassured, exhausted, I capitulate. I pause, one hand on the kitchen doorknob, on my way out.

'Just one more thing, Giles. No. Two more things.'

'Oh, God, Rina, can't they wait?' he cries, at last exasperated.

No. I am inexorable. He has finished our marriage and negated my hopes. He can at least answer my questions.

'The first is a message from Josh.'

He slumps down again. There are bruised shadows beneath his eyes.

'Josh said to give you his love. But he did ask me to

put in a word about going to Jefferson's next month. He wants to know if you would reconsider and let him go to a local school instead.'

Slowly, Giles shakes his head. He looks older, sterner, and in complete control. Transformed into the schoolmaster again. 'The reason I originally decided on Jefferson's was that it would allow him sufficient freedom while encouraging him to be self-reliant. That's even more important now than it was when we made the decision. In a situation like this the boy's better away from home.'

I cannot refute his reasoning, though I am sorry for it.

'And what was the other matter?' Giles asks. Brisker, now that he is on familiar ground.

But I am about to cast him out into the deeps again. 'Giles, why didn't you get in touch with me as soon as you got back from Switzerland? I left messages on the answering machine. You must have known I was concerned. You could have telephoned the Gages to let me know that everything was all right.'

He is slightly testy now. 'I still don't understand what all that fuss was about. I didn't get back until the early hours of Sunday morning. You'd rung me four times before I could pull myself together, and I did try Trenoweth on Monday afternoon but there was no reply. I rang on Monday evening and that dumb-bell Dagmar said everyone was out and put the phone down. And I was going to ring again yesterday evening, but by that time you'd turned up here.'

Temporarily revitalised, he asks 'Why on earth did you drive up out of the blue like that? You're not the sort of woman who panics easily. You must have known that no news is good news. And, for God's sake, you're due home at the end of next week, anyway.'

I remember the reason I came, the plans I made, the script I wrote, and the white lie I concocted. They are all pointless, even ridiculous.

I answer factually. 'I was worried about us. I thought I could put things right. I wanted to talk things out.'

Giles looks away, sheepish.

Having the last word, I say sardonically, 'Well, we seem to have done that, at any rate!'

Our bedroom is full of images.

Giles lying on the bed, bronzed and lithe and naked, talking to someone else in a caressing tone he never used to me. A young god steps with shy dignity from the shower room. Hair like damp gold fleece. Dimple in chin. My scarlet towel embracing his youth and beauty.

I change the sheets, take two Alka-Seltzers to combat the amount of acid in my stomach, sleep fitfully for an hour and a half, and wake at five o'clock, having conserved enough energy to leave. The scarlet towels are still hanging on the rails in our bathroom. I bundle them into the laundry basket with hands that shake. I find more towels and take a long slow ruminating bath. I dress and make up carefully. I have no hangover, and am amazed to see my reflection looking reasonable.

I am glad that Giles is still asleep. Downstairs I make myself tea and leave him a note. I hesitate over the beginning, because we have darlinged each other easily and affectionately for years, but I cannot take the name of darling in vain. I compromise with his name only.

Giles, We shall be home on Saturday week around six o'clock. If you need me for anything please contact the Gages, who will give me a message. I shan't telephone you otherwise. I think we've said everything of importance.

I hesitate over the end, but again cannot send love. He is not my love, and I have no love for him at this moment. Nor will I use his pet name for me. I sign it *Marina*.

FOURTEEN

I take the low road, for a change, and breakfast in an eighteenth-century hostelry just over the border of Dorset, attracted by smells of wood smoke and frying bacon. At nine o'clock I use mine host's private telephone to communicate with Trenoweth, not without a tremor in case Conrad answers. But it is Harriet, whose tone changes from general cordiality to relief when I say my name.

'Marina! That is good. Your son was worried about you – It is your mamma, Joshua! – but I tell him that you and Giles are talking, talking, and do not remember the time until it is too late!'

I put my super-self forward to cover for me: light, bright and impersonal.

'Absolutely right, and I'm terribly sorry, Harriet. The clock struck three and we said in a chorus, "Heavens! Is *that* the time?"'

She gives a great, 'Aah!' of satisfaction and delight. 'So all is now well?'

I have decided not to confide the true situation

to anyone, but can hardly keep up the pretence that Giles and I are in rapturous concert, and must somehow account for my sudden return. I compromise.

'It was certainly the right thing to do – and I do thank you, Harriet, for giving us the opportunity. But we seem to have sorted everything out for the moment, and I'm able to come back earlier than I thought.'

'You come back together?' Hopefully.

'No, by myself. Giles has had enough travelling for the moment, and he's got heaps of things to do before term begins. I may as well leave him to it.'

She is concerned again. 'But why should you do that? No, stay,' she pleads. 'Stay with your husband. Joshua is happy now you have telephoned. You have no need to worry about him. Do stay.'

My voice sounds as thin as my story. 'Truly, Harriet, we've said all we need to say, and there's no point in my hanging around here.'

'I understand,' she says. Her tone is now resigned, reserved. She has drawn her own conclusions.

'So when do we see you, Marina? Tomorrow?'

I realise then, of course, that I cannot tell her I am already on my way and in Dorset. If Giles and I are in amicable agreement then why should I have hared out of London at the crack of dawn after a couple of hours' sleep? Neither Harriet's friendship nor her credulity must be stretched too far. I realise also that I am light-headed with tension and exhaustion. A day by myself, with a night's sound sleep to follow, would give me time to recharge my batteries.

'Yes,' I say brightly, 'I'll be back tomorrow.'

She does not say or convey that she will be glad to see me.

'You will eat supper with us?'

I swerve away from the invitation. Too much, too soon.

'Bless you, Harriet, but I'd rather make a leisurely

start and eat on the way. I'll be with you in time to pick Josh up and whisk him off to bed.'

She does not demur, as formerly she would have done. The invitation has sprung from her innate sense of what is due to me, not what she wants.

'It shall be as you wish,' she says, relieved of my presence at her table.

Then, trying to whip up a little enthusiasm for my dead marriage, 'Give our love to Giles, and enjoy your day together. You wish to speak with Joshua?'

I nerve myself to be cheerful with my son. 'Yes, that would be nice!'

She calls his name. In the background I hear a halting explanation from Dagmar. Poldy calls, 'Hello! Goodbye! Ha, ha, ha!' into the mouthpiece.

'Marina? – Poldy, be silent! – Marina, Joshua has run out with the girls. They are here one minute and the next gone. Shall Dagmar bring him back?'

'No, don't bother. Just give him my love, and say I'm sorry I worried him.' I endeavour to cover all eventualities. 'And, Harriet, I shan't ring again tonight. We shall probably be out, painting the city bright pink.'

She does not laugh, does not respond. She has divined the true state of my marriage, certainly realised that Conrad is interested in me, possibly guessed that he has made an offer. Is she now taking an intuitive leap into the future, deciding that I intend to have an affair with her husband to make up for the failure with mine? And, to be truthful, hasn't that thought occurred to me, though dismissed every time it rears its seductive head?

Harriet says, as to a stranger, 'Goodbye, Marina. Have a nice day and a safe journey.'

With stoicism and regret I think, that was my friend. That was.

I pay for my breakfast and telephone call and move

on. To where? In the heat of late August the Dorset coastal towns will be crowded, and accommodation will be nil.

Betjeman chants in my head, 'Ryme Intrinsica, Fontmell Magna, Sturminster Newton and Melbury Bubb,' and I am filled with unexpected exaltation; for no one knows where I am, and no one expects me to emerge on the scene and play my part until tomorrow evening. During my adult life, mostly spent running against the clock, I have had no time to stand and stare. Now I find myself in a state of non-being, suspended in space, with all the time in the world. I drive carefully, being tired, and yet without a care, being free. I drive wherever my fancy takes me and stop when I feel like it. I am in the world but not of it; and I see Marina Meredith from a great distance as if she were at the wrong end of a cosmic telescope, a puppet who has made her own costume, written her own part, manipulated her own strings and kept herself in bondage.

These green and pleasant roller-coaster hills are tranquil. Sheep graze, the wind stirs in the grass. From this height I sit and view my temporary queendom: arms clasped around my knees, chin resting on them, as Sarah used to sit when she was thinking. She is here somewhere, chasing but not capturing the errant butterflies, keeping me silent and harmonious company. And I can see so far on this bright day that the whole of the world and my life lies before, behind, beyond and below. Were I to stand up, to take one step out into the void, I should not fall but soar.

At this moment I understand and am made whole. There have been others. The black-haired girl embracing her army officer in the night train at Penzance was one such.

I know them. I am them. I have been and shall be this.

That was what I felt, but could not express, at four years old, sitting in my mother's lap, as they laughed together out of pure joy.

And another. Winning a scholarship to high school, which would cost Ethel blood in the way of a uniform and still deny me access to the charmed circle we were seeking. Yet in the moment of knowing I had won, I thought, Here I am. Where I was supposed to be.

Escaping from Salford was another. Ethel crying on a Manchester station platform, because her headstrong daughter had found a job in the wicked metropolis, and was probably heading straight for white slavery and the embrace of a black sultan – actually, into the motherly arms of a YWCA hostel and a respectable estate agent's office.

I had registered, and was sorry for my mother's grief. I embraced her as warmly as she could have wished, and far more warmly than I felt. I talked down her fears with poor promises.

'I'll ring you up as soon as I get there, and write to you every Sunday, and send you lots of postcards, and come home for Christmas.'

But when the whistle blew and the train lurched my heart leaped, and I waved so enthusiastically that my arm ached for quite a while afterwards. And all the way down to Euston the train wheels drummed *Iamfree Iamfree I am* FREE *free free free free, Iamfree Iamfree, I am* FREE!

Other moments.

Looking down on the twins, who had always been meant.

Finding the house near Richmond, which had always been mine.

Seeing myself in Sarah: a second self with a more privileged start in life, born into a prosperous era, rich in opportunities. O my daughter.

So why were the promises, so clearly stated, never

fulfilled? I wonder, musing on a green hill. And since the results of past actions still frame and constrain the present, how can I begin to improve the future?

Changing position I recline on one elbow, and in pondering and remembering droop closer and closer to the earth, until at last I fall asleep with my cheek pressed to the grass. And wake to find that the ramparts have thrown a vast shadow over the fields below, and my questions remain unanswered. But I remember that tomorrow I must buy roses for Harriet, which have supposedly been grown in my London garden.

Something has happened at Trenoweth during my absence. At eight o'clock the following evening Joshua is sitting on the gate at the head of our lane, rucksack on back, for once without his attendant harem of ash-blonde girls. As I turn the bend he shouts and waves, rejoiced to see me.

Stopping to take him aboard for the last few hundred yards I say jokingly, 'What's all this, then? Have you been chucked out?'

He shakes his head vehemently. 'No, but Aunt Harriet and Uncle Conrad have gone out for a meal, and Dagmar's given us our tea, and the girls are going to bed. So I said I might as well be off.'

He is not telling me everything. He pushes his glasses back on his nose and asks politely, 'How's Daddy?'

'Very well, very brown, and very busy!'

He is worried, and I speak playfully to make sure that he is not worried about us. For one of the props has fallen away from Joshua's magical tree-house of a summer, and it leans at a perilous angle. Nevertheless, he imitates my buoyant tone.

'Just his usual self in fact!' he says, and then less hopefully, 'Mum, did you ask him about Jefferson's?'

I temper Giles's reaction. 'Yes, and he's sympathetic, but he thinks you should give it a try.'

Joshua slumps in his seat. 'Thought so. Oh, well. Did you tell him about old Webster?'

I have to admit that I forgot.

'You forgot to ring us up, too,' says Joshua reproachfully.

I accept the rebuke and apologise again. He sighs down his nose.

'What was rotten old London like?'

'Too hot.'

He is restored by my answer and the sight of home. 'Cheers! There blows Hendra! Aren't you glad to be here, Mum?'

In my imagination I feel that the cottage has an air of being slightly offended, small grey back hunched against our absence. Affection for her surges like the sea. 'Very glad,' I say, 'and isn't it lovely that we've still got another week and a bit? We must make the most of it.'

Joshua does not answer at once. He waits until I have unlocked the door and opened the windows before he shares his news.

'We'll be by ourselves, Mum. The Gages are going home on Saturday.'

I am glad, and sorry, and apprehensive. To still the apprehension I pour myself a large Scotch.

He stuffs both hands deep into the pockets of his shorts. They are brown, like his face and body. The two of us are an advertisement for the beauty and efficacy of the Cornish Riviera. Photograph us on arrival and as we are now. Before and after. And talk about transformation!

Yet we are both perturbed. I move restlessly from kitchen to parlour and back again, discarding my headscarf and shoulder bag, steeping the roses in a deep jug of water, tidying my hair in the oval mirror over the mantelpiece. My image speaks to Joshua's image, hovering behind me. 'I thought they were staying until the end of the month. Like us.'

'They were, but Aunt Harriet decided to go home a week early and sort things out ready for school. They've been here longer than we have, of course.' He is looking for a good excuse and can find none.

I say, 'Oh, well, we'll walk over tomorrow morning, and take Harriet her roses.'

He looks dubiously at the florist's blooms. 'Where did you get *those* from?'

I make a confession. 'Actually, I forgot to pick some from the garden, so I bought these instead because I'd promised Harriet. Why, what's wrong with them?'

'They look too stiff and too much alike to come out of our garden.'

With his brows drawn together and his judicial purse of the lips he bears an uncanny resemblance to Giles.

'It seems to me,' he says reproachfully, 'that you forgot a lot of important things. Anyway, there's not much point in giving them to Aunt Harriet now, is there? She won't want to cart them all the way back to London, will she?'

I am piqued by his observation, and say, 'Nevertheless, I did promise her, and I shall take them.'

From the manner in which Joshua lags behind me I can tell that the atmosphere of Trenoweth has changed. The sun may shine blissfully outside but inside storm clouds glower and threaten any moment to burst.

I hesitate on the threshold, but will not play the coward at this stage in our friendship, so knock briskly on the door and enter, crying, 'It's me, Harriet! Marina! Offering gifts!'

And instantly connect the words with their origin. I fear the Greeks, even when they offer gifts. I hope Harriet does not know this, and walk boldly through the empty rooms, looking and calling for her, who has been my dear friend and stalwart colleague all these summer weeks.

She is upstairs, organising the packing with ruthless efficiency. A list of household contents is in her hands. She consults it from time to time, while she and Dagmar sort out Gage possessions from those of Trenoweth. Poldy plays with his truck on the floor, humming in a subdued monotone. Elisabet, cross-legged in the window-seat, sings softly to her doll. Bibi and Karin are packing their own cases, obediently, neatly. None of the children speaks, and Conrad is nowhere to be seen. Joshua, sensitive to atmosphere, retreats, saying he will wait downstairs.

I enter, carrying my armful of roses, and Harriet lifts her head.

'Ah, it is you, Marina,' she says abstractedly. 'You see we are busy? We leave today.'

'Good Lord! Josh said it was Saturday!'

'Yes, but then I remember that Saturday is a bad time to go. There is much shopping to be done, and the house to open up again. We leave this afternoon. We eat high tea at Little Chef. The children sleep in the car. We are home by midnight. I have all weekend to sorting myself out.'

She ignores my roses until I hold them out foolishly, saying, 'These are for you. Won't you take them? I've bashed the stems and wrapped them in wet cotton wool. They'll survive the journey.'

She stops in the midst of her operations, regards me with dignity, and answers with blighting politeness. 'I thank you for them. They are very beautiful. But I think not. You have them, Marina. You are here longer.'

I feel that she is waiting for me to go, but I cannot believe it. 'Can't I help in any way?' I ask.

'No, I thank you. Dagmar helps me. Also the children help.'

I swallow my terror of Conrad, whom she has probably subdued also.

'Then why don't you all have lunch at Hendra before you leave?'

'No, I thank you. We have sandwich here. It is more quick.'

'Coffee afterwards, then? To save you washing up the cups.'

'I thank you, but we are wise to go as soon as we can.'

Her hostility is tangible. I can feel it pushing me politely but inexorably out of her vicinity.

Still I pursue my course, as if it were a part I must play, as if there were lines I must say: pretending that all is still well between us. 'Then we must meet again in London.'

She does not answer me immediately, saying to Dagmar, 'All these towels belong here and must go in laundry bag.'

Yet she is too kind, too graciously reared, to snub me completely. She says, 'Sometime I ring you, perhaps.'

There is a long pause while she pretends to consult the list and I see that she is almost crying. Without looking at me, she says in quiet desperation, 'Marina, do you, please, excuse us now? We have so much to do.'

I hear my voice answer flatly, void of emotion, accepting that something is very wrong. 'Yes, of course. Goodbye, everybody. Have a safe journey.'

Harriet answers to the space beyond my left shoulder, 'Goodbye, Marina. Please to say goodbye to Joshua from us all.'

The children look up now, perturbed that their summer playmate should be dismissed so lightly, but they do not protest or defy their mother in this particular mood.

I come downstairs with my rejected roses, feeling

as if the breath had been knocked out of me. My son interprets my expression, sticks his hands in his pockets, and trails dejectedly home behind me.

On Hendra's threshold, I say to him incredulously, 'Harriet didn't even want to say goodbye properly. What on earth's gone wrong?'

To which he replies miserably, 'I don't know. But she was really mad at Uncle Conrad. That's why he took her out to dinner. Is she still mad?'

'Yes,' I say, 'I believe she is. They're not even staying until Saturday. They're going this afternoon, and he seems to be keeping out of the way.'

'Cripes,' says Joshua. 'Shall we be seeing them in London, Mum?'

'I don't know. Harriet wouldn't commit herself. Wouldn't even come for a cup of coffee or let me help her. She seemed to want to be rid of me.'

I feel guilty, and yet I am not guilty. She is condemning me in advance.

'I wonder what Uncle Conrad did wrong?' says Joshua.

I endeavour to strike a lighter note. 'He can be pretty maddening at times!'

'I suppose so,' says Joshua slowly. 'But I always thought he was great. And she never got vexed with him before.'

He stands thoughtfully, hands in pockets, head held a little to one side. He is young and vulnerable, suffering loss; his mouth is full and soft and sweet. He lifts his face to me in appeal.

'*He* wouldn't go without saying goodbye to us properly, would he?'

'I don't know,' I reply, and smooth his hair. 'I simply don't know, Josh.'

'Oh, well, it was good while it lasted,' he says stoically.

He sets his florid mouth into a sterner line and

reaches for his bucket and spade. The tide is up, but on the turn. 'Better grab a spot before the grockles arrive!' says Joshua, and trots off.

He has no one now, and I wonder if he will revert to Sarah. From time to time I look through the window, but he is building his fortress unaided, absorbed in his task, and resolutely alone. My son is growing up.

I hope that I am.

Conrad throws a shadow across the threshold, and I gasp with shock.

'Sorry!' he says. 'I thought you could hear me.'

He is subdued as I have never seen him. His pause on the threshold is not to draw attention to his presence but to ask me, silently, whether he might come in.

'Yes, Conrad. Do,' I answer, as if he had spoken.

He holds out both hands and I clasp them. We stand looking at each other, wordless and sad.

Then he says, 'I couldn't leave without saying goodbye. I see that Josh is on the beach. I'll go down and make my farewells to him in a minute, but I'm afraid I must be quick about it.'

I have grown through my disturbing habit of pouring with tears at unexpected moments, and I was never a very crying person, but I should like to cry now. And must not. And will not.

As subdued as he, I say, 'Harriet's out of tune with me, and I've done nothing to wrong her. I tried to put my marriage right so that Harriet shouldn't be hurt. Oh, and for its own sake and mine, of course.'

'And it isn't right?'

'It isn't even a marriage. Giles is in love with someone else.'

A curious expression crosses his face. He says carefully, sounding me out, 'He likes women but he's not really interested in them, you know, except as friends and companions.'

'I know that. I know it now, anyway. I didn't.'

It seems disloyal to mention Timothy Mungus. Instead, I say, 'I've met the person he's in love with.'

Conrad surveys the tips of his Gucci shoes. He would love to hear details but understands that this is not the moment. So he purses his lips and says, 'Hard on you. Not the usual situation. How will you cope?'

'One day at a time, I expect. As with everything else that's happened over the past couple of years.'

'No, no. I meant – are you thinking of a divorce?'

'Not without a specific reason on one side or the other.'

We are both down to the bare bones of ourselves, without pretence or defence or provocation.

I say, 'Giles and I have a good relationship in many ways. A good working arrangement. Neither of us wants to break it up at the moment.'

He homes in on what concerns him.

'So you're free to do as you please? What about us, Marina?'

I shake my head slowly, and say, 'I don't know. I don't know what to do about anything. It all seems to be happening without me.'

He has made up his mind and takes the lead. Naturally.

'Shall I drive Harriet and the children home, and come back?'

I am shocked, thinking of Joshua, and say, 'No!' vehemently.

'Why not? No Cornish eyebrows need be raised, if that's what you're worrying about. I can stay at Trenoweth. The rent is paid until the end of the month. I shall tell Mrs Martin, whose village shop is the equivalent of a local radio station, that I'm working on a television script. A documentary about Cornwall's seaside towns. I shall say it's based on the Lizard. It sounds plausible even if it's not true. Mrs Martin won't know the difference.'

For the first time that sad but honest day the actor raised his head, always hopeful with possibilities.

'Actually, there's been an idea like that in the pipeline for quite a while. Just a question of getting someone interested who can raise the money.'

I sigh, and ask, 'But what will you tell Harriet?'

He turns and looks out of the kitchen window as he answers me. 'There's no need to tell her anything. I shall simply say that I'm going away for a few days. We understand each other in this situation. She'll draw her own conclusions and accept the inevitable.'

My throat is full at the thought of such a gain and such a loss. 'She was my friend.'

He answers over his shoulder, quietly, without histrionics. 'Yes, and you were hers. And I'm sorry. But that's one of the prices to be paid if we're to live life instead of denying it. The summer was good. Now it's over. We must move on.'

I say to his hunched back, 'Ironically, I feel not the slightest desire for you right now.'

He turns round and laughs in genuine amusement. 'Nor I for you. But, believe me, that could be altered in a moment. The reason I'm keeping my distance is because we must know where we are with each other. I'm not making a return trip in order to play fool to your conscience or your sense of propriety.'

'Speak now, or be for ever silent?' I ask sardonically, and we both laugh.

He is easier now, lighter of heart, full of hope. 'I promise you that no one's feelings will be ruffled, nor their suspicions roused. Above all, those of our Josh. So what is it to be, Marina?'

He holds out his hands and I clasp them. He has won his lady. We smile at each other in mutual accord.

I am still smiling to myself when he walks down to the beach. Over the distance I hear him hail my son, faint but clear. And fainter still, over the distance, comes Joshua's shout of joy as his hero descends.

FIFTEEN

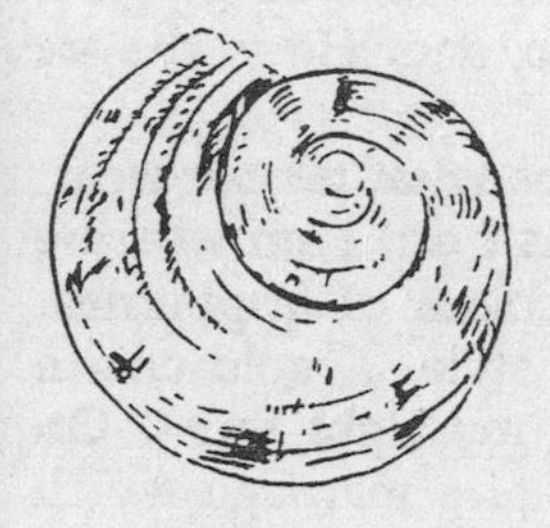

October

That final week in August, the last of our Cornish summer, seems a world away and a long time ago. I am in London again, in a state of suspended animation which only Conrad can bring to furious life. After that week of almost perfect freedom, of which even our chaperone Joshua was a treasured part, we are tailoring our love affair to the dictates of city life and other people's timetables.

At the moment Conrad is resting, as they say. So he has offered his services free, in an advisory capacity, to a fringe theatre group. As a temporary member of this new generation he feels young, avant-garde. As an experienced and established outsider he feels mature and wise. Meanwhile he draws the dole and lives on his summer earnings.

I am not working just yet. Wonderful words: *just yet*. They cover a multitude of reasons. My firm allowed me six months' paid leave while Sarah was dying. After her death I applied to be out of work for a year. The year is not up until February, and so I am on the dole, too.

I choose to stay that way so that I shall not miss a moment of this love affair.

On Thursdays we are able to meet regularly because Harriet is taking an upholstery course at evening class. Otherwise we meet whenever and wherever we can: to make love if possible, or simply to see each other, touch hands and lips, and talk. My present life is centred on Conrad. He is its deepest meaning. He is all my past moments of exaltation rolled into one. He is the *we* of me.

For him, since he always notices what people wear, and loves dressing up as much as I do, I am wearing this dress of fine red wool, the colour of raspberries. I have done my hair in Spanish style. A gold charm bracelet glitters and chatters on my right wrist. On my left hand gleams the symbol of a marriage which is no longer golden. My earrings, huge jet tear-drops, are the colour of mourning. I sit for a few minutes and turn over the pages of a magazine. I get up and consult my image in the glass or the weather through the window. But I can do no more with the one and nothing at all with the other. I pace the long room from end to end, sit down again, read my horoscope in the *Evening Standard*, and don't believe a word of it. For what am I waiting? I am waiting for the telephone to ring and release me.

There is a dream-like quality in our present existence. Giles and I live in double complicity: he preoccupied with his love, and me with mine. Our home is a small hotel from which we emerge to live our lives elsewhere. Our hospitality, on the wane since Sarah's illness, has not waxed again. Charitably, friends interpret our neglect of them as part of our readjustment, which in one sense it is. We encourage them to do so. We fulfil necessary public engagements, show a united front to the world, and take care not to offend each other.

Like prisoners forced to share a cell, we have laid

down rules to make life bearable. Neither of our lovers is allowed to come here, nor are they mentioned. Scrupulously, we notify each other when we are going out and say when we are likely to be back. Arrangements for meals at home, no longer taken for granted, are made in advance. If something unexpected happens we leave a message on the answering machine. There is an art in a married couple being unfaithful to each other at the same time.

But whereas I do know that Tim exists, my husband does not wish to know that I have a lover. He can read all the signs but prefers to hide from the situation rather than to acknowledge it. And I am no better than he at facing unpleasant truths. Joshua is at boarding-school, and though he does not complain, I sense from his weekly letters that he is unhappy. But his daily presence would further complicate our private lives, and so long as he does not appeal directly to my mother self I can ignore his situation. The ruthlessness of love appals and enthralls me.

The telephone rings. I am too quick to pick it up, and so draw a deep breath before I answer, and silently damn my eagerness, because this affair is both war and peace, and my dearest love can also be my deadliest opponent.

Conrad keeps his working life strictly separate from his personal life. His descriptions are so vivid, his mimicry so exact, that I imagine I know his fellow-actors. Actually I have met none of them, and don't expect to do so. In the background I hear a hubbub of farewells, in which he joins intermittently. Rehearsal is over and has apparently been successful.

'Ma-ri-na? Sorry to bc latc, but tonight is Gaudy Night! Ken will lend us his flat for a couple of hours – Oh, goodbye, darling, see you tomorrow! – We can go straight there and make the sun run. Love first and then we'll eat out. I've found a new Italian restaurant which is not yet as popular as it will be – See you, Daniel! – I'll give you Ken's address, and his telephone number in case you get lost. It's a tricky place to find. – *A bientôt*, Maria! – A mews cottage. I thought you'd like that, though it bears no resemblance whatever to Hendra! See you there, then, as soon as possible? Can't wait. Can't wait. Ma-ri-na!'

His voice is light and music. We shall have a scintillating evening, leading to love-making of a high order. Conrad is never half-hearted about anything, never deals in half-measures. It is all or nothing with him. Totally committed in heart and flesh, I follow in his wake. Only my mind stays single and observant, and my intuition tells me to fulfil every moment. I cannot tell when or why or how this affair will end, but its end was implicit in its beginning. In a few months or a year at most, depending on temperament and circumstance, I shall be alone again.

But at this moment life has shot up to high fever level. Hurriedly I scribble a note for Giles. *Food in fridge if you need it. Home around midnight. Marina.*

Driving pell-mell down the road I pass Sue Goddard's car, laden with children. At the risk of hurling them all over the back seat she brakes, rolls down the window, shrieks my name and flags me to a halt. The demand is not to be ignored or denied. I reverse to draw level with her.

'Hail, total stranger! Whither away so fast?'

'Important appointment,' I say, guarded, smiling, impatient. 'Late for it.'

She laughs, but her pale green eyes do not. They are my enemies, shining naked lights from the centre-ceiling of her face.

'But, darling! You're always dashing off somewhere else these days, and never, never coming to see poor old us! And I must say you're looking marvellous on whatever it is you're doing. Darling, if I didn't know you so well I'd say you had a lover . . .'

I laugh. I am brilliant. I should have been an actress.

'Transcendental meditation,' I say. 'You should try it sometime!'

And salute her, and drive off before she can ask me about it.

'Transcendental meditation?' says Conrad, an hour later. And laughs.

He is walking about the living room of Ken's flat, which is not large. Five strides to one wall. Four to the other. He is pleased with himself and me. I recognise the pleasure we are feeling at the moment. It is not sexual but mental. I have found another inspired teacher, this time an expert in *affaires de coeur*, eager to transmit his knowledge. And Conrad has found a pupil ardent to learn.

'How are you going to back that statement up?' he asks idly, amused.

I have already thought of that. 'Oh, I shall find a transcendental meditation class and go to it now and again. It will probably do me a world of good, and I need a sound excuse for being out of the house, anyway.'

'Ma-ri-na, your capacity for deception astonishes even me!'

His mood is changing from admiration to desire. His arms round me he says, 'There's a hint of the Spaniard about you this evening!'

He does not allow me to talk. Only he must be the master of ceremonies, the commentator. And how easy it is to let him have his own way. To let him be. To let me be. To let everything happen.

The kisses grow longer and deeper.

He says, 'How I love to destroy creations!'

Takes the pins from my hair, none too gently. Zips

my dress open, so suddenly that I cry out, 'Careful! It's new.'

'So much the better,' says Conrad, grinning fiendishly. 'Quick now!'

I undress as rapidly as he, for he is quite capable of ripping clothes in his impatience. Conrad is not a gentleman, nor a gentle man, in bed. And in bed we suddenly are: a bed which has been, as Ethel would say, pulled up warm over the wrinkles. Fastidiousness, for myself and its owner, makes me ask in a funny little high voice, 'But does Ken mind us using his—' before the gag of Conrad's mouth comes down and silences it.

Sometimes we voyage to the Isles of the Blessed. Sometimes we take a jolly boat ride in a choppy sea. And once in a while we head smack into a gale. This is Force Ten night. I gasp, protest, struggle against him, hit him, shout at him, and finally fight through with him.

We are cast up on a silver shore and lie there, spent, sweating, breathless, and tingling with life. Lazily, incredulously, we turn our heads and smile at each other. He runs one finger down my nose.

'Still furious with me?' he asks.

I hunch one shoulder, as if to say, 'Does it matter?'

And we close our eyes, and lie on the white-gold sand in a white-gold mood, as we did on our first night together in the moonlit cove.

Later, much later, we remake Ken's bed, leave a bottle of wine for him on the mantelpiece, and go out to eat.

Conrad is wearing the black slouch hat and a belted mackintosh which make him look like a gangster. He calls this outfit his disguise, and on the whole it works, but there are always enterprising fans who would recognise him under three layers of black paint and dressed in a straw skirt. They are likely to dart upon him from unexpected places, at inconvenient times, and ask worshipfully for his autograph.

When this first happened I tried to become invisible, shrinking into the shadows, turning away to look in a shop window, fearful of their curiosity. Then I realised that I was not sufficiently important to hold their attention. He was Conrad Gage. As his companion, though an object of envy, I was nobody and they chose to ignore me.

This evening he is accosted with self-conscious impudence by a couple of teenage girls dressed in shining black leather from peaked cap to boots. Their breasts move tenderly behind blouses unzipped almost to the waist. Their kidney-length tangled manes are streaked psychedelic pink and orange. The strut of their young buttocks promises everything.

Piqued, I watch him flare into life for them. He signs his autograph with a flourish. Jauntily takes my arm and walks me away.

'And how did you manage to impress *that* generation?' I ask waspishly.

'Probably as the middle-aged satyr who seduces young girls in *Road Riders*, judging from their appearance,' he answers. 'I never enquire too closely. My vanity is easily punctured.' Then he laughs and says, 'What a bore it all is!' and does not mean it.

London on a fine autumn evening is the perfect background for a love affair which goes very deep but cannot last very long. There is an ephemeral air about the season and the place, a sense of time passing, which matches our mood and our stage of life. Youth is over, middle age is upon us. From now on we can only grow older and less attractive. The edge of love-making will become dulled. The ability to take fire will fade. Standing on Chelsea Bridge, looking down at the lights in the river, we know simultaneously that we are fully alive and already dying. These moments are to be seized and savoured, for they will never come again to the two of us.

Conrad quotes MacNeice's words from *Autumn Journal*.

> '"*You* are one I always shall remember,
> Whom cant can never corrupt
> Nor argument disinherit."'

We do not remain quite so harmonious.

'How long can we stay?' I ask.

'My darling, I must get back by eleven tonight. Harriet will be waiting up for me.'

I am angry with us both because we are betraying his wife. I hear my voice drawl, 'And where does she imagine you are tonight?'

He shrugs, moves slightly away from me, folds his arms on the parapet, broods. The angle of his hat hides his face.

My voice loses impact, becomes softer, sadder. 'Harriet's very important to you, isn't she?'

He shrugs again, and replies frankly. 'She's my only reality.'

Desolated, I ask, 'Then what am I?'

'A dream I like to dream. Do I seem any more real than that to you?'

To answer that truthfully would be an admission too great to risk. I fall back on worldly wiseness. 'How can anyone tell what's real and what isn't? The only clear view one has is in looking back.'

He refuses to pick up that cue, and says, 'When Harriet and I die I shall certainly go to hell, and she will just as certainly fly up to heaven. But I know that she will let down a silver thread of forgiveness to pull me up.'

Cruelly I make a suggestion. 'Suppose she decides to have a little peace and quiet in preference to being plagued in heaven as well as on earth? Suppose she decides, for once, not to let down her silver thread of forgiveness?'

He laughs and says, 'Then I'm doomed and damned, my dear.' Conrad, like the rest of humankind, does not care for too much reality. He looks at his watch and says abruptly, 'Shall we go?'

Hurrying me along, he is thinking how to hurt me. I hone the sword of my tongue. For to love Conrad is to battle with him. Only Harriet conquers him with goodness and mercy. Well, he will get no mercy from me, even though the arrows I aim at him pierce my heart also.

'Ma-ri-na,' he begins with silky softness, and squeezes my arm, 'did I ever tell you a tale of deathless love? A true story?'

'No, you never did, but I'm sure I'll adore it,' I remark disbelievingly, and he laughs because I have divined his intention.

He draws me closer to him and smiles cat-like into my face, as once I have seen him draw Harriet to him, and smile as he prepared to torment her.

'As you probably know, the top echelon of film people can lead glamorous lives in which love affairs appear as regularly as bread and butter. But this amazing experience happened to a producer's secretary, a lady in her middle thirties, of modest appearance and impeccable character, married to a man as forgettable as herself, and having three innocuous children. I am recounting this tale at second hand. I didn't know her at the time. Anyway, in the midst of her humdrum, but no doubt pleasant enough life, she was swept off her feet by this great love. Not merely transformed, but transfigured. The actor who told me said that the entire studio watched the process taking place, and in astonishment they realised that this man and this woman were not only desirable human beings but also beautiful, intelligent and in every way extraordinary. Love had carried them, as it were, far beyond their usual level.

'The price of fulfilment was high. Her lover was a studio technician, also married with children. After, one presumes, cloud-bursts of tears and daggers of remorse, they decided that love should conquer all. They persuaded their respective partners to divorce them. They took on the burdens of guilt and finance which usually accompany such transactions of the heart, and offered these sacrifices at the altar of their god.'

He pauses, and we walk on more slowly. My whole being is set against him. Had we still been standing on Chelsea Bridge I would have pushed him over. I refuse to ask what happened to the lovers, and after a while he begins again. I will say this for Conrad, nothing defeats him.

'It was a poignant story, a gallant story if you like, and I was greatly intrigued by it. But to tell you the truth I didn't entirely believe it, because my friend had a tendency to exaggerate, and sometimes even to lie spendidly from start to finish.

'Imagine my surprise when we met again during a television production and he told me that the lovers were still there, still working for the same producer, and still – some twenty years later – together. I insisted on viewing these aged acolytes of the blind god, so we lunched in the canteen and looked out for them. And what do you think I saw?'

I reply coldly, 'I really don't care!'

He laughs and says, 'Oh, but you should care, Marina, because this is a true tale with a moral.'

And continues it.

'What I saw was a man and a woman, not too far from retirement, eating at the same table. They had nothing to say, and were far more interested in their food than in each other. There was no glow about them, no air of fulfilment. Physically, emotionally, spiritually, they were finished. Love had turned to dust, ashes – and habit. I looked and looked, but sensed nothing apart from a tremendous *ennui* with themselves and life.'

He pauses awhile before appending the moral.

'Love, Marina, is essentially of the moment. Once we try to capture it, to tame it, to adapt it to our daily lives, it flies away.'

His smile this time is that of friend to friend: regretful, sympathetic.

He says gently, 'End of story.'

He has made a point that did not need making, and I withdraw my arm from his. Perhaps this is the end of our story, too? Perhaps from now on only transcendental meditation will lift me above the sorrow and dreariness of my present existence. I must try it.

I say in my most acerbic tones, 'You underestimate me, Conrad. Only a very silly female, or a woman of Harriet's forbearance, would hope for a permanent relationship with you. I'm neither so stupid nor so patient. You should know me better than that.'

The faintest shadow glides across his face. This has gone further than he intended. I take it further still.

'I gave you more credit for perception than you deserved. There's a tremendous difference between crossing swords with someone and hitting them over the head with a cudgel. I didn't know you could be so – gross.'

I walked away with such a sensation of relief, and yet such a savage sensation of loss, that I feared I should fall into two distinct halves. He did not call my name or follow me, and I was glad of that. After a while the walking and the solitude brought me to myself again. By the time I got into the car and headed for home I had recovered my little shadow, who always stayed away from me when I was with him.

Conversationally, I said over my shoulder, 'All right in the back, Sarah?'

She did not answer, of course, but she was there. I could feel her presence in the dark, relaxed and smiling.

He did not ring for a week, but even the Conrad Gages of this life must run out of ladies and entertainment sometime, and Harriet's evening class no doubt reminded him that this was Thursday and our regular night.

Giles, answering the telephone, sounded nervously affable, and handed the receiver to me as if it were something too hot to handle. I realised then that he knew and minded about Conrad, but had no reason to complain and no defence. In one way I was sorry, because I didn't want to hurt him. And in another way I was glad, because he had hurt me. I thanked him and accepted the call composedly, though my heart leaped at my throat.

Giles, walking quickly into the kitchen so that he need hear nothing, closed the door and effaced himself.

'I said, 'Yes, Conrad?'

And waited for some clever remark about the complaisant husband, to which I intended to reply, 'Sorry, wrong number! and put down the receiver.

He was not stupid. He had decided to be straightforward. 'Marina, I'm sorry we quarrelled.'

I endeavoured to strike the right note, reasonable but not submissive. 'I'm sorry, too. We should know each other better by this time.'

Slightly cheered but still wary, he said hopefully, 'It's Thursday, Marina,' and then caught up by his own eloquence he declaimed, 'and the name of Thursday is Marina.'

'Do I hear echoes of that old black magic?' I asked, but not unkindly, and he laughed and said my name over to himself as if it were a mantra.

'Marina, Marina, Marina. You're the most maddening and obstinate woman I know. How on earth should I manage without you? Is it possible for us to meet and talk? We shall have to content ourselves with good food, good wine and good company because I've found nowhere for us to lay our heads tonight. Nevertheless I believe I have a temporary solution to that problem which may well please you.'

Now I felt I could relax my guard, and spoke as joyfully as I felt. 'Oh, my dear Conrad, it doesn't matter – well it *does* matter, but it's not the end of the world! – that we've nowhere to lay our heads tonight. I'd love to see you, anyway, my darling. Where shall we meet?'

SIXTEEN

'Is that Mrs Harvey?'

''Es?' cautiously.

I had forgotten how elderly Cornish people wait for a telephone to explain itself. None of your city slickness with name, number and what can I do for you. Just – ''Es?' cautiously.

The long hot summer days return in that one word, and a ridiculous rush of affection assails me. 'Mrs Harvey? This is Marina Meredith speaking. Do you remember me? I rented Hendra from you from May to the end of August this year.'

The voice becomes animated. Evidently the memory is an agreeable one. 'Oh, Mrs Meredith, is it? Yes, I remember you, my dear, and your liddle boy. Joseph, wasn't it?'

'Joshua – but it doesn't matter! – Mrs Harvey, what's the position with regard to Hendra now? I mean, are you letting it, altering it, selling it or what? Because I'd like to come down for a month.'

I am being much too quick for her. She picks her way across the stones of my sentences.

'Joshua! That's it. Knew it was a biblical name. Nice-mannered liddle boy. He's well, is he? That's all right then. Hendra, you say? Well, I don't want to let him nor nothing till he's smartened up.'

'But I don't mind about Hendra being smart, Mrs Harvey. I like Hendra the way it is. Truly.'

She ignores my plea, gathers momentum, and advises me for my own good. 'Oh, you don't want to come down here this time o' year, Mrs Meredeth. Since we put the clocks back it gets dark some early. And all they cafés and such have closed down for the winter. You should've come for the 'Arvest Supper last week but one. My 'usband won a bottle of whisky in the raffle. But now there aren't nothing happening nor nothing to see.'

'Mrs Harvey! I'm not coming down to amuse myself. I was hoping to rent Hendra for four weeks in November.'

She is puzzled. I can hear it first in her silence, and then in her voice. She speaks as to a fractious child with the wrong notion in its noddle. 'You don't want do that, Mrs Meredeth. Hendra's shut down for the winter. There aren't been no one there since you left in August. And I'm having him smartened up.'

My spirits falter.

'John 'Enery Tozer be going to do him d'reckly.'

My heart lifts. *D'reckly* means any time that John 'Enery happens to get round to it. Now I try to impress her in order to convince her of my sincerity.

'Mrs Harvey, I'm going back to my job early next year, and they've given me some work to do beforehand. I need a nice quiet place in which I can study. I thought perhaps . . . ' Third time lucky?' . . . you'd let Hendra to me for the month of November?'

Another pause. We have entered the realms of the possible. Apparently I am not driving from London to the Lizard in search of a heavy night life.

'Oh, doing some studying are you? You bringing Jonas with you?'

'Joshua? No, he's at boarding-school.'

'You bringing your 'usband with you?'

This is hard going.

'No, Mrs Harvey. My husband's very busy at *his* school. I'm coming by myself.' I adopt the Cornish habit of repeating information two or three different ways to make matters perfectly clear. 'I have some studying to do before I go back to work. I need somewhere quiet to study. I have to be by myself in a quiet place to do this work for my firm.'

'Oh, I see. To do some studying.'

Mr Harvey, passing through the hall, is persuaded by his wife to have a polite word with me. He clears his throat, hopes I am well, and informs me that he won a bottle of whisky in the Harvest Supper raffle. I remember to ask him how his mother is, and he tells me at length. Then Mrs Harvey interrupts us to explain my situation to him in detail, while I cradle the telephone between ear and shoulder and pour myself a sustaining Scotch. They discuss the chances of Hendra being smartened up before Christmas, but Mr Harvey has no more faith in John 'Enery than I have, and advises her to do business with me instead. When she speaks again her tone has changed.

'That'll be all right, then, Mrs Meredeth. But my 'usband says this time of year the range have to be lit, and kept in night and day. And you'll be using some 'lectricity, with it being darker and colder. So he think we should charge the same rent as summer, to cover the cost of 'eat and light, Mrs Meredeth. Now would that be all right?' Hesitantly.

The sum had been minimal, anyway.

'Perfectly all right, Mrs Harvey. I'll send you four weeks' rent in advance.'

'You will? Well, then!' Surprised and pleased. 'We'll

have him all warm and comfortable for you, Mrs Meredeth. And my daughter'll clean him up. If you write me an order for Mrs Martin at the village shop my 'usband'll take it to her and see it's delivered. When might you be coming, Mrs Meredeth? So's I can have tea ready when you do arrive . . .'

We have worked this holiday out so carefully, Conrad and I, to combine his work with our delight. The television documentary, which he used as a fictional excuse to cover his presence during the last week of August, has emerged from its pipeline and become fact. He will now be conducting and commentating on a tour of Cornish holiday resorts, to be called *Out of Season*. He reckons that this will take about a fortnight in the middle of November, and he and the team will be based first at Bodmin and then at Penzance.

What I have done is to overlap that period generously, so that I shall not miss a possible moment of our being together. He will be working throughout the short days, of course, but the most of the evenings will be ours and a few of the nights.

We shall be clever, discreet. We shall eat out in different places, and never on the Lizard. Trenoweth, our nearest neighbour, is locked up and shrouded, dark and silent until its owners return for Christmas. There is no one within a mile who can check up on the comings and goings at Hendra. *Not a mouse shall disturb this hallowed house*. I shan't meet the team and they won't know about me. They may guess that Conrad has a personal interest elsewhere, but guesses are not proof. And as all his visits will be by car in the dark it is unlikely that he will be recognised in the village. I know, as my mother always says, that it's the unexpected which happens, but we seem to have covered most contingencies.

Meanwhile, to make sure that I don't spend my days waiting for him, I am working on a personal project. (I have lied to you, Mrs Harvey, my firm knows nothing about the study I am about to undertake.) The idea has arisen from eighteen years of professional buying and selling, amateur renovating, and general learning about houses. If I had capital I would invest in a small house or cottage on the Lizard and turn it into its old self again, carefully modernised so that the visitor could enjoy its charm without undue deprivation. Josh and I would have first choice of holidays, of course, but in between we could let the place to Londoners at London prices, and so cover its expenses. In time I reckon I could make a profit, even resell at a higher price and reinvest in something larger. This is no fanciful notion dreamed up on a boring afternoon. I have done my homework.

The Lizard, I was amazed to discover, is not the most popular place in Cornwall, but there are schemes afoot to bring it to the public attention. Next year there will be an Aero Park in Helston, to fetch in a wide range of tourists and their children. On their own initiative Kerrier Council has decided to produce a tourist's guide for 1976 which will concentrate on the Lizard coastline. And this, if my nose for business does not mislead me, will only be the beginning. I reckon that the peninsula is on its way up and probably not yet aware of its future potential. Now would be the time to buy, if I had the money.

So I shall survey old properties on the Lizard which are for sale, collect information, take photographs, compile a dossier, cross my fingers, and hope for a windfall. The purchase of a second home here would provide me with a degree of freedom I have not enjoyed so far, as well as a link with Cornwall and an escape route from the situation at home. I had thought about taking out a bank loan once I got back to work, but Giles and I run such a tight budget that I doubt if I would dare to borrow money. But even if it comes to nothing, as is more than likely, I shall have explored a dream instead of brooding over Conrad's absence.

In the meantime, I shall have four weeks of Hendra. My little shadow will keep me company during the days, and Conrad will illuminate the nights. What more could I ask?

Dear Mum,

I wish I was coming with you to Cornwall. While your away do I have to write to you and to Dad seperetely, or shall I just write to you and you can pass the news on? Uncle Conrad writes to me now and then. He doesn't exackly write regulally but his letters are ace and he is my friend.

Love, Josh

P.S. Say hello to old Webs's gost for me, will you? Do you think his gost hunts the gosts of the mice he killed?

On our second Saturday evening together Conrad and I arrive early at Desdemona's in Falmouth and sit at a table in the window overlooking the bay. So far, the Cornish documentary is going well, and our relationship flowers in consequence. I am reminded of Harriet saying, 'Always he is what he does. He can be very moody, very difficult.'

I am fortunate in his present occupation. Conrad's mood tonight is mild and slightly melancholy: an echo of the seaside towns in their autumnal state of desertion. He picks up my hand and kisses it, smiles into my eyes.

'What have you been doing all day?' he asks tenderly, as he might ask Harriet.

But I am not Harriet. In the first place, though I

am besotted by the beauty of his mouth in repose, I don't tell him what I have really been doing, only a superficial part of it. 'Oh, wandering round the Lizard, revisiting favourite places. Taking photographs of the churchyard at Lizard Town. Reading names on the gravestones of sailors who perished at sea. Eating lunch in the pub, surrounded by pictures of shipwrecks. Cornwall shows its dark and sombre side at this time of year. I loved it in the summer, but I feel at home with it in the autumn.'

'You have a dark and sombre side yourself, Marina!' he remarks.

The waitress, smiling on both of us, but more on him, gives us two menus.

'Like Webster, you are much possessed by death,' he remarks to me, while courting her with his eyes, 'and see the skull beneath the skin.'

She looks confused, gives a shy smile, and disappears.

He remembers that my daughter died nine months ago and I am mourning her, that our cat was called Webster and is dead also. He is instantly and sincerely sorry. So sorry that I forgive him before he apologises. We put out our hands at the same time, and clasp them in understanding, in amity.

He says, as Joshua once did, 'I wish we could stay here for ever.'

And again I feel sad, as I felt sad for my son, because it is impossible to make the moment stand still.

We are finishing dessert and thinking about coffee when two weathered hands plant themselves firmly on the table between us, and a weathered face turns from one to the other of us in recognition.

'Now you may not remember us, but my wife remembers you,' the man says, and meanders into a long explanation. 'Funny thing. We don't hardly go out nowhere these days. And we never been here before. Never heard of it until my cousin told us. But tonight is by way of being a celebration. Esther and me, we been married forty years . . .'

He pauses long enough to accept our congratulations.

'And my cousin said, "Never you mind sitting at 'ome, eating a pasty. You ought to treat her to a meal at Desdemona's! That's what you ought to do!" So we did. We don't hardly ever stir beyond Helston, and we never thought to see someone we knew. But my wife says to me just now, she says, "Why, isn't that those visitors that was down near us in the summer and their boy was trapped on the cliff! Rescued him by helicopter, they did." We was taking the dog for a walk on the beach that evening – he be shut in the kitchen tonight while we come out! – so Esther sent me over to ask how you are and how the boy be. And there she be, at the table over there.'

Devastated, we smile and lift our hands in greeting. And the lady whose hair has been waved and curled for this occasion, and who is wearing her best navy blue silk dress, smiles and waves back vivaciously.

'Some night that was,' says our old acquaintance. 'Thought the boy was done for, I did. With that tide coming in. All right now, is he?'

Yes, we assured him. Joshua was very well.

'And now you'm all on holiday here again,' he pursued.

No, we said, Joshua was at boarding-school.

'Haven't I seen you on the television?' he asked, nodding at Conrad.

And without being invited he settled down in the chair between us, ready for an evening's conversation.

'Hadn't you been making a film when you was on the Lizard?'

Conrad still smiles, though the smile is taut. He answers casually, 'Yes, that's right. And now I'm down here again to make a documentary.'

The man's eyes narrow, summing us both up. 'You had a little girl, too, as I remember. Fair liddle maid.'

'Yes, that's right.'

'She away at school, too?'

As we murmur something inconsequent about Bibi the waitress hovers, saying, 'Shall you be wanting coffee, sir?'

I look at Conrad, beseeching, despairing. He takes the hint. 'Actually,' he says, turning the full power of his charm upon her, 'we *won't* have coffee. As it happens we've promised to meet some friends and we're already rather late.'

I pick up his cue. 'We really should go as soon as possible, Conrad. They'll be waiting for us.'

'*Would* you mind giving me the bill?' he asks.

But our acquaintance pursues us relentlessly. 'I never forget a face. My wife says, "You never forget a face, Samuel!" There was a foreign young man with you, and a foreign lady. Friends of yours, were they?'

'What an excellent memory you have,' says Conrad smoothly, smiling, paying, tipping.

'Because my wife wondered if the lady might be a relative to one or t'other of you. With her looking so like the liddle maid.'

' . . . and as you so rightly remarked,' Conrad continues, as if he had not felt this probe, 'it was some night.'

In unison, we rise and say, '*So* nice to have seen you again!'

And repeat the smiling lie to his wife as we pass her table. And escape ignominiously, and drive far, far away so that we shall not see them again.

* * *

It seemed as if Cornwall, having seduced us, now tired of us. Our second week was fraught with coincidence.

On Sunday I rang Giles, who reported that Harriet had just telephoned, hoping to talk to me. And he had told her that I was staying at Hendra.

'What did she say? Did she leave a message?' I asked apprehensively.

'She just said she would get in touch with you another time.'

On Monday I met Mrs Harvey in the village, who greeted me with a look which was both knowing and disapproving.

'I b'lieve you met Samuel and Esther, night before last, in Falmouth!'

She had a way of saying Falmouth which made it sound like Sodom and Gomorrah rolled into one.

'At Desdemona's?' I said brightly. 'Yes. Quite a coincidence. They recognised Mr Gage, of course. He's making a television documentary about Cornish seaside towns. His wife,' I improvised, using whatever material came to mind 'rang my husband up, hoping to speak to me. And he told her I was at Hendra. So they thought we should meet while Mr Gage was in this part of Cornwall. I didn't realise that Mr and Mrs . . . ' Damn them for not introducing themselves properly! ' . . . were friends of yours.'

'They didn't seem to know who you was neither,' said Mrs Harvey grimly. 'Samuel thought you was Mrs Gage. I told Esther when they come to tea yesterday. I said, "That's not Mrs Gage. That's Mrs Meredeth who be staying in Hendra."'

'Well, it was all rather confusing. We didn't know them, you see, and we were in rather a rush. No time to sort things out.'

'I said to Esther, "Mrs Gage is a foreign lady, and don't look like Mrs Meredeth one bit!" But she said,

"The way they was chatting together I thought they was married."'

'Well, I'm sorry there was some misunderstanding,' I said helplessly.

But Mrs Harvey stuck fast to the new opinion she had formed of me. 'Known Esther since I was a liddle maid,' she said grimly, looking at me as if I had changed into something nasty. 'Lovely woman, Esther. Never known her tell a lie nor hide nothing from nobody. And she never looked at no man after she married Samuel. And though Samuel have his faults – like the rest of us! – he do think the world of her.' This eulogy was not so much for Esther as against me.

I said as pleasantly as I could, 'They certainly seem to be a devoted couple. Mr – er – Samuel told us that they were celebrating their fortieth wedding anniversary. Forty years! That's quite a time, isn't it?'

''Es,' says Mrs Harvey contemplatively. 'Aren't many marriages going to last that long, these days. The way things be.'

Conversation dwindled to nothing after that. I enquired as to the correct method of making Cornish pasty but Mrs Harvey did not intend to humour me or to be humoured. She excused herself on the grounds that she had to go home and cook her husband's dinner. She also added that, in case I was thinking of calling, she would be out every afternoon this week. Politeness forced her to add vaguely, 'What with Christmas coming. And Mr Harvey's mother being out o' sorts!' But I knew that I had received a massive social snub. And lost another friend, of course.

The grapevine had been working overtime. At the village shop I was served hurriedly, with an embarrassed smile, by Mrs Martin. Behind my back three women, who had stopped speaking when I entered, now whispered and laughed together. One of them, bolder and older than the others, spoke up in a false-friendly voice while I packed my shopping bag.

'You the lady that's staying at Hendra?'

I am many sorry things, but a coward is not one of them. I faced her and answered easily and directly. 'Yes, that's right. And I remember you from the summer. You had a boy round about my son's age.'

Maternal pride threw her off course only for a moment, then she returned to the straight and narrow with zest. 'Some dark and lonely you must find it down there, this time of year.'

'No. I rather like it.'

'I'd be feared of somebody knocking at the door that meant no good.'

'I don't worry about things like that. It's much more dangerous living in London than in Cornwall.'

Her cronies joined in.

'Pity that the folk at Trenoweth won't be back before Christmas.'

'For if you was took bad, or anything should happen, how would us know? Down there, all by yourself.'

'We shall just have to hope that I stay unmugged and healthy,' I remarked, and picked up my bag firmly and wished them good morning.

There was a brief silence after I left. But while I was still within earshot one of them said, 'Some nice woman Mrs Gage was!'

And was answered, 'Pity there aren't more like her!'

I am being ostracised. And although I have expected nothing more than a friendly nod or a few words from the villagers when we meet – and the feeling that at worst they do not mind me, and at best quite like me – I am sore and angry and afraid when they shut me out. Added to the fact that I have a bad conscience about Harriet, anyway, there is something unnerving about this silent censure. The atmosphere subtly undermines me.

I make sure that I drive rather than walk down the lane in the early evening. I no longer venture outside the cottage after dark. I find myself drawing curtains that formerly I left open, locking doors and windows to which I never gave a second thought, listening to sounds inside and out. When Conrad knocks I always cry, 'Who is it?' And my first question when he comes in is, 'Did anyone see you come here?'

In short our second honeymoon has been brief and anxious, and my summer haven has become a wintry prison.

Sympathetic, in his offhand way, Conrad says that we will make up for all this nonsense when the documentary finishes at the end of the week. I must give Mrs Harvey my notice, tell her to keep the rent I owe, pack up and walk out. That will show them! Then the two of us, openly, beautifully, caring not a feather or a fig for the world's opinion, will drive off to Devon or Dorset or Somerset, somewhere in the West Country where nobody knows us, and find an old inn where we can stay under an assumed married name. And make love for a week.

I hear the theatre in every mellow word.

'What shall we call ourselves?' he asks, enchanted with this new idea.

But luck has deserted us, and this daydream receives the same rough treatment as our original plan. Conrad's agent telephones him to say he must return to London as soon as possible. There is a wonderful part for him in a play which, the backers say, will run for ever.

Since I cannot compete with the offer of fame-for-eternity we are reduced to one last night together.

SEVENTEEN

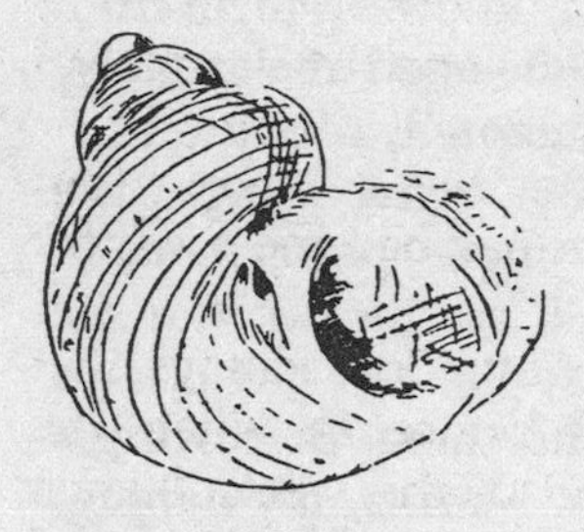

Hendra has stood up to this wild weather for more than a century and a half, and providing her roof and woodwork are sound she will stand for centuries more. Those who built her were a hardy breed, and made no provision against the wind wailing down the chimney and knifing under the doors. Used to central heating, draught-proofing and double-glazing, I am doubly aware of the noise and the cold, and grateful for reasons other than love when Conrad spends his last night with me.

Huddled together in the brass bedstead, under all Mrs Harvey's spare blankets, listening to the elemental buffeting and howling outside, we preserve the perfect silence of true fellowship for a while. The bedside light, romantically shaded with an orange scarf, softens the starkness of the walls and holds the night at bay.

Conrad whispers, tickling my ear with his lips and his voice, 'I grow old! I grow old!' and kisses the lobe gently.

A sign that at the moment he is feeling loving rather than bent on further love-making.

I whisper back, 'You will never grow old.'

Marvelling at his needs. For I, too, fear the years and watch their encroachment, and this is what he should be saying to me. But there is a deep streak of female in Conrad, which may be the reason why he is so fiendishly clever about women, knowing them from the woman within him. In middle-aged melancholy, Conrad must be courted, complimented, reassured.

He repays me for saying the right thing. 'We must find somewhere a little more permanent in London, when we are both back, so that we can see each other more often. The gipsy life can pall after a while. A couple of hours here and there. Borrowing a friend's flat for the afternoon . . . Marina, my darling, when do you go back to work?'

Lest I perceive the design beneath the question he holds me closer and strokes my hair, but I leap lightly to his conclusion. So far he has found our meeting-places. Now he means to make this my responsibility. He believes that as I deal in property I shall be able to find some jewel of a *pied-à-terre* at the price of a bauble, and probably pay my share of it. Well, I will deal with that problem later. The warmth of his body seeps into mine. I am relaxed and languorous with love-making.

'After Christmas,' I reply lazily. 'February. But it will be . . . even more difficult to meet . . . then. Your hours and mine . . don't coincide.'

Living and planning only one day at a time, as he does, he answers lazily, 'Oh, we shall manage somehow.'

Stroking my hair and planning. Kissing my fingers and thinking.

The mention of Christmas reminds me that this will be the first one without Sarah, and my mind begins to turn again on its wheel.

Last year we made Christmas round her bed at home, and Joshua decorated a miniature tree for her table, and made paper hats for the bears. This year promises to be quietly bloody. I needn't ask how Conrad will be celebrating the festival, and Giles will almost certainly leave us as soon as he decently can, both men, in their different ways, enjoying themselves. But we shall be alone, my son and I, and I still more alone keeping Giles's secret.

'Why's Daddy going out this evening?'

'Oh, something wildly important to do with work! What else?'

We exchange understanding smiles. Daddy is behaving as usual. Except that I know he is not. Let's pull another cracker, shall we? Happy Christmas!

'How are Giles and the boyfriend?' Conrad asks.

I can tell by his voice that he is smiling, he is amused in the twilit room.

Blast him!

'More fortunate than ourselves,' I reply, rather pettishly, 'they've established a regular routine and a permanent meeting-place.'

'I wonder if they'll settle down together eventually?' Conrad purrs, treading cat-like among my buried fears.

Heart and tone hardening, I say, 'I haven't the slightest idea. They seem to be perfectly happy as they are.'

'But what would you do, my darling, if they did?'

'Say good riddance and set up by myself.'

His pause is long enough to suggest that he is considering this statement seriously, and I could kill him. He pads round my predicament, eyes gleaming. 'But wouldn't that upset everybody's apple cart? Yours, theirs, Joshua's?'

I am wide awake. There will be no more love-making now, and it is his fault, perhaps even his intention.

'That's my business, Conrad, and *I'll* manage it, if you don't mind.'

He is in a teasing mood. Stepping softly, softly. Purring. Claws freshly sharpened, ready to pounce.

'But I *do* mind, Marina. I'm concerned for you, my darling.'

'Oh, why don't you go to hell and stay there?' I say with savage emphasis, and push him away from me.

Outside, the storm smites Hendra's walls and bellows for entrance.

Or I'll huff and I'll puff and I'll blow your house down!

Inside, Conrad laughs aloud at my display of temper.

'My dear, you are a lady of your time,' he says. 'The girls of today would tell me to piss off. Born in a more gracious era, you send me to hell!'

The wind roars like a pride of lions, and the light goes out.

'Power cut!' says Conrad gleefully. 'Where are the matches, Marina?'

'On the washstand with the candlestick.'

He is out of bed in an instant, seeking to illuminate our quarrel. My quarrel, I should say, for Conrad never quarrels. He only provokes. He needs rising temperatures, clashing personalities, tempest and hysteria about him. Other people's emotions nourish him, give him energy, give him copy. He remains an amused, even a grateful, spectator.

Of course, if his vanity is outraged or his security breached, he erupts in fury, pouring a lava of rage on the offender; and having reduced him or her to ashes, becomes tranquil again. When it pleases him he can out-tantrum any prima donna. But he never allows anyone to argue with him. He would not permit such equality.

Softened by the thought of my bonds, enjoying his relative freedom, Conrad says in his nicest, frankest fashion, 'And I'm not much use to you either, leaving you all by yourself in this wilderness, with the gossips snapping at your heels. What will you do when I've gone, my darling?'

Probably leave too, and find an old inn in a place where nobody knows me, and lick my wounds. But given a chance to have the last word, I take it. Saying sweetly, 'Once you're gone they'll have nothing to gossip about. So I shall stay here until the end of the month, as I planned – and love every minute of it. I came here for Cornwall's sake as much as yours,' and add in a tone as silky as his own, 'my darling!'

As soon as I pick up my morning post I know that this is all bad news. I recognise the handwriting on all four envelopes, and all of them have first-class stamps: a sign of urgency and importance. A coward, I turn to the correspondent least likely to cause me trouble. Giles.

Marina dear,

Just a note from me to you. Nothing to worry about, but I do need to talk to you. I know it's quite a trek to the telephone, but would you be very sweet and ring me either tonight or tomorrow evening between six and seven? If this is not convenient then could you ring as soon as possible and leave a message saying when we can talk?

Love, as always, Giles

I wonder, with a failing heart, whether he has quarrelled with Timothy Mungus and wants to be reconciled to me.

I turn to Joshua's espistle.

Dear Mum,

I am writing to you speshially becaurse its no use asking Daddy. I have tried to like Jefferson's becaurse of Uncle Conrad saying to be brave and do things I don't like but he also said there was such a thing as bitter limmertashions and Jefferson's is one of them. I want to leave here for good and if you don't let me I shall run away to Uncle Conrad who is my best friend next to you and Daddy. I have saved up enoufh money for the train fare and I know where he lives. Please let me know very quikly.

Your loving son, Josh

'Oh, well done, Conrad!' I say, in barren disbelief. 'Never a dull moment!'

Ethel's letter, I realise as I open it, is not from Ethel. I have been misled by the backward-sloping hand and the Lancashire postmark.

Dear Mareena,

I speak as a neighbour of your mother's for many years, and as one that knew you when you was young. Your mother is very poorly and has been poorly ever since Sarah's funeral which broke her heart whatever she said. I took the liberty of calling in the doctor yesterday, owing to her cough that she never got rid of and is now worse. He says she is to go into hospital today and she wants me to write and tell you and cover it up like, saying as its nothing much to worry about, but as a honest woman and good neighbour I think you should come home like a good daughter and look after your mother as has been a good mother to you and is now badly. I am looking after the shop while she is away and I am getting your bed ready and expect to hear from you soon. I just hope she hasnt left it too late.

Yours truly,
Mrs Charlotte Greenhalgh

The fourth letter I have deliberately kept to the last. Although she has written to me only once in our brief deep friendship, I recognise the hand of Harriet. Though not quite ten o'clock in the morning, I pour myself a double Scotch before opening the envelope.

Dear Marina,

I telephone you at your home as my friend of the summer to tell you good news, but Giles says that you stay at Hendra again, so instead I write you. I expect fifth baby – What handsome family, as Mrs Harvey says! – late June next year . . .

I work out its time of conception on my fingers. Late September?

I should hardly have thought, with our affair in full swing, that this was the right time to have a new baby. Did Conrad agree to it on purpose to provide himself with a let-out clause, or did Harriet take the decision herself in order to bring him back to the family fold?

. . . and I am so happy, but poor Poldy will be sad! Conrad is working away and I have no address of him, so I say to myself I will tell Marina. The girls speak of you and of Joshua so much. Dagmar sends greetings. She has make a pen-friend in Australia but I hope she does not leave me to find him. I ask her to stay one more year and then she go with my blessing. Dagmar is not lucky in love. I think she will be wise to stay here where she is happy.

I think of our friendship, Marina. Perhaps some day we meet again. My love to you and Joshua.

Harriet

Does she really not know where Conrad is working? Is this meant as a warning to him, through me, that he has come to the end of his rope? Or is she hoping to appeal to my sense of decency? Giving me a graceful order to move out of the way because Family Comes First?

Automatically I arrange the letters in order of importance, and make a note of them as I would if I were at the office.

1. Ring Mrs Greenhalgh and tell her I'm coming up as soon as I can
2. Ring Giles and tell him I'll be home tomorrow afternoon, and we'll talk when I get back
3. Write to Joshua and tell him to hold his horses until the end of term while I look after Ethel
4. Write to Harriet and congratulate her
5. Call in on Mrs Harvey and tell her I'm leaving tomorrow morning
6. Start packing

I lock the door of Hendra behind me and mentally say goodbye to her. For I am changed, and she will be, and considering all the circumstances we are unlikely to meet again.

Though disclined to sentimental gestures I do walk down to the bottom of the garden and take farewell of Webster's grave, which looks sodden and forlorn in the wild wet winter weather, its wooden cross awry and the lettering obliterated. And as I drive past Trenoweth I stop for a minute in yet another silent leavetaking, because that summer and those people have gone for ever.

My interview with Mrs Harvey yesterday was maddening. Although her politeness never faltered it was plain that she did not believe my reasons for going, and considered that I felt too ashamed of my behaviour to stay. Nor was she grateful when I said, 'Of course, I don't expect any money back,' but replied, 'Well, no, t'wouldn't be right, seeing we agreed on four weeks.'

Today she is full of quiet triumph as I arrive to hand over the keys. The fact that this is early morning and she is consequently in *dissabell* doesn't seem to worry her in the least, even though a handsome, heavy, middle-aged Cornishman is warming himself by the Rayburn. In fact she introduces him with considerable pride and pleasure.

'This 'ere is John 'Enery Tozer, Mrs Meredeth.'

He is not what I expected at all. Quick black eyes, an assured manner, and an air of knowing exactly what he is about.

'Some trouble I've had over that cottage,' Mrs Harvey confides in me, shaking her head. 'Not knowing what to do for the best. I didn't want no hinderment, but some told me one thing, and some another. And some was jealous because Father left him to me. But now John 'Enery be going to buy 'Endra outright. And that way I don't have to smarten him up, nor nothing. For he's been more trouble to me than Father, I can tell you.'

Mr Tozer agrees with this statement sympathetically and indicates that her troubles are now over, and she can enjoy the money while he shoulders the burden. Rubbing his hands and smiling, giving me swift sidelong glances, assessing me as coolly as I assess him, he addresses me frankly. 'They tell me you been looking at properties round here, Mrs Meredith.'

Foolish of me to think that I could hide anything at all. They probably knew when I blew my nose.

'Ah! Who told you that?' I ask, cordial but firm.

'My wife's cousin lives at Chyteg. Pretty liddle place. And I been looking over Tregatreath myself. Shouldn't think about Nansawsan if I was you. He needs a new roof. If they don't sell him soon he'll fall down.'

He gives a great grin, knowing he has surprised me. Still, the grin is full of fun rather than triumph, and his eyes admire me.

Mrs Harvey looks bemused, and I don't blame her. Evidently John Henry sees me in a different light.

'That was my opinion, too,' I reply. 'But I would expect a fair amount of decay in any old property.'

'You looking for holiday homes for your London firm, are you?'

'No. I was looking for a place for ourselves. I haven't got the capital together yet. My house-hunting is at the dreaming stage, to be honest.'

Mr Tozer feels in his waistcoat pocket, finds a business card, and hands it to me with an inclination of the head which is almost a bow.

'When you buy him you'll need a builder,' he says. 'I do a good job and charge a fair price. Anyone'll tell you that.'

The word *d'reckly* hovers wickedly in my mind, but does not seem to apply to this shrewd Cornishman. I cannot help wondering whether he intended to buy Hendra all along, and I am sure he will eventually make a handsome profit out of the investment. But that makes him no better and no worse than myself.

So I thank him, and slip the card in my handbag with a little glow of hope, and take my farewell of them both.

EIGHTEEN

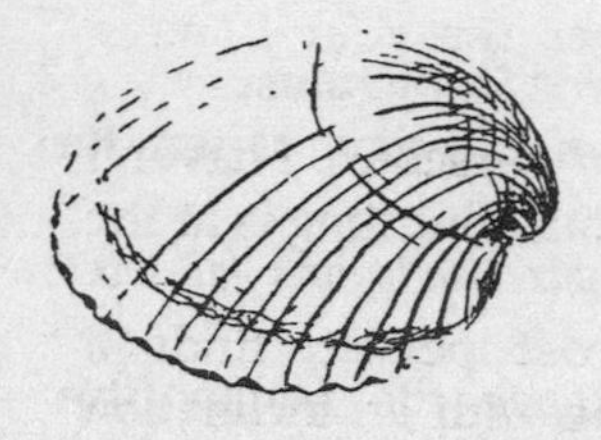

Giles has taken the afternoon off so that he can be home to greet me. I see a casserole simmering behind the glass door of the oven. A drinks tray is set up and waiting. He is genuinely pleased to see me, kisses my cheek like an old friend, and fusses round, bringing in my bags, asking me if I want a shower or a drink first, what time I should like to eat, what sort of journey I had.

'I'll have an old-fashioned first,' I say, 'then a shower, and then dinner.'

It is a different scenario this time, though based on the same theme, and the element of shock is missing, which makes it easier on the nerves. Still, the situation is a ticklish one, and Giles has set the stage and plays the first scene with care.

Woman-like, he feeds and wines me into semi-insensibility before he begins to confess, eyes cast shyly down, turning his coffee-cup in his hands, consulting its liquid depths as if he were reading someone's fortune. He is relying, as a woman would, upon my manly decency, and has rehearsed his lines well. They come too pat to be spontaneous.

Slightly smug, innocently incredulous of the joy that has befallen him, my husband has progressed from the dicey delights of an affair to the hallowed status of a permanent relationship. Giles is not merely desired, he is needed by a partner who may be younger but is infinitely stronger than himself. Tim and he have decided to declare their relationship and set up house together.

I am so tired that I see his words in pictures.

'Tim is telling his parents on Sunday, when he goes to tea . . '

Two little old dolls throw up their hands and fall over backwards.

' . . . and he's prepared to leave the family firm and find work elsewhere, if that's necessary.'

A stick figure, spotted bundle swinging from the end of his rolled umbrella, walks on a wild heath.

'I have an appointment to see the headmaster on Monday, and I shall be perfectly frank with him.'

Headmaster claps one hand to his brow, and with the other bids Giles go forth and never darken the doors of the school again.

'We both know that if we accept ourselves as we are, and confess what we mean to each other, we may well make enemies, but more importantly we shall find real friends. At the moment we have no friends because nobody really knows us . . . '

A cast of thousands divides like the Red Sea into two groups: one booing, the other cheering. Tim and Giles march down the middle, looking neither to left nor right, heading for the Promised Land.

' . . . except you, of course, Rina.'

At the sound of my name I wake with a jerk and spill my coffee.

'That's enough for one evening,' says Giles kindly,

repentantly, mopping up. 'You're tired out. Upstairs to bed with you and have a good night's sleep. Oh, Tim and I thought it would be a good thing if the three of us talked things over together, since we're all involved. And he's invited us both to dinner at his flat tomorrow night.'

My old sarcastic self surfaces for a moment.

'Now won't *that* be jolly?'

But this is Custer's last stand and we know it. Up the curving stair we go, as we used to in the early years of marriage: arms round each other's waist, my hand trailing on the rail, Giles supporting me.

Outside our bedroom door, now my bedroom door, he says very sweetly, almost anxiously, 'You half expected this would happen, didn't you, Rina? Better to sort things out properly, don't you think?'

As well as Joshua's school, my mother's health, and the affair with Conrad.

'Oh, yes, why not?' I mumble. 'Bring on *all* the clowns!'

Giles chuckles. He is perfectly content. 'I shall miss your acerbic tongue, Rina.'

I am yawning wide enough to swallow all the trouble in the world.

'And we're still good friends, aren't we?' he asks anxiously.

I hear my voice say clearly and rather sadly, 'Oh, yes. We've always been the best of friends.'

Left to myself I fall on the bed and sleep in my clothes until four o'clock in the morning, at which time I undress, take a bath, and then lie awake juggling with all my problems until Giles brings me a cup of tea at half past seven.

On this Saturday morning I ring Ethel's doctor, the hospital, and Mrs Greenhalgh. Giles hovers at my elbow, reminding me that he ordered a bouquet to be sent to her from Interflora yesterday, and has she received it yet? Asking his questions and mine, and trying to disentangle the answers, I gather that my mother is comfortable and not in immediate danger but my presence would be greatly appreciated. I arrange to drive up on Monday.

'So whatever we have to talk about must be done tonight,' I warn Giles.

Then I telephone Joshua at school.

He speaks to me from Matron's room, and Giles is within earshot of me, still sending messages and asking questions, so there is an undercurrent of anguish in our conversation because neither my son nor I can speak openly. But Josh has had my letter and my promise to help him, and says he is sorry Grandma is ill, and to give her his love, and say that he will write to her this weekend.

He manages to send one message that only he and I will understand. 'Do you remember me holding on, when I got stuck on that cliff, Mum?'

I say, 'Yes, my love – and I remember you being rescued, too.'

My eyes are full of tears, but there is no time for crying. I have to unpack one set of clothes and repack another, check the car for oil, water, petrol, tyre pressures. And go out to dinner with the happy couple, of course. Of course.

As for the rest, Harriet must be content with a cordial note which commits itself to nothing. All Conrad will know, via a letter through his agent, is that my mother is ill in hospital, I am with her, and I shall contact him later. I have not been able to decide anything else.

'Yes, we must do all our talking today,' I say to Giles.

Life continues to astonish me, pleasantly and unpleasantly by turns. I spent a delightful social evening in the company of my ex-husband and his lover. Despite the boyish fleece of hair and obvious youth, Tim was a formidable character. From start to finish he directed the dinner party subtly and stylishly, intending us all to be at ease and enjoy ourselves. He declined to entertain any of the negative moods which tend to permeate such occasions: rivalry, hostility, chagrin, self-pity. He was punctilious in his behaviour to me, and as if he and Giles had decided this course of behaviour beforehand neither of them made a display of their relationship. The affection they felt for each other was subtly evident in tones and glances, never overt. And though I pride myself on being a realist I had to admit that what my eyes didn't see my heart wouldn't grieve over.

Besides that, Tim and I had much in common. He had gone to immense trouble with the meal and its presentation, even to the choosing and arranging of flowers. His small flat was no bachelor's pad but a work of art, appearing larger and more gracious than it was in fact.

One wall of the dining area was a mirror, and behind my host I could see the room reflected, looking twice its length. I had used a similar effect in the narrow hall of our first home, and we began to talk about the use of space, and then of buying and renovating property. I entertained them with my tales of inspecting old houses and cottages on the Lizard, embroidered and exaggerated to meet the occasion. There was a surprising amount of laughter, considering the circumstances.

I thought that were he not Giles's lover he and I could be friends. But since their first love and loyalty was to each other, and I merely a third party, that was not possible. So I remained sociable, civil and appreciative. Nor did I nourish any illusions as to the reason for this meeting. I could, in my role as doubly injured wife, be a dangerous and expensive adversary.

Whereas, if we arrived at an amicable agreement they would sustain less damage to their self-esteem and to their pockets.

Tim led the discussion discreetly. I kept my head, reminded myself of my own worth, and was careful not to drink too much.

The general plan was very broadly outlined. We agreed that there should be no public airing of dirty linen, which would hurt all of us.

Giles was for half measures, of course: a legal separation on grounds of incompatibility. Whereas, in my mind, I favoured divorce because that was decisive and clean-cut. In either case I should have custody of Joshua, with Giles given reasonable access.

None of us could agree on how much of the truth our son should be told and when. Giles was for concealment until Josh was in his mid-teens. Tim thought that if Joshua were to meet him soon as his father's friend, and be able to look on their flat as a second home, he would accept them for themselves and arrive at their true relationship gradually. I pointed out that Josh was a child of the seventies and a great deal more sophisticated than they realised. I suggested that he be given a year's grace before meeting Tim and meanwhile be told that Giles was staying with friends.

As to the date of parting, Giles thought we should wait until Joshua had gone back to school for the spring term. But Tim and I, being impatient and decisive people, overruled him and said we should start our new lives as soon as possible. I wanted my son to be at home with me when he was told, and I intended to monitor the situation in order to spare Josh, who would now be faced by another major domestic crisis. Which brought us to the next question.

I took precedence when it came to talking about property. It was obvious that our present house would be too large and expensive to keep up, nor did I want to live within sneering distance of the Goddards and their ilk. A new home is a new beginning. I suggested that we put our dream house up for sale: the deposit to remain mine, since I had earned it, and the profits to be divided equally between Giles and me so that I could buy something smaller which would be my own.

Tim's problem was the opposite. His flat was too small for the two of them, and they would have to look for a larger one.

'I'm perfectly prepared,' he said, turning to me, 'to buy our new place myself so that you can have *all* the money from the sale of your house.'

For the first and last time that strange evening Giles and I looked at each other directly, nodded, and spoke up turn by turn in mutual support and agreement.

I said, 'That's very generous of you, Tim. And what Giles decides to do with his share of the profits is his business. But as far as I'm concerned he should have them.'

Giles said, 'Marina and I both worked throughout our marriage, and we've always split expenses down the middle. Except when the children were born, of course,' he added in a lower voice, 'and during Sarah's illness, and after her death – but those were extraordinary circumstances.'

Our marriage had made itself manifest, and though Tim was too self-possessed to be dismayed by this spectre he did survey it with some surprise.

I said, 'Giles and I always believed that each of us should be able to support him- or herself. It's sad that society judges people by how much they earn rather than what they do, but it's a fact of life.'

Giles said, 'I don't want to be financially dependent on you in any way, Tim. That principle worked for Marina and me. It must work for us, too.'

The statement was intended as a compliment to the

partnership we were dissolving. I accepted it as such, even drew a measure of cold comfort from it.

Tim accepted our decision gracefully, and Giles and I slipped back into our new roles. There didn't seem much to say after that, and I was still feeling the effects of yesterday's journey and had another one ahead of me. So we made our excuses and I thanked Tim, who bowed over my hand and said that he hoped this would be the first of many meetings.

Giles lingered behind me for a few moments on the way to the car, and I realised miserably that he was saying goodnight to his lover.

It wasn't jealousy I felt. Just envy. And emptiness.

NINETEEN

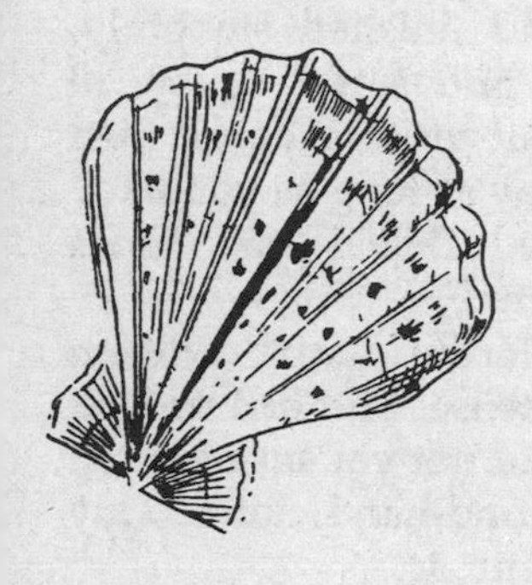

My mother's bed had been moved to the end of the ward, next to the nurses' room. Through its broad window someone could always keep an eye on her. She was dozing when I arrived. I would not let the nurse wake her, putting one finger to my lips and sliding quietly into the visitor's chair. But even my presence acted as an instant alert. She opened her eyes and turned on me a smile of such radiance that I was humbled.

'Eh, I'm glad you've come,' she said. Then rallied to deal with the occasion, speaking as briskly as she could. 'You needn't mither yourself. It's only a touch of bronchitis. I'll be up and about again in no time.'

For the next ten minutes she drove herself to enquire about my journey, my holiday, Giles and Joshua, the shop and Mrs Greenhalgh. I answered her brief questions at length to spare her the effort of talking. She listened and watched my face, satisfied, then fell asleep. When I was sure she would not miss me I went into Sister's office.

'Would it be all right if I went home now, Sister, and unpacked and had something to eat? I've only just arrived, and I came straight here. I'd like to speak to the lady who's running the shop, and generally settle in.'

'Oh, there's no immediate danger, Mrs . . . ' she glanced down at her notes and finished smoothly, 'Mrs Meredith. Yes, go home and settle in, by all means. You needn't worry about visiting hours. Just come whenever you like, and stay as long as you like.'

A fearful curiosity demanded that I ask, 'Does she know that she won't get better?'

Sister was a middle-aged North-Country woman with a fund of sound common sense. She had not yet made up her mind about me, had not yet surmounted the barriers of my first-class second-hand clothes, my acquired accent and my competent air.

'Oh, I think she knows,' she said thoughtfully, 'but I don't think she wants to admit it.'

I wrote down my telephone number at the shop. 'And would you be kind enough, please, to ring me the moment she wants me – or if you think I should come?'

She understood that I meant this, and warmed towards me slightly. 'Right, Mrs Meredith,' she said. 'I will.'

'Tell her, if she wakes up, that I'll be back at eight o'clock.'

Monday. I had forgotten the smell of Lancashire on a Monday evening at six o'clock. November. Fog sifting, sinking into the lungs. A coldness which is both bitter and stimulating. On the air float savoury smells of left-over meat, minced and fried with onions; of burned toast and stewed brown tea; of salty fish and chips deep-fried in lard at corner shops, for those too idle, or too poor, to cook anything for themselves. Appetites sharpen, stimulated by a long day's washing and mangling, or working in mill and pit, or yawning through inky, milky, concrete playgrounded schooldays. At the table, laid with cloth or newspaper, the family fall to, for once united. Nothing has changed, except that afterwards they will squabble over a choice of television programmes, whereas in my young days they could only beg the price of a cinema seat or play in the streets until it was dark.

One sniff, and I am back in my childhood: fatherless, thin-skinned, intelligent, proud as Lucifer, saddled by my mother with a name which causes eyebrows to rise and derisive tongues to comment, and a destiny that no one less than a duchess could fulfil. Her ambitions for me are matchless. My own ambitions, I must acknowledge, were mainly to get out of this rut and away from her. Which I did. And am now drawn home again, to see it and her for the first time.

Tuesday. Starching and ironing. My grandmother had a wooden wash-tub, a metal poncer and a scrubbing-board. She used dolly-blue to make the whites whiter; mixed starch in a basin, like cornflour pudding, and added it to the final rinsing water; heated her flat-irons on the hob, holding each one near her cheek to gauge the temperature. Now housewives have washing-machines and steam-irons with thermostats, and starch is sprayed from a tin.

Wednesday. Baking. We baked our own bread. Even I, the budding duchess Marina, was initiated into the mysteries of setting yeast to froth, kneading dough into an elastic ball and producing a crusty miracle from the oven some hours later. In our neighbourhood, then, to bake bread was prestigious: the mark of a good housewife who possessed both skill and time, for most of them drudged in factories all day and bought white sliced on the way home. Yet Ethel warned me, before my marriage, that a lady never troubled herself with such matters. How wrong she was. Alone among my fashionable friends I am regarded with something of the reverence accorded to a guru because I have mastered this humble, basic craft. Once I spent a precious Saturday instructing three of them in Sue Goddard's magnificent fitted kitchen, and was secretly delighted to discover that they found it difficult. Pride has always been my major sin.

Thursday. Cleaning. How my grandmother worked: scrubbing her floors, donkey-stoning her doorsteps, beating her carpets, washing her windows, polishing anything that could shine. 'And do you know the best polish in the world, my girl? Elbow grease!' She and Ethel both laughed when I asked if we stocked it in the shop.

Friday. Shopping. Judicious lists made out, with prices pencilled beside them, and something crossed reluctantly off if cash and list did not coincide. 'Pennies saved will turn into pounds, my girl!' I can guess how she would have reacted to mortgages, loans, hire-purchase and easy payments. 'What I can't afford to buy I go without!'

Saturday and Sunday. A holiday for men and children. More work for women. And so to Monday when the week starts all over again.

Now I have thinking time, and a sharp sweet time it is, with all subjects ending in death. Death of a daughter, death of a marriage, death of a mother, death of a love affair. I have two ghosts, but they are jealous of each other and will not appear together. Sarah stays with me at the hospital, which seems fitting, for she has walked this valley before and has returned to guide the new traveller.

Ethel talks about her often, and once in that twilight state between waking and sleeping she said to me, 'That little lass is here all the time. I can hear her running about and playing.' Then she looked worried and added, 'But ask her not to make so much noise, Marina. Sister won't like the patients being disturbed.'

So Sarah keeps watch with us. But once I step out into the evening street, and in the shop and through the night, Conrad is with me. Most often alone, and most life-like, sometimes loving, sometimes infuriating, though the infuriation makes me laugh now. I miss his flicking wit, his superb vanity, his ability to transform even this dark city into realms of gold. We should not have done badly together, Conrad and I. He would never have had Giles's patience with me, Giles's pride in me; and I should not have worshipped and spoiled him as Harriet does. Our relationship was always on the point of bursting into flames of one kind or another. But burned with life.

Sometimes Harriet smiles her way into my dreams, carrying the new baby. And I, not by nature a maternal woman, am filled with envy and delight. But Conrad's children are not for me. And Conrad is not for me. And I am bereft.

My mother is a long time dying.

Each morning I brace myself to cope with Mrs Greenhalgh's arrival directly after breakfast. *D'reckly,* that Cornish measure of time, has a different meaning in the industrial north. Here it means at once. Not next week, next month, next year, or whenever I happen to be available. Mrs Greenhalgh's *d'reckly* means sharp on the stroke of eight. Knock, knock, knock. Three raps of doom.

'Mornin', M'rina. Not such a good mornin'. Still, this time o' year you can't expect t'much, can you?'

Ping, clash. Shuts the door behind her. Takes off her headscarf and unbuttons her stout grey coat which resembles an army blanket.

'And how did you leave your mam last night? Much

the same? Ah, dear me. It's sad. It's very sad. Well, yes, I would like a cup o' tea.'

All week I have trekked off to the hospital at nine o'clock and stayed there most of the day. The nurses are very kind. They offer me meals with the staff. I accept tea from the ward trolley, but prefer to slip out for a snack and a break at lunch-time. Then back again, to leave at six in the evening when supper is served, and Mrs Greenhalgh must be relieved of her duties.

My mother was always patient and obedient. Sucked down by life. The approach of death frees her in small strange ways. She now arrays herself in the fashionable scarlet nightgowns I gave her years ago, wears a lacy Shetland shawl round her shoulders, and uses French perfume. The whiff of Mothaks is not quite overridden by Madame Rochas. On her wrist she displays the gold watch which Giles and I gave her for her sixtieth birthday. On her bedside table is a travelling clock and a gilt desk calendar. And in the locker, ready for any occasion, is a small collection of our presents which until now have remained in their wrappers.

She is always sitting up when I arrive, freshly washed and gowned, expectant, waiting for my compliments.

'Goodness, you *are* looking smart today!' I cry, and embrace the little bag of bones she has become.

'I didn't want to let you down,' she replies. 'And, then, coming into hospital you don't want folks turning their noses up at you, do you?'

'Of course not!'

I believe there is another and deeper reason beside these two conventional ones. Unconsciously, Ethel must feel that life owes her something, and is using her treasures on earth while she can. Of the treasures she has amassed in heaven she says not a single word, and seems reluctant to claim them. She continues to play the role of an invalid who will soon be better. To soothe her, I take on the part of a devoted daughter who happens to be staying in the neighbourhood for a few days.

We develop a routine. She sleeps for an hour or so, while I write the painful letters which are going to alter my life yet again, and then wakes up ready for a chat. This is not a child's death, flowing trustfully forward on dark waters, marvelling still at the immediate. My mother has a long history to unravel, a long past with which to come to terms. Salome-like, she is unveiling herself as one world merges imperceptibly with the next.

'I dreamed last night that your father was sitting in that chair. Funny thing. I haven't dreamed about your father for years.' She smooths the top sheet with both hands, smiling, musing. Then the old look of self-doubt returns. She pinches her lips together, pinches the sheet reflectively. Almost querulously she says, 'I often wondered whatever made him bother with *me*. He was a good-looking man and folk liked him. Dark as a gipsy and tall as a house. Like you, Marina. You get your looks from his mother's side. I never knew her. Dead years since. I didn't like his father. Rough. Very rough. Ted wasn't rough but he was a great one for going down the pub and having a drink and arguing about politics. It worried me and your grandmother.'

I began to listen attentively at this point. My father had always been presented to me as a silent knight in armour, cut down in his prime.

'He was against everything as we stood for. Law and order and religion, and the gentry governing the country. Well, it's only right, isn't it? They know better than us.'

She did not wait for me to answer. I was there to receive, not to give.

'But he wouldn't have it. Ted the Red, they called

him. The police kept an eye on him, you know. He was warned more than once for holding meetings as he shouldn't. Folk said he'd have gone far if he'd lived, because the Labour people got voted in after the war, and all the things he'd talked about happened.

'He'd taken his time about marrying. He was in his thirties when we met. And so was I. On the shelf. "You're on the shelf, Nellie!" Mother said. I was too shy to be aught else. And, any road, she frightened men off.

'Your father wasn't feared of her. He used to come into the shop for his cigarettes and joke with me. He made me laugh. He started courting me. Took me to the pictures on a Saturday night, and walking on a Sunday. I'd never been out with a man before. Your grandmother didn't like it. Didn't like him. But I did. I thought the world of Ted. Thought the world of him.'

She pauses, and says in wonder, 'What did he want of *me*?'

Like Henry the Fifth at point of death, my mother is on trial. She has accusers who must be answered, and is anxious to produce all the evidence that her internal tribunal might demand.

'I've got his letters and papers,' Ethel says.

She motions towards the bedside cabinet. Surely they are not in there? No, the gesture reveals a key to unlock secrets. She hesitates, but time is not on her side and reparation must be made.

'They're in a box on the top of the wardrobe in my bedroom. You can read them. The letters'll mean more to you than they did to me, I daresay.'

She rallies herself. Marriage, made in heaven and presided over by an all-seeing and all-knowing God, must not be demeaned by such a heretic as honest observation.

'Not that I needed *them*,' she says stoutly. 'I had *him*, didn't I?'

* * *

When the shop is closed and Mrs Greenhalgh has gone home, having wrung every drop of drama out of Ethel's situation, I begin the discovery of my father. All these years we have remained mere acquaintances, for the wedding photograph on the sideboard revealed nothing more than a dark face, a sporting moustache, and the anonymity of uniform. Details of his life and death had never been forthcoming.

'A hero, that's what he was,' my grandmother would say when asked. 'That's what your father was. An unsung hero.'

She must have heard the phrase somewhere. She liked it sufficiently to repeat it every time she mentioned him. *An unsung hero*. And yet, according to Ethel, she had neither cared for him nor approved of him. How we comfort and delude ourselves with cant and jargon.

The letters, which Ethel must have read in bewilderment and kept out of reverence for the dead, are a revelation to me. Self-taught, passionate, argumentative, searching. To whom did he write? Not to his wife. He must have known that. Not to posterity, for posterity did not acknowledge his existence. Not to God, in whom he did not believe. To himself, perhaps?

He was articulate to a fault, and army discipline had not curbed his desire or ability to speak out. The blue pencil of the censor erased several sentences, which I am sure were not about gun emplacements and suchlike, but the galling stupidity of those in authority. My father, like the Irish, was against authority on principle.

They were not lover's letters, though at the end of each one he spoke tenderly of me, urged Ethel to wrap up well, and sent a row of kisses.

They were not the letters of a traveller, though he wrote vividly of Alexandria and Cairo, of the people and their customs, and of the desert which became his home.

They were the sermons of a mad wise prophet, hampered by lack of education, imprisoned by circumstance, yet forever learning, observing, questioning. The man who was my father created himself anew on these old pages. Flying off at a tangent in pursuit of ideas, losing the thread of his argument, explaining explanations, hammering home his doubts.

A singularly good but sadly untutored mind, Giles would have said.

Certainly, Ethel would have no idea what he was talking about. Probably she skipped whole passages, and in return wrote of what she did know: the bad weather, my milk teeth, and the difficulties of rationing. I hoped that the very ordinariness of her letters might comfort him a little: a lull in the rages of personal and professional war. And though my lot has been more fortunate I understand his rage. I am his daughter.

Among the papers two shocks await me. The first of joy. For my father's birth certificate gives the name, surname and maiden surname of his mother as Kerenza Ainsworth formerly Pascoe. Inwardly I shall claim her as my birthright to some patch of Cornish earth. Outwardly I shall proclaim her when I next cross the Tamar. Nonchalantly, but with pride. Kerenza Pascoe.

My mother's marriage certificate is a different kind of revelation. According to the dates she must have been three months' pregnant when Ted made an honest woman of her.

I sit for a long time with that information in my hands, imagining what my mother must have suffered then and now. As with Giles, once the vital piece of information is given everything begins to make sense. A daughter named after a duchess, and kept apart. The polite fiction about a hero father. Our social isolation, in spite of the fact that we served a small community. The constant propitiation to an all-seeing and unforgiving God. A woman's life burned out in one bright flare of lust.

I return the secrets to their hiding-place, lock them up, and put the box back on top of Ethel's wardrobe.

She was waiting for me as if I were Judgement Day. Lying on her side, fingers picking at the coverlet, eyes downcast, a splotch of shame on each cheekbone. When I put my arms round her she clung to me and gave a short deep gasp.

'Have you read everything?' Ethel asked tremulously. And as I nodded, 'What did you make of it all, then?'

I said, 'I wish I'd known years ago. About everything. I'd have been a lot nicer to live with.'

Relieved that I was not outraged and estranged, she said, 'You couldn't have been any nicer if you tried. You've always behaved like a *lady*.'

Then sadly to herself, 'I never seemed to make much sense of life except for you.'

And suddenly fell asleep.

I stroked her hand and thought of my father's unused talents and wasted life, and their love affair. But even if he had survived the war he was too big for Ethel's corner-shop world. Ungovernable, he would have burst his marriage bonds, wounding her more deeply in life than he had in death. I could not imagine them being happy together. Like so many people they would have begun by feeling at one, and then, betrayed by time, emerged as total strangers.

My letter to Conrad must have been drafted a dozen times before I satisfied myself with the result. I kept it brief: loving but not desperate, truthful but not reproachful. He had boasted of his freedom, acted as if he were a free agent, but this was yet another illusion. Harriet allowed him out on a long rein, but only for short distances. Our affair had been countenanced for a while, but time was up. Soon she would turn his head for home.

The woman in me was about to suffer a second rejection, and with the separation or divorce from Giles I should have to face a public as well as a private failure. But if I waited until Harriet and Conrad decided I was dispensable I should also lose my dignity. So I took the initiative and told him I should not be seeing him again. And now I was truly alone.

On the second Monday, just as the early-evening smells of minced meat and fried onions begin to pervade the air, and I prepare to go, Ethel puts out her hand and clutches mine. Her eyes are asking for help. She makes the first starkly honest request that I can remember.

'I might die tonight and I might not. Just sit with me.'

Further words are unnecessary. We have communicated. I draw my chair up closer, kiss her cheek, and hold her hand until she falls asleep. As if she had read the scene aright through her window the night nurse pads silently, alert and smiling, to the end of the bed, and whispers a question.

I say, 'Yes. My mother wants me to stay with her all the time now. Would you be kind enough to ring Mrs Greenhalgh at the shop, and tell her the situation? Say that I'll keep in touch with her. She has a key and knows what to do.'

Nurse nods, feels Ethel's pulse, smooths the sheet, and goes.

My mother and I begin the long night together. I am used to such nights. In the last year I have had a lot of practice. You could say I was no novice with deathbeds.

At two o'clock in the morning nurse invites me to share cocoa and digestive biscuits with her. We sit in front of her window: sipping, dipping, talking, keeping our eyes on the sleeping ward. Other nurses join us, padding silently in on rubber-soled shoes, exchanging news in lowered voices. The atmosphere is relaxed and harmonious. They like my mother, who demands no more in dying than she did in living. They call her 'Our Ethel' between themselves, and discuss her case as if I were not present.

'Our Ethel's not one to make a fuss, and there's no resistance in her. She'll slip off nice and quietly.'

'I'm not so sure about that. These little scraps of things can hang on.'

'Yes, I'm with you there. Our Ethel's tougher than she looks.'

Then they catch themselves up, smile apologetically at me, feeling they need to excuse this familiarity.

'We've grown fond of your mother. She's quite a character, isn't she? Let's hope she sleeps herself out,' they say.

I resume my watch. I am past questioning. I accept what comes.

As dawn breaks, Ethel's eyes open and focus on me.

She says in wonder and self-congratulation, 'I'm still alive, love!'

Her pleasure and triumph are to be short. A respite is not a reprieve. Later she will fret at her unexpected strength.

'There's a lot of life in this body yet – don't you think?'

Resent good nursing.

'I can't make head nor tail of it. Why won't they let me slip away?'

Be impatient with herself.

'I'm making a right mess of this job. I can't get across.'

Be fearful that I might lose patience.

'You won't go, will you? I feel everything's right when you're here.'

And so we labour through the second week together. She hovers between this world and the next. The long-dead come alive again, fantasy merges with reality, and I coast along with all of it.

'Marina, have you told the Queen about me?'

'What do you want me to say to her?'

'Obviously dying.'

I stay at the hospital all the time now. They have a narrow white bed in a narrow white room where I sleep for a few hours while she is resting.

Mindful of her beliefs, thinking of her spiritual comfort, I ask the vicar if he will call round, which he does, kindly bringing a bunch of draggled chrysanthemums from the vicarage garden, and a card of good wishes signed by members of the congregation. Engrossed in her task, she refuses to look at him and speaks to me as though he were not present.

'He's been round twice already, and that's enough. I'll be all right! He needn't fret himself – and you needn't either!'

Said in a tone of high dudgeon.

Unsnubbed and smiling, the vicar assures me that he will come whenever he is wanted, and I can call him at any time. Still I am puzzled. I had expected her to be anxious for her salvation.

'Oh, never fear, Mrs Meredith,' he says, friendly and confiding, 'your mother is in the hands of God, and closer to Him than either of us.'

When I return from seeing him off the premises Ethel is nursing a grievance. She speaks with a certain asperity, sounding uncannily like me. 'I don't want anybody else visiting me. I've got too much to do. You can tell them all to stop away and keep their flowers to themselves!'

She is no longer frightened of dying, simply puzzled how to accomplish the act.

Sister says, 'Most people come to terms with death

once they face it. I've known very few who were afraid. It's a natural process, after all.'

And I remember Sarah's patient acceptance of what appalled us.

Yet in the early morning, propped up on her pillows to soldier through another day, Ethel looks lost. She is no longer eating, and her frail bones peak the flesh. Nurse, out of kindness, brushes her long grey hair into a bun at the top of her head and ties a scarlet ribbon round it to match the Welsh flannel nightgown. The ribbon looks rakish, ridiculous, out of place. My mother has become an ancient little girl.

Pitifully she asks me, 'Why am I still here?'

TWENTY

On that second Saturday evening, as I sit and watch her dozing her life away, the nurse comes tiptoe on her soft-soled shoes and aburst with excitement, to tell me that a gentleman is asking to see me.

I wonder muzzily whether Sue Goddard or her ilk, sniffing out all sorts of trouble, have sent a husband to spy on me.

But she cries, exalted, 'He just gave his name as if he was an ordinary person, Mrs Meredith, but we all recognised him straight away. It's Conrad Gage. And he's brought such a beautiful bunch of flowers for your mother, and asked ever so nicely if you could have a word with him. Conrad Gage! Oh, Mrs Meredith, I've seen all his films, but I never thought to see *him*. And he's sitting in Sister's office, chatting away – just like anyone else!'

Only shock prevents me from saying acidly that Conrad is an ordinary human being, and only too human at that. But, in any case, she would not listen. I recognise the fanatic glow of an admirer. She casts a professional eye on the patient and says, 'Your mother seems comfortable enough, Mrs Meredith. I'll keep an eye on her while you have a word with him.'

So I rise wearily, warily, putting both hands to my hair to smooth it, and am even guilty of applying powder and lipstick surreptitiously in the corridor, outside Sister's room. The reactions are automatic. So is that vaulting leap of the heart when I see him. He looks as pale as I feel but is keeping up appearances rather better, though he stands up and bows as if to a queen, and waits humbly for recognition, which seems to me to be overdoing the family friend act.

I put out my hand and he clasps it, murmuring something about being so sorry, so very sorry.

Sister, who has evidently been charmed and well primed, says, 'Mr Gage was hoping to take you out for dinner, Mrs Meredith, and I think that would be a good idea. You've been mewed up here for nearly a fortnight. If you give us a telephone number we can always contact you should there be any change in your mother's condition.'

Then she offers us the privacy of her room while we have a few words, and goes out smiling.

At the end of my tether, I blurt out, 'It's no good, Conrad. We can't go on. Harriet's expecting another baby – and in this day and age I really should like to know *why* you both decided to have a fifth child . . . '

But he holds my hands in both of his and lifts them to his mouth and kisses them, and whispers, 'Hush, Marina. Hush, love.'

And I do hush, because I am standing at the edge of one world and peering into the next, and nothing matters, anyway. We stand close together, hands clasped, and stare as if we could swallow each other up.

His very presence is enough, but at this moment Conrad represents far more than himself and a precious part of me. He is life and hope and the moment, as opposed to death and resignation and looking back. His vitality warms me. I believe that he brings with him an answer to all my troubles, and will shortly dispel them.

'Yes,' I say, hypnotised, 'I should love to come out to dinner with you.'

The spell is broken and we move away, aware that we are in Sister's office and she will soon return.

'Have you come by train?' I hear my voice ask quite normally.

'By train from Euston to Manchester, but I've hired a car. So we can go anywhere you please. Anywhere you suggest.'

I regress to a child-like self, crying, 'I want to get right out of here. I've had too much of sickness and dying. How far are you prepared to drive? Sixty miles? There's a lovely restaurant at Matlock.'

'Then we'll go there,' he answers peaceably. 'Should I book a table?'

Momentarily I cover my mouth as if it has sinned. I strive to be a sensible adult again.

'No. I can't go as far as that. If she woke up and asked for me I couldn't get back quickly. Besides, I don't want a lot to eat.'

'Then we'll stop at the nearest reasonable place we find, shall we? The background doesn't matter, does it, so long as we can talk?'

I shake my head vehemently.

A florist's shop of roses is glowing in shades of ruby, topaz and pearl on a side table.

He picks them up, saying, 'I brought these for your mother – that imaginative lady who named you after a duchess. The idea has always intrigued me. Might I give them to her? Or,' perceiving that Sister has returned and is smiling in the doorway, 'is Mrs Ainsworth not well enough to receive visitors?'

Sister answers for me whether I like it or not. 'Oh, she'll be thrilled – won't she, Mrs Meredith?'

I lift my hands and drop them, in assent, in despair.

'If you wouldn't mind waiting a few minutes, Mr Gage,' says Sister. 'I think we'd better prepare her!'

And whisks out again.

'What's this then, Conrad?' I ask, soft and savage, 'a busman's holiday?'

Very soberly he answers, 'You misinterpret me, Marina. A whim, if you like, but not a performance.'

And I feel ashamed, which is hardly fair.

When we are finally allowed in I see that Nurse has alerted the entire ward. The female patients are all sitting up, twittering, faces turned to the swing doors, waiting for his entrance.

Conrad's appearance, though brief, does not disappoint them. He pauses, smiles slightly, inclines his head at the scatter of handclaps, and disappears behind the curtains which divide the living from the dying.

The invalid has been tidied up and propped up to meet the great man. Her thin grey hair is brushed into a topknot, graced by the girlish scarlet ribbon. Nurse has trimmed her nails, and Ethel spreads her fingers in front of her on the tight white coverlet, bemused. She says to me wilfully, pettishly, 'I don't *like* having my nails cut!' I reassure her. 'But they look so nice now, and so do you!' And then, 'Mother, this is Conrad Gage, the actor. Do you remember my writing and telling you that he and his family were on holiday with us in Cornwall this summer?'

She is not sure of herself or him, and extremely worried in case she says the wrong thing and lets me down. But Conrad has never lost a member of the public yet. He picks up one of the newly manicured hands and kisses it. He offers his tribute of roses with a bow and a courteous explanation. Ethel takes them into her arms, and revives.

She says accusingly to me, 'Met him on holiday, indeed! What a story! Why, I know this gentleman. I've seen him on the television.' Then, with a shy smile for Conrad, 'It's very good of you to come, sir. I wish I could offer you some refreshment but I'm not in charge here.'

'I need nothing,' he says simply. 'I wanted to see how you were for myself.'

She motions him to sit down. He draws the chair close to the bed and asks her how she is feeling, as if he had known her for years, as if they were old and dear friends. They both ignore us.

Transformed, my mother has become young enough to match the hair ribbon, and I now see that once she was pretty.

She confides in him, 'I'm not dead yet, you know. I think I'll last until Tuesday, but I don't want to be here Wednesday.'

'Now what sort of talk's that when a famous gentleman comes to see you?' Nurse demands cheerfully, and swoops on the roses. 'Oh, what lovely flowers! Shall I put them in a nice vase for you, Ethel?'

Never taking her eyes from Conrad my mother answers with annihilating dignity.

'My *name* is Mrs Ainsworth! And yes, you *may* put the flowers in water but Mr Gage and I wish to have a private conversation.' And to him, with regal splendour, 'I believe I've put up with this familiarity quite long enough.'

Nurse raises her eyebrows at me. My own eyebrows rise in reply. And we retreat, leaving the stage to the two principal characters, who wish to play this final scene alone.

Ethel is very bright and pleased with herself when we leave, and inclined to patronise the nursing staff, a harmless fault which they accept with great good humour. Indeed we are all delighted with her, though Sister feels she must warn me that this is not a sign of improvement, only a momentary rise in spirits. Nevertheless I go with a light heart, and kiss my mother goodbye with genuine affection.

Her little claws clutch my sleeves as I bend over her. She says, 'Eh, I do love you. I always did.'

Her fingers stroke my winter coat of cocoa-coloured suede, touch the thick fur collar and cuffs. She tells me to stand back so she can get the full effect, though she has seen it dozens of times.

'Right smart!' she says. 'Is it from that fancy second-hand shop?'

'No, it was new last winter, from Peter Robinson's.'

Her spurious self-confidence, invoked by a quarter of an hour with Conrad, gives tongue. 'I wouldn't mind a coat like that myself, when I get better.'

'Then I'll buy you one for your birthday.'

She beckons me to come close so that she can whisper. Her warm sour breath flutters on my cheek. Her tone is roguish. 'Isn't it lucky you were here when Mr Gage called on me? You wouldn't have met him, else!'

'Very lucky!' I say solemnly.

'Mind you behave yourself!' she warns, as she used to when I was a child.

On that ironic note we part. And Saturday evening comes in sharp and foggy, with sulphurous haloes flaring round the lamp standards.

Mildly elated, Conrad and I drive across the border into Cheshire and find a carefully preserved old inn on thc banks of a river. My appetite for food, life, and – yes! – Conrad, has rushed back. I am delighted with him, admiring of him, in love with him, because he has transported Ethel to magical regions, and turned the common straw of events into gold.

'Am I allowed to ask what you and my mother talked about?'

He smiles and twirls the stem of his glass.

'Oh, of shoes and ships and sealing-wax . . . '

'And cabbages and queens?'

He laughs, and thinks aloud. 'The human mind is a fascinating thing. On the edge of dissolution it plays extraordinary tricks. Your mother was sometimes lucid and sometimes confused. Following her through the maze was an extraordinary privilege.'

Our table is by the window, overlooking a night garden hung with coloured lanterns. On the starched white cloth candles illumine strawberry globes. The atmosphere is hushed and intimate.

'What did we talk about? Mainly you. She was concerned about your position in the world. I assured her that you moved in the most exclusive circles, and were regarded as the peer of many royal personages. I embroidered her dreams and made them come true.

'When she spoke of her illness I dismissed it as being an unpleasant, but necessary, precursor to greater health and happiness than she had ever known. And I promised her a box at the theatre for my latest production.'

He pauses, and smiles a little to himself.

'We got on pretty well,' he says modestly. 'But, then, I am used to the world of illusion.'

We don't speak again until mine host approaches to explain the particular subtleties of the hand-written menu. Proudly he tells us that his wife cooks the food, and has drawn favourable comments from Egon Ronay. His tone is reverent and adds savour to each dish. As they all sound delicious we choose different ones, so that we can share and taste.

Conrad consults the wine list as if our lives depended on it, and orders a bottle which is brought up from the cellar in state, cradled like some dark and dusty foundling about to be handed over to adoptive parents. Waiters, scenting our mood and his generosity, converge upon us, smiling, tempting. This will be an expensive meal but Conrad's attitude towards money is casual and stylish. When he has plenty he spends it. When he has none he doesn't worry. He sits loose in the bonds of life, and has loosened mine also, though the cost has been great, and the loss of him will be greater still.

He lifts his glass to me and says, 'To knowing you!'

Lifting my glass I reply sincerely, 'And to having known *you*!'

His pause is not deliberate, but natural. He is thinking the statement through. When he answers his voice is light and humorously wary. 'I detect an elegiac note in your voice, Marina. Are you really thinking of saying goodbye to the pair of us?'

In the last ten months I seem to have said goodbye to all those I love. This year is the end of a lot of things. But I mustn't be ponderous.

'My dear Conrad, I thought I'd done so already, but you seem not to have read my letter!'

He leans across the table and speaks persuasively. 'The letter made its point, I grant you, but let me put it another way. Yes, Harriet is pregnant, and will need a greater share of my attention and reassurance than usual. You, too, have family problems which will demand extra time and emotional energy. But surely we are not required to give up everything? Does it not seem to you – beset as we both are and shall be – that we deserve a little joy occasionally? Why go to extremes? Why say *never again* when it could be *now and again*? Why, doing our duty by those who require it of us, should we deny ourselves entirely, Marina?'

'The last twist of the knife!' I say, only half laughing at his persistence. 'What a perfect devil you are!'

He catches my hands in his and gives them a little shake.

'Ma-ri-na. Listen to me. I'm perfectly serious. What disturbs Harriet most is never knowing where I'll be or with whom.'

'Lord, what an unreasonable woman she is!'

'No, darling. Don't mock. Listen. Suppose I give up the chase? I'm three and forty, after all. Supposing I were to settle down for good with you as my one and only mistress? How could Harriet – given time – be hurt by that?'

Fervently he expounds this new philosophy. 'Certainly, such a situation couldn't be hidden and would cause reactions, favourable or unfavourable, among our various friends and acquaintances. But after a year or so we should be old news to everyone but each other. We could settle down together, and you and Harriet and I would be complete.'

I open my mouth, whether to cry or laugh I am not sure.

'No, let me finish,' he says earnestly. 'Harriet knows and likes you. You could be friends again. She need never worry about other women. And you needn't worry about finding another husband. In fact, Marina, you shouldn't try to find a husband. You're better suited, temperamentally speaking, to the role of a mistress. It frees you to pursue your own course.'

He gives my hands another little shake and says, 'What do you think?'

His face is alight with the beauty of this idea. He shines with sincerity. And I am fearfully tempted because I want him so much, and am terrified of suffering the loss of him, and because I need a haven of any sort.

I say slowly, 'My darling Conrad, it sounds wonderful in theory, but in practice I suspect it would fall down rather hard – and hurt itself and us.'

'Why? Why should it.' For once he is involved, is wounded, is arguing with me.

I try to treat him as carefully as the waiter treated the wine. 'I can't imagine Harriet sharing you with another woman. And I don't blame her.'

'But she shares now! She shares with the world!'

'No, she puts up with your affairs because they're on a temporary basis. Other women pass by, but Harriet remains. That is her privilege and her strength. She would *never* allow another woman to share you permanently. And you know that, Conrad, if you think about it.'

He broods over his wine, not looking at me. And I look my fill of him because I am not going to see him again until we are old and cold and our love affair stirs neither hearts nor loins.

I ask him frankly, 'Was the new baby Harriet's idea?'

'Oh, yes. In fact, Harriet's *fait accompli*. She deals with that side of our life. I have no say in the matter. I am not asked. I am told!' Then he glances at me sheepishly, and adds, 'But, of course, I love them, too. I like to look down the table and see a row of little heads, and play the great papa.'

I don't hide my smile, answering, 'I know you do. I've seen you in action.'

'Are you wondering whether Harriet became pregnant in order to get you out of the way?'

'It had occurred to me. She knows what my reaction would be.'

'And she was right?'

'Yes, my dear. She was.'

And here we are, at the end of us. But how does one end the end?

Ah, life knows! With the waiter gliding up to tell us that there is a telephone call from the hospital. With Sister's voice telling me urgently, sympathetically, that my mother's condition has deteriorated and she would advise me to return as soon as possible. With Conrad driving furiously through the wet black North-Country night, neither of us speaking. Yes, life knows how to end everything.

Hurrying down the corridor I say to Conrad, 'I want to see her by myself.'

'Of course.'

'But you will wait for me, won't you?'

'Of course.'

Sister intercepts my progress, coming quietly out of her office to speak to me before I can hurry to Ethel's side.

'I'm so sorry, Mrs Meredith, but your mother died soon after I telephoned. Very peacefully.'

'Did she ask for me?'

I think she is gauging what my reaction will be, rather than telling the truth, but her hesitation is minute.

'No, Mrs Meredith. She never recovered consciousness.'

Hospitals, like shows, must go on. The patients have been settled down to sleep. The nurses are drinking tea behind the broad window, looking out on to the ward. Only the curtains drawn round my mother's bed denote death. And, after all, death is part of hospital life.

Nurse rustles forward and whispers, 'Would you like to see her?'

A shrunken child, claws clasped in the position of prayer, mouth closed in hurt, jaw bound up, is my mother. Was my mother. For minutes I cannot speak. Then I turn away, saying to them, 'Thank you for all you've done.'

And to Conrad, 'Would you mind taking me home?'

He stayed with me all night, and we made love because we wanted to, and because we should never make love again, and because old age and death would put an end to it, anyway.

I expect that the neighbours saw us both arrive, and some of them must have observed Conrad leaving after breakfast. But that was not important, because Ethel wasn't living there any more and I had left a long time since.

TWENTY ONE

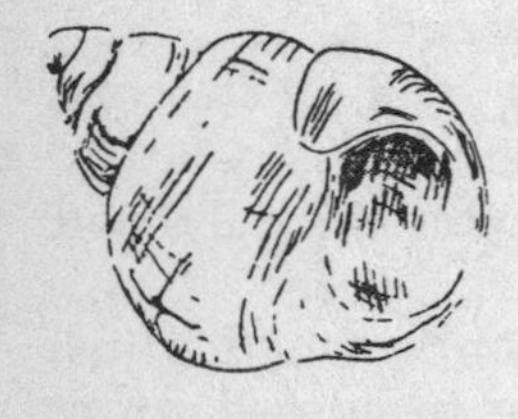

The funeral is over. We have buried Ethel North-Country style, in a windy churchyard on a bleak December day, and invited the neighbours in for a funeral tea, at which a vast baked ham played the leading role. Left to ourselves, Joshua and I have washed up and tidied round, and now sit together before a fire which is probably heating half of Salford. Night is drawing in. The living room is close and cosy and smells of apples. It is the hour of remembrance, and of confidences. I do not mind the one, but am so dreading the other that I have provided myself with a double Scotch.

Sprawled in his armchair, Joshua has been watching me and gauging my mood while supposedly reading the *Dandy*, but now puts his comic down and prepares for conversation. My son has grown up in both senses. His best grey suit, bought for Sarah's funeral, is tighter. His wrists poke beyond his cuffs. When we stand up together his head advances past my shoulder. He holds himself well, speaks clearly, thinks before he speaks, and says what he means.

Evading his curiosity, I remark, 'That suit's too small for you already. How much have you grown?'

'I don't know. I haven't measured myself. A lot, I expect,' he answers briskly, and moves straight on. 'Mum, how long have you known Tim?'

'Only a little while, but he's been friendly with Daddy for about two years. They play squash together on a Thursday.'

Joshua thinks this over. I keep my cool.

'By the way, Josh, did he ask you to call him Tim or is that just you being over-familiar?'

'Nope. He asked me. He's a very friendly sort of bloke, isn't he?'

Before I can answer he moves on again. 'It's just that I'd never heard of him before he turned up at school on Tuesday, with a letter from Dad to introduce him. Matron had told me about Gran on Sunday, and said I'd be going up for the funeral, but I thought Dad would collect me. The next thing I know I'm zooming up the motorway with a total stranger in a blooming Porsche.'

'What fun!' I cry, withdrawing my legs from the blaze.

The uninvited guest at Sarah's interment had made himself indispensable in the past five days: driving Giles up from London to deal with the business of death; returning to collect Joshua and ferry him to the funeral; keeping discreetly apart yet always ready to help; and conducting himself throughout with the utmost tact and delicacy.

'Oh, I'm not complaining, Mum. It was terrific. And we talked a lot, and ate a lot. But it seemed a bit sudden, if you know what I mean.'

'Oh, well. Daddy tends to be absent-minded about anything except education. I was at the end of my rope. And the decision was rather taken out of my hands. But it worked very well, I thought.'

I had used Ethel's upstairs parlour for the funeral tea, warming it with an electric fire for two days beforehand to make it fit for company. We were all chilled from the churchyard, which acted as a natural wind-funnel, and the atmosphere was lugubrious.

Joshua walked round, serving glasses of sweet sherry to our guests. Giles was drawn into conversation with Mrs Greenhalgh. The other neighbours whispered together in a shy tight knot. And by the prick of my thumbs I became aware of Timothy Mungus at my side.

I had realised over the last few days that Tim was a young man who wielded considerable power. My objection to his meeting Joshua had been overruled in the nicest possible way, and Giles had been pressed into my service despite himself. Consequently I felt angry and grateful at once.

He began conversationally, courteously.

'Do you remember, that evening at my place, talking about renovating an old property in Cornwall, and letting it? Were you serious, or just chatting?'

'I was perfectly serious. In fact I have a short list of three properties ripe for conversion. But it would take quite a bit of capital to renovate even one of them, and I haven't got it. And I should have to drive down to Cornwall on a Friday night and come back on a Sunday afternoon, for months, to keep an eye on everything. And deal with workmen who say *d'reckly* when they mean sometime or never!'

He laughed and said, 'I remember you were very amusing about that.'

'Actually, I wasn't being entirely truthful. I know a builder who seems to be excellent. If ever I need him. But *d'reckly* makes a better story.'

I added, for his presence made me uncomfortable, 'I think I'd better mingle – as they say.'

But the neighbours, feeling more at home with Joshua than with us, were questioning him. And Mrs Greenhalgh was laying down the law to Giles, who twisted his glass between his fingers and kept on smiling.

Tim said firmly, reassuringly, 'Oh, they'll be all right for five minutes. And I promise to relieve Giles of the lady-with-the-chin afterwards. Look, Marina, suppose I lend you the money to convert your property? At a fair rate of interest. As a business proposition.'

I was startled, but could not resist the ironies of the situation. 'And suppose it turned out to be a failure and I couldn't pay you back? Wouldn't that make life peculiarly difficult for the three of us?'

He smiled and said, 'Oh, I doubt if you'd lose money on it. You might, at a pinch, simply break even. But my belief is that you'd make enough to buy another holiday cottage or three and do rather well with all of them.'

My pride and suspicion must have been showing.

He looked me straight in the face and said, 'I'm not offering to lend you the money out of guilt or sentimentality but because I know you're a good bet. And I think you deserve a backer.'

'*How* do you know?' I asked caustically. 'What *can* you know of me, after so short and fraught an acquaintance?'

He refused to be wounded, annoyed, or thrown off course.

He really is a surprising young man.

'I know you through Giles, and because of Giles.'

He judged my possible response to what he was about to say, and risked it. 'We're very alike, you and I. Pushy people – if I might be forgiven the expression – who know exactly what they want and where they're going.'

Ah, you were right once, I thought. But you're wrong, now. I'm looking into a dark glass and finding no reflection at all.

'Giles, on the other hand, is the retiring type. An academic who likes the stimulus of the outside world but needs protection from it.'

Since I could not contradict him on this point he ventured further still. 'Marina, it's purely the luck of the draw that Giles is attracted to men rather than women. Otherwise you'd probably have celebrated your silver, gold, ruby and diamond wedding anniversaries together.'

The dark glass cleared momentarily. I saw and understood a little more, minded a little less, nourished a little hope. Though I said nothing.

He hesitated again, but decided to be brave. I will say that for him. He is brave.

'The money-lending is purely business. On the personal side I'd like us to be friends if we could, Marina. I don't see why we can't be. I'd like to have known you, anyway, quite apart from the accident of meeting through Giles. But that's a decision I must leave to you.'

I took time to reply, to answer truthfully and without sourness.

'I haven't surfaced yet, Tim. I mean from everything that's happened this year, not just from you and Giles. It may well be possible when I've settled down and sorted myself out.'

He inclined his head.

Under the influence of a second glass of sherry the neighbours were venturing towards me, and Mrs Greenhalgh made a beeline for Tim, smiling like a crocodile.

'Do tell me the name of this determined lady,' he whispered. 'And please do think about the loan, Marina. I'm perfectly serious. The offer's there any time you feel like taking it up.'

* * *

Now that the funeral was over, and they had done their duty by us, the two men wanted to be together. Giles had already told me that he would be returning at once with Tim, and from the way he avoided plans for the coming weekend I guessed that most of it would be spent away from us.

Remembering this, I cover for the happy couple. 'Tim's a stockbroker, and he's been advising Daddy on investments . . . ' That will be the day. Giles knows nothing about investments and has nothing to invest. ' . . . so I'm afraid we shan't see much of him this weekend because they'll both be busy.'

'What's new?' says Joshua automatically, having more important matters on his mind. 'Mum, I don't want to worry you, after all the trouble with poor old Gran, but have you had time to talk to Daddy about Jefferson's?'

Yes, and other things. Our marital affairs are to be put in the hands of separate solicitors after Christmas. Giles's luck is holding. His headmaster, he told me, showed remarkable understanding. And Tim's parents, though not yet prepared to meet Giles, had behaved in an exemplary fashion.

So as everything was going his way I had taken advantage of the moment.

'Yes,' I say drily, 'he's agreed to let you leave . . . Joshua! Joshua! Stop whooping about. Sit down, for heaven's sake. The school will need a full term's notice, and I can't imagine Daddy paying fees for nothing, so you'll have to soldier on until Easter.'

'I don't give a feather. I don't give a fig!' Joshua cries, hopping from one leg to another. 'I'm leaving rotten Jefferson's. I'd like to dance a jig!'

'Not now, if you please. I've had enough disturbance to last me a lifetime!'

He hugs me swiftly, spontaneously, and then turns

shyly from me saying, 'Thanks, Mum. Gosh, only two weeks until Christmas!'

I think this is a good time to introduce the first of the glad tidings I have been left to impart. 'So it is! What excitement! And lots of exciting things will be happening after Christmas. We're going to move house, Josh.'

He looks over his shoulder, startled. 'Why? When? Where to?'

'I don't know yet. I think we'd better find a good day school for you first, and then plan the house round that.'

He is frowning, concentrating. Firelight winks off his spectacles.

'Will it be bigger than the one we've got?'

'No. Smaller.'

He sticks his hands in his pockets and kicks Ethel's rag rug gently.

He says, face averted, 'Is Daddy coming with us to the new house?'

I parry this one. 'Why do you think he wouldn't?'

Coward!

Joshua gives me a look so long and deep that excuses fail me. 'No, Josh. He isn't. That's the other thing I was coming to.'

While I am taking a long swallow of Scotch, and drawing breath, Josh aims a question directly at me.

'Are you and Daddy getting divorced?'

I pull myself together and say, 'Not yet. For the moment we're separating.'

There is silence between us for a while, then Josh aims again. 'Is it because of Uncle Conrad?'

'Oh, dear God, Josh! Why should it . . . ?'

No, don't go into that maze! And don't pretend.

I say sharply, forbidding further discussion on this subject, 'No, it certainly is not! Conrad has his family to look after. Harriet wrote to tell me that she's expecting another baby in June.'

He gave me another long deep look. 'But we shan't be seeing them. Right?'

'I shan't be seeing them. But *you* can. And Conrad told me that he will keep in touch with you. He said you were his friend.'

Josh nods to himself, pleased and sad. And then aims again. 'If Daddy isn't coming to live with us, will he live with Tim?'

'Well. Yes. He will,' I answer in surprise. And add diplomatically, 'Just while he looks around.'

Again Josh nods to himself. I have apparently supplied a vital piece of information which is slotting everything into place, but whether he comprehends the whole truth I cannot be sure.

He blurts out, 'Am I living with you, then?'

'Yes, Josh.' I attempt lightness. 'I hope you don't mind!'

He shakes his head, not looking at me.

'You'll see lots of Daddy, of course.'

'Well, that'll make a change,' he mutters to himself.

His tone is sulky, resentful. I don't blame him. I try to reassure him.

'Daddy and I are still friends. Just because we're separating . . .'

He swings round on me, and I have a glimpse of Joshua as he will be in his maturity: dark, impassioned, and dedicated to the truth as he sees it.

'Oh, don't give me that!' he cries. 'Don't give me the spiel about both of you loving me just as much, even if you don't love each other any more. Don't tell me not to worry because everything's going to be great. Because it isn't. It's never going to be the same again. I shall have to learn to live with two sets of people in two different places. I know boys with divorced parents. I've heard what they say – once they've got over it enough to talk. I know what it's all about. So you can forget *that*!'

Sorrowfully I watch him struggle with himself, realising I must say and do nothing. Until he turns and throws his arms round me, and thrusts his head into my shoulder and breaks his heart.

I let him be until his sobs are transformed into the occasional sorry hiccup, and hold him close and stroke his young black silky head. And when I judge that the time is right I begin to tell a tale to solace him.

I speak frivolously.

'You know how keen Grandma was on good behaviour and doing the right thing? Well, when she was dying she decided to bring all the family skeletons out of the cupboard – and did they rattle! That solemn young soldier, whose photograph is staring at you from the sideboard – your grandfather – was a pre-war socialist called Ted the Red!'

Joshua likes that. He gives a snort against my shoulder, sits up, wipes his eyes, blows his nose. He says, 'Ted the Red! You're making that up, Mum!'

I hear my voice lilt on. 'No, truly. Your grandfather was a very clever, courageous and original person. But he never had the chance to achieve anything. He was killed during the last war, in Southern Italy in 1943. I've got a boxful of his letters that Grandma gave to me. You might like to read them when you're older. You could read them now if you liked, but I think you'll find them a bit prosy. So, think on, as Grandma used to say. And when you're feeling down in the mouth you can say to yourself, "Part of me is Ted the Red!"'

And part of me too, I thought.

'And guess what, Josh. You'll love this! He was half Cornish!'

The news goes down very well indeed. His eyes

snap wide open. He polishes his glasses furiously and puts them on in order to see me better.

'And your great-grandmother's maiden name was Kerenza Pascoe!'

His mouth, which is less beautiful and more masculine than it used to be, flowers into a grin. 'Why, we're one of them!' he says joyfully. 'No wonder we liked staying there!' He is filled with light. 'Mum! Can we go to Hendra for Easter?'

Floundering slightly under yet another loss, I say, 'I'm afraid Hendra's been sold, and I don't know what's happening to it yet. But not to worry. We can find somewhere else to stay on the Lizard. And I'll let you into another secret. I'd like to buy a cottage for us when I've got some money together. So that we have a place of our own there . . .'

Joshua is completely restored. And as I have carried my research round with me like a talisman I bring out photographs of all three properties to show him, and confide my hopes and plans.

'I loved Chyteg. Dear little duck of a place! And Nansawsan is truly beautiful but it's in a bad state. Tregatreath is really too big for us, but it's the best bet of the lot. More like a home than a holiday cottage, and easier to rent out because it will house more people.'

'How will you pay for it?' asks Joshua, practical.

'There are two possibilities. I know someone who is prepared to lend me the money, but we shall have to settle into our new house first and work out our finances. And I shall get some money for this shop. The whole terrace is due for demolition. The notice came through while Grandma was in hospital.'

In such dry documents does our future lie.

'Fortunately she didn't need to know, and I didn't tell her. But I'll be given compensation for both the house and the business.'

'How much?' Josh asks, interested.

'As little as they can get away with, I expect. And it will take a fair time to come through. But I shall have it eventually, and then I can use it.'

'Good old Mum! But that means we can't buy Tregatreath.'

'We don't know that. It may come on the market again. The money may come sooner than we think. Anything can happen. What I do know is that we shall get the house we're meant to have, however long it takes.'

His silence is appreciative. Then he begins again. 'What does Tregatreath mean?'

'The house near the sea. And it is. Near Lizard Town. Chyteg means the pretty house. Nansawsan is the Englishman's house – which I thought would be rather appropriate!'

'No, it wouldn't,' says Joshua positively. 'We're Cornish.' He purses his lips, thinking. 'Mum! Could I bring my friend Daniel down at Easter? He's the only decent thing about Jefferson's. He's just your sort, Mum. An absolute nutter.'

'So that's how you see me!' I murmur, not displeased. 'Yes, bring Daniel by all means. We can have him over in the Christmas holidays if you like. It will be nice for you to play together.'

'Play?' says Joshua scornfully. 'Play? Mum! Do you think I'm a baby?'

'Well, whatever it is that you say now. Someone to have adventures with?'

He accepts this, and moves on to the next question. 'Mum, can we have another cat?'

I recognise that the conversation has moved into the realms of Mum-is-feeling-guilty-let's-see-how-far-I-can-go time. And begin the ascent to earth.

'Not until we've moved house and settled in. Then we can.'

'Thanks, Mum. A proper cat. Not a posh one. Not

like that Persian powder puff next door. I want a real cat. Like old Webs.'

'You shall choose your own alley cat, Joshua, and I shall go along with it.'

His look is half wistful, half judicious.

'Mum! I've just had a wonderful idea. Why don't we buy Tregatreath for our new house, and go down to live in Cornwall altogether?'

I am on firm ground once more.

'No, Joshua. One step at a time. And now, guess what, *I've* had a wonderful idea. It's nine o'clock. How about going to bed?'

In solitary state, I mend the fire and refresh my whisky. The evening's revelations have gone surprisingly well. There will be others, less happy. There will be some that are downright bloody.

'And you must take care of yourself and keep healthy,' I tell myself aloud. 'So that you can run like hell to stay in the same place!'

But I can run, and have run, and will run, and I stand a good chance in the race.

I think of my mother, who remained on the starting line all her life, whose only satisfaction came from watching me forge ahead. Like so many women she made her mistakes out of love and paid for them with self-sacrifice. Her story could be told in three words: drudgery, duty, bewilderment. That will not be my lot. It would not have been Sarah's lot.

I try to sense my daughter's presence, but having lingered a while she has at last taken her leave.

So I go to bed, and join her in the lesser death of sleep and dreams.

On this brisk North-Country morning the neighbours have come out to see us off. Mrs Greenhalgh speaks first, eyes screwed up against the winter sunlight, tone bantering and slightly contemptuous.

'That car o' yours must have seen more miles than I've eaten bread puddings! Eh, you haven't half done some traipsing about this year, M'rina.'

I forestall her next remark with astringent Lancashire humour. 'Yes, I have. Let's hope it gets me somewhere!'

She gives a short sharp bark of a laugh, and says, 'Aye. I hope you're right. Well, have a safe journey. And a merry Christmas.' And stands back, hands folded in her apron.

As the others shake hands their comments reflect my thoughts.

'My word, it's been hard on you, the last nine months, M'rina. First your little lass and now your poor mam.'

'But wasn't your mam proud of you? Doing so well for yourself.'

'And hasn't that little lad grown up?'

And finally, 'Eh, but weren't it a grand summer? We shan't forget that in a hurry, shall us?'

The light is clear and cold and gold.

A good day for a long journey.